DR. G. A. LAZENBY, JR.

CLARE VICTOR DWIGGINS

SALAMMBÔ

A ROMANCE OF ANCIENT CARTHAGE

BY

GUSTAVE FLAUBERT

WITH AN

APPENDIX

CONTAINING NOTES OF THE CONTROVERSY
OVER THE ROMANCE

———

VOLUME IV.

SIMON P. MAGEE
PUBLISHER
CHICAGO, ILL.

ILLUSTRATIONS

———

SALAMMBÔ

(CONTINUED.)

X.

THE SERPENT.

THESE clamourings of the populace did not alarm Hamilcar's daughter. She was disturbed by loftier anxieties: her great serpent, the black python, was drooping; and in the eyes of the Carthaginians, the serpent was at once a national and a private fetish. It was believed to be the offspring of the dust of the earth, since it emerges from its depths and has no need of feet to traverse it; its mode of progression called to mind the undulations of rivers, its temperature the ancient, viscous, and fecund darkness, and the orbit which it describes when biting its tail the harmony of the planets, and the intelligence of Eschmoun.

Salammbô's serpent had several times already refused the four live sparrows which were offered to it at the full moon and at every new moon. Its handsome skin, covered like the firmament with golden spots upon a perfectly black ground, was now yellow, relaxed, wrinkled, and too large for its body. A cottony mouldiness extended round its head; and in the corners of its eyelids might be seen little red specks which appeared to move. Salammbô would approach its silver-wire basket from time to time, and would draw aside the purple curtains, the lotus leaves, and the bird's down; but it was continually rolled up upon itself, more motionless than a withered bindweed; and from looking at it she at last came to feel a kind of spiral within her heart, another serpent, as it were, mounting up to her throat by degrees and strangling her.

She was in despair at having seen the zaïmph, and yet she felt a sort of joy, an intimate pride at having done so. A mystery shrank within the splendour of its folds; it was the cloud that enveloped the gods, and the secret of the universal existence, and Salammbô, horror-stricken at herself, regretted that she had not raised it.

She was almost always crouching at the back of her apartment, holding her bended left leg in her hands, her mouth half open, her chin sunk, her eye fixed. She recollected her father's face with terror; she wished to go away into the mountains of Rhœnicia, on a pilgrimage to the temple of Aphaka, where Tanith descended in the form of a star; all kinds of imaginings attracted her and terrified her; moreover, a solitude which every day became greater encompassed her. She did not even know what Hamilcar was about.

Wearied at last with her thoughts she would rise, and trailing along her little sandals whose soles clacked upon her heels at every step, she would walk at random through the large silent room. The amethysts and topazes of the ceiling made luminous spots quiver here and there, and Salammbô as she walked would turn her head a little to see them. She would go and take the hanging amphoras by the neck; she would cool her bosom beneath the broad fans, or perhaps amuse herself by burning cinnamomum in hollow pearls. At sunset Taanach would draw back the black felt lozenges that closed the openings in the wall; then her doves, rubbed with musk like the doves of Tanith, suddenly entered, and their pink feet glided over the glass pavement, amid the grains of barley which she threw to them in handfuls like a sower in a field. But on a sudden she would burst into sobs and lie stretched on the large bed of ox-leather straps without moving, repeating a word that was ever the same, with open eyes, pale as one dead, insensible, cold; and yet she could hear the cries of the apes in the tufts of the palm trees, with the continuous grinding of the great wheel which brought a flow of pure water through the stories into the porphyry centre-basin.

Sometimes for several days she would refuse to eat. She could see in a dream troubled stars wandering beneath her feet. She would call Schahabarim, and when he came she had nothing to say to him.

She could not live without the relief of his presence. But she rebelled inwardly against this domination; her feeling towards the priest was one at once of terror, jealousy, hatred, and a species of love, in gratitude for the singular voluptuousness which she experienced by his side.

He had recognised the influence of Rabbet, being skilful to discern the gods who sent diseases; and to cure Salammbô he had her apartment watered with lotions of vervain, and maidenhair; she ate mandrakes every morning; she slept with her head on a cushion filled with aromatics blended by the pontiffs; he had even employed baaras, a fiery-coloured root which drives back fatal geniuses into the North; lastly, turning towards the polar star, he murmured thrice the mysterious name of Tanith; but Salammbô still suffered and her anguish deepened.

No one in Carthage was so learned as he. In his youth he had studied at the College of the Mogbeds, at Borsippa, near Babylon; had then visited Samothrace, Pessinus, Ephesus, Thessaly, Judæa, and the temples of the Nabathæ, which are lost in the sands; and had travelled on foot along the banks of the Nile from the cataracts to the sea. Shaking torches with veil-covered face, he had cast a black cock upon a fire of sandarach before the breast of the Sphinx, the Father of Terror. He had descended into the caverns of Proserpine; he had seen the five hundred pillars of the labyrinth of Lemnos revolve, and the candelabrum of Tarentum, which bore as many sconces on its shaft as there are days in the year, shine in its splendour; at times he received Greeks by night in order to question them. The constitution of the world disquieted him no less than the nature of the gods; he had observed the equinoxes with the armils placed in the portico of Alexandria, and accompanied the bematists of Evergetes, who measure the sky by calculating the number of their steps, as far as Cyrene; so that there was now growing in his thoughts a religion of his own, with no distinct formula, and on that very account full of infatuation and fervour. He no longer believed that the earth was formed like a fir-cone; he believed it to be round, and eternally falling through immensity with such prodigious speed that its fall was not perceived.

From the position of the sun above the moon he inferred the predominance of Baal, of whom the planet itself is but the reflection and figure; moreover, all that he saw in terrestrial things compelled him to recognise the male exterminating principle as supreme. And then he secretly charged Rabbet with the misfortune of his life. Was it not for her that the grandpontiff had once advanced amid the tumult of cymbals, and with a patera of boiling water taken from him his future virility? And he followed with a melancholy gaze the men who were disappearing with the priestesses in the depths of the turpentine trees.

His days were spent in inspecting the censers, the gold vases, the tongs, the rakes for the ashes of the altar, and all the robes of the statues down to the bronze bodkin that served to curl the hair of an old Tanith in the third ædicule near the emerald vine. At the same hours he would raise the great hangings of the same swinging doors; would remain with his arms outspread in the same attitude; or prayed prostrate on the same flag-stones, while around him a people of priests moved barefooted through the passages filled with an eternal twilight.

But Salammbô was in the barrenness of his life like a flower in the cleft of a sepulchre. Nevertheless he was hard upon her, and spared her neither penances nor bitter words. His condition established, as it were, the equality of a common sex between them, and he was less angry with the young girl for his inability to possess her than for finding her so beautiful, and above all so pure. Often he saw that she grew weary in following his thought. Then he would turn away sadder than before; he would feel himself more forsaken, more empty, more alone.

Strange words escaped him sometimes, which passed before Salammbô like broad lightnings illuminating the abysses. This would be at night on the terrace when, both alone, they gazed upon the stars, and Carthage spread below under their feet, with the gulf and the open sea dimly lost in the colour of the darkness.

He would set forth to her the theory of the souls that descend upon the earth, following the same route as the sun through the signs of the zodiac. With outstretched arm he showed the gate of human generation in the Ram, and that of the return to the gods in Capricorn; and Salammbô strove to see them, for she took these conceptions for realities; she accepted pure symbols and even manners of speech as being true in themselves, a distinction not always very clear even to the priest.

"The souls of the dead," said he, "resolve themselves into the moon, as their bodies do into the earth. Their tears compose its humidity; 'tis a dark abode full of mire, and wreck, and tempest."

She asked what would become of her then.

"At first you will languish as light as a vapour hovering upon the waves; and after more lengthened ordeals and agonies, you will pass into the forces of the sun, the very source of Intelligence!"

He did not speak, however, of Rabbet. Salammbô imagined that it was through shame for his vanquished goddess, and calling her by a common name which designated the moon, she launched into blessings upon the soft and fertile planet. At last he exclaimed:

"No! no! she draws all her fecundity from the other! Do you not see her hovering about him like an amorous woman running after a man in a field?" And he exalted the virtue of light unceasingly.

Far from depressing her mystic desires, he sought, on the contrary, to excite them, and he even seemed to take joy in grieving her by the revelation of a pitiless doctrine. In spite of the pains of her love Salammbô threw herself upon it with transport.

But the more that Schahabarim felt himself in doubt about Tanith, the more he wished to believe in her. At the bottom of his soul he was arrested by remorse. He needed some proof, some manifestation from the gods, and in the hope of obtaining it the priest devised an enterprise which might save at once his country and his belief.

Thenceforward he set himself to deplore before Salammbô the sacrilege and the misfortunes which resulted from it even in the regions of the sky. Then he suddenly announced the peril of the Suffet, who was assailed by three armies under the command of Matho — for on account of the veil Matho was, in the eyes of the Carthaginians, the king, as it were, of the Barbarians, — and he added that the safety of the Republic and of her father depended upon her alone.

"Upon me!" she exclaimed. "How can I——?"

But the priest, with a smile of disdain said:

"You will never consent!"

She entreated him. At last Schahabarim said to her:

"You must go to the Barbarians and recover the zaïmph!"

She sank down upon the ebony stool, and remained with her arms stretched out between her knees and a shivering in all her limbs, like a victim at the altar's foot awaiting the blow of the club. Her temples were ringing, she could see fiery circles revolving, and in her stupor she had lost the understanding of all things save one, that she was certainly going to die soon.

But if Rabbetna triumphed, if the zaïmph were restored and Carthage delivered, what mattered a woman's life? thought Schahabarim. Moreover, she would perhaps obtain the veil and not perish.

He stayed away for three days; on the evening of the fourth she sent for him.

The better to inflame her heart he reported to her all the invectives howled against Hamilcar in open council; he told her that she had erred, that she owed reparation for her crime, and that Rabbetna commanded the sacrifice.

A great uproar came frequently across the Mappalian district to Megara. Schahabarim and Salammbô went out quickly, and gazed from the top of the galley staircase.

There were people in the square of Khamon shouting for arms. The Ancients would not provide them, esteeming such an effort useless; others who had set out without a general had been massacred. At last they were permitted to depart, and as a sort of homage to Moloch, or from a vague need of destruction, they tore up tall cypress trees in the woods of the temples, and having kindled them at the torches of the Kabiri, were carrying them through the streets singing. These monstrous flames advanced swaying gently; they transmitted fires to the glass balls on the crests of the temples, to the ornaments of the colossuses and the beaks of the ships, passed beyond the terraces and formed suns as it were, which rolled through the town. They descended the Acropolis. The gate of Malqua opened.

"Are you ready?" exclaimed Schahabarim, "or have you asked them to tell your father that you abandoned him?" She hid her face in her veils, and the great lights retired, sinking gradually the while to the edge of the waves.

An indeterminate dread restrained her; she was afraid of Moloch and of Matho. This man, with his giant stature, who was master of the zaïmph, ruled Rabbetna as much as did Baal, and seemed to her to be surrounded by the same fulgurations; and then the souls of the gods sometimes visited the bodies of men. Did not Schahabarim in speaking of him say that she was to vanquish Moloch? They were mingled with each other; she confused them together; both of them were pursuing her.

She wished to learn the future, and approached the serpent, for auguries were drawn from the attitudes of serpents. But the basket was empty; Salammbô was disturbed.

She found him with his tail rolled round one of the silver balustrades beside the hanging bed, which he was rubbing in order to free himself from his old yellowish skin, while his body stretched forth gleaming and clear like a sword half out of the sheath.

Then on the days following, in proportion as she allowed herself to be convinced, and was more disposed to succour Tanith, the python recovered and grew; he seemed to be reviving.

The certainty that Schahabarim was giving expression to the will of the gods then became established in her conscience. One morning she awoke resolved, and she asked what was necessary to make Matho restore the veil.

"To claim it," said Schahabarim.

"But if he refuses?" she rejoined.

The priest scanned her fixedly with a smile such as she had never seen.

"Yes, what is to be done?" repeated Salammbô.

He rolled between his fingers the extremities of the bands which fell from his tiara upon his shoulders, standing motionless with eyes cast down. At last seeing that she did not understand:

"You will be alone with him."

"Well?" she said.

"Alone in his tent."

"What then?"

Schahabarim bit his lips. He sought for some phrase, some circumlocution.

"If you are to die, that will be later," he said; "later! fear nothing! and whatever he may undertake to do, do not call out! do not be frightened! You will be humble, you understand, and submissive to his desire, which is ordained of heaven!"

"But the veil?"

"The gods will take thought for it," replied Schahabarim.

"Suppose you were to accompany me, O father?" she added.

"No!"

He made her kneel down, and keeping his left hand raised and his right extended, he swore in her behalf to bring back the mantle of Tanith into Carthage. With terrible imprecations she devoted herself to the gods, and each time that Schahabarim pronounced a word she falteringly repeated it.

He indicated to her all the purifications and fastings that she was to observe, and how she was to reach Matho. Moreover, a man acquainted with the routes would accompany her.

She felt as if she had been set free. She thought only of the happiness of seeing the zaïmph again, and she now blessed Schahabarim for his exhortations.

It was the period at which the doves of Carthage migrated to Sicily to the mountain of Eryx and the temple of Venus. For several days before their departure they sought out and called to one another so as to collect togeth_r; at last one evening they flew away; the wind blew them along, and the big white cloud glided across the sky high above the sea.

The horizon was filled with the colour of blood. They seemed to descend gradually to the waves; then they disappeared as though swallowed up, and falling of themselves into the jaws of the sun. Salammbô, who watched them retiring, bent her head, and then Taanach, believing that she guessed her sorrow, said gently to her:

"But they will come back, Mistress."

"Yes! I know."

"And you will see them again."

"Perhaps!" she said, sighing.

She had not confided her resolve to any one; in order to carry it out with the greater discretion she sent Taanach to the suburb of Kinisdo to buy all the things that she required instead of requesting them from the stewards: vermilion, aromatics, a lin_ girdle, and new garments. The old slave was _ azed at these preparations, without daring, however, to ask any questions; and the day, which had been fixed by Schahabarim, arrived when Salammbô was to set out.

About the twelfth hour she perceived, in the depths of the sycamore trees, a blind old man with one hand resting on the shoulder of a child who walked before him, while with the other he carried a kind of cithara of black wood against his hip. The eunuchs, slaves, and women had been scrupulously sent away; no one might know the mystery that was preparing.

Taanach kindled four tripods filled with strobus and cardamomum in the corners of the apartment; then she unfolded large Babylonian hangings, and stretched them on cords all around the room, for Salammbô did not wish to be seen even by the walls. The kinnor-player squatted behind the door and the young boy standing upright applied a reed flute to his lips. In the distance the roar of the streets was growing feebler, violet shadows were lengthening before the peristyles of the temples, and on the other side of the gulf the mountain bases, the fields of olive-trees, and the vague yellow lands undulated indefinitely, and were blended together in a bluish haze; not a sound was to be heard, and an unspeakable depression weighed in the air.

Salammbô crouched down upon the onyx step on the edge of the basin; she raised her ample sleeves, fastening them behind her shoulders, and began her ablutions in methodical fashion, according to the sacred rites.

Next Taanach brought her something liquid and coagulated in an alabaster phial; it was the blood of a black dog slaughtered by barren women on a winter's night amid the rubbish of a sepulchre. She rubbed it upon her ears, her heels, and the thumb of her right hand, and even her nail remained somewhat red, as if she had crushed a fruit.

The moon rose; then the cithara and the flute began to play together.

Salammbô unfastened her earrings, her necklace, her bracelets, and her long white simar; she unknotted the band in her hair, shaking the latter for a few minutes softly over her shoulders to cool herself by thus scattering it. The music went on outside; it consisted of three notes ever the same, hurried and frenzied; the strings grated, the flute blew; Taanach kept time by striking her hands; Salammbô, with a swaying of her whole body, chanted prayers, and her garments fell one after another around her.

The heavy tapestry trembled, and the python's head appeared above the cord that supported it. The serpent descended slowly like a drop of water flowing along a wall, crawled among the scattered stuffs, and then, gluing its tail to the ground, rose perfectly erect; and his eyes, more brilliant than carbuncles, darted upon Salammbô.

A horror of cold, or perhaps a feeling of shame, at first made her hesitate. But she recalled Schahabarim's orders and advanced; the python turned downwards, and resting the centre of its body upon the nape of her neck, allowed its head and tail to hang like a broken necklace with both ends trailing to the ground. Salammbô rolled it around her sides, under her arms and between her knees; then taking it by the jaw she brought the little triangular mouth to the edge of her teeth, and half shutting her eyes, threw herself back beneath the rays of the moon. The white light seemed to envelop her in a silver mist, the prints of her humid steps shone upon the flag-stones, stars quivered in the depth of the water; it tightened upon her its black rings that were spotted with scales of gold. Salammbô panted beneath the excessive weight, her loins yielded, she felt herself dying, and with the tip of its tail the serpent gently beat her thigh; then the music becoming still it fell off again.

Taanach came back to her; and after arranging two candelabra, the lights of which burned in crystal balls filled with water, she tinged the inside of her hands with Lawsonia, spread vermilion upon her cheeks, and antimony along the edge of her eyelids, and lengthened her eyebrows with a mixture of gum, musk, ebony, and crushed legs of flies.

Salammbô seated on a chair with ivory uprights, gave herself up to the attentions of the slave. But the touchings, the odour of the aromatics, and the fasts that she had undergone, were enervating her. She became so pale that Taanach stopped.

"Go on!" said Salammbô, and bearing up against herself, she suddenly revived. Then she was seized with impatience; she urged Taanach to make haste, and the old slave grumbled:

"Well! well! Mistress!—Besides, you have no one waiting for you!"

"Yes!" said Salammbô, "some one is waiting for me."

Taanach drew back in surprise, and in order to learn more about it, said:

"What orders do you give me, Mistress? for if you are to remain away——"

But Salammbô was sobbing; the slave exclaimed:

'You are suffering! what is the matter? Do not go away! take me! When you were quite little and used to cry, I took you to my heart and made you laugh with the points of my breasts; you have drained them, Mistress!" She struck herself upon her dried-up bosom. "Now I am old! I can do nothing for

you! you no longer love me! you hide your griefs
from me, you despise the nurse!" And tears of
tenderness and vexation flowed down her cheeks in
the gashes of her tattooing.

"No!" said Salammbô, "no, I love you! be comforted!"

With a smile like th grimace of an old ape,
Taanach resumed her task. In accordance with
Schahabarim's recommendations, Salammbô had ordered the slave to make her magnificent; and she was
obeying her mistress with barbaric taste full at once
of refinement and ingenuity.

Over a first delicate and vinous-coloured tunic she
passed a second embroidered with birds' feathers.
Golden scales c'ung to her hips, and from this broad
girdle descended her blue flowing silver-starred trousers.
Next Taanach put upon her a long robe made of the
cloth of the country of Seres, white and streaked with
green lines. On the edge of her shoulder she fastened
a square of purple weighted at the hem with grains
of sandrastum; and above all these garments she
placed a black mantle with a flowing train; then she
gazed at her, and proud of her work could not help
saying:

"You will not be more beautiful on the day of
your bridal!"

"My bridal!" repeated Salammbô; she was musing
with her elbow resting upon the ivory chair.

But Taanach set up before her a copper mirror,
which was so broad and high that she could see herself completely in it. Then she rose, and with a light
touch of her finger raised a lock of her hair which was
falling too low.

Her hair was covered with gold dust, was crisped

in front, and hung down behind over her back in long
twists ending in pearls. The brightness of the candelabra heightened the paint on her cheeks, the gold
on her garments, and the whiteness of her skin;
around her waist, and on her arms, hands and toes,
she had such a wealth of gems that the mirror sent back
rays upon her like a sun;—and Salammbô, standing
by the side of Taanach, who leaned over to see her,
smiled amid this dazzling display.

Then she walked to and fro embarrassed by the
time that was still left.

Suddenly the crow of a cock resounded. She
quickly pinned a long yellow veil upon her hair, passed
a scarf around her neck, thrust her feet into blue
leather boots, and said to Taanach:

"Go and see whether there is not a man with two
horses beneath the myrtles."

Taanach had scarcely re-entered when she was descending the galley staircase.

"Mistress!" cried the nurse.

Salammbô turned round with one finger on her
mouth as a sign for discretion and immobility.

Taanach stole softly along the prows to the foot of
the terrace, and from a distance she could distinguish
by the light of the moon a gigantic shadow walking
obliquely in the cypress avenue to the left of Salammbô, a sign which presaged death.

Taanach went up again into the chamber. She
threw herself upon the ground tearing her face with
her nails; she plucked out her hair, and uttered piercing shrieks with all her might.

It occurred to her that they might be heard; then
she became silent, sobbing quite softly with her head
in her hands and her face on the pavement.

XI.

IN THE TENT.

HE man who guided Salammbô made her ascend again beyond the pharos in the direction of the Catacombs, and then go down the long suburb of Molouya, which was full of steep lanes. The sky was beginning to grow grey. Sometimes palm-wood beams jutting out from the walls obliged them to bend their heads. The two horses which were at the walk would often slip; and thus they reached the Teveste gate.

Its heavy leaves were half open; they passed through, and it closed behind them.

At first they followed the foot of the ramparts for a time, and at the height of the cisterns they took their way along the Taenia, a narrow strip of yellow earth separating the gulf from the lake and extending as far as Rhades.

No one was to be seen around Carthage, whether on the sea or in the country. The slate-coloured waves chopped softly, and the light wind blowing their foam hither and thither spotted them with white rents. In spite of all her veils, Salammbô shivered in the freshness of the morning; the motion and the open

air dazed her. Then the sun rose; it preyed on the
back of her head, and she involuntarily dozed a little.
The two animals ambled along side by side, their feet
sinking into the silent sand.

When they had passed the mountain of the Hot
Springs, they went on at a more rapid rate, the ground
being firmer.

But although it was the season for sowing and
ploughing, the fields were as empty as the desert as
far as the eye could reach. Here and there were
scattered heaps of corn; at other places the barley
was shedding its reddened ears. The villages showed
black upon the clear horizon, with shapes incoher-
ently carved.

From time to time a half-calcined piece of wall
would be found standing on the edge of the road.
The roofs of the cottages were falling in, and in the
interiors might be distinguished fragments of pottery,
rags of clothing, and all kinds of unrecognisable utensils and broken things. Often a creature clothed in
tatters,with earthy face and flaming eyes would emerge
from these ruins. But he would very quickly begin
to run or would disappear into a hole. Salammbô
and her guide did not stop.

Deserted plains succeeded one another. Charcoal
dust which was raised by their feet behind them,
stretched in unequal trails over large spaces of perfectly white soil. Sometimes they came upon little
peaceful spots, where a brook flowed amid the long
grass; and as they ascended the other bank Salammbô
would pluck damp leaves to cool her hands. At the
corner of a wood of rose-bays her horse shied violently
at the corpse of a man which lay extended on the
ground.

The slave immediately settled her again on the cushions. He was one of the servants of the Temple, a man whom Schahabarim used to employ on perilous missions.

With extreme precaution he now went on foot beside her and between the horses; he would whip the animals with the end of a leathern lace wound round his arm, or would perhaps take balls made of wheat, dates, and yolks of eggs wrapped in lotus leaves from a scrip hanging against his breast, and offer them to Salammbô without speaking, and running all the time.

In the middle of the day three Barbarians clad in animals' skins crossed their path. By degrees others appeared wandering in troops of ten, twelve, or twenty-five men; many were driving goats or a limping cow. Their heavy sticks bristled with brass points; cutlasses gleamed in their clothes, which were savagely dirty, and they opened their eyes with a look of menace and amazement. As they passed some sent them a vulgar benediction; others obscene jests; and Schahabarim's man replied to each in his own idiom. He told them that this was a sick youth going to be cured at a distant temple.

However, the day was closing in. Barkings were heard, and they approached them.

Then in the twilight they perceived an enclosure of dry stones shutting in a rambling edifice. A dog was running along the top of the wall. The slave threw some pebbles at him and they entered a lofty vaulted hall.

A woman was crouching in the centre warming herself at a fire of brushwood, the smoke of which escaped through the holes in the ceiling. She was half hidden by her white hair which fell to her knees; and unwilling to answer, she muttered with idiotic look words of vengeance against the Barbarians and the Carthaginians.

The runner ferreted right and left. Then he returned to her and demanded something to eat. The old woman shook her head, and murmured with her eyes fixed upon the charcoal:

"I was the hand. The ten fingers are cut off. The mouth eats no more."

The slave showed her a handful of gold pieces. She rushed upon them, but soon resumed her immobility.

At last he placed a dagger which he had in his girdle beneath her throat. Then, trembling, she went and raised a large stone, and brought back an amphora of wine with fish from Hippo-Zarytus preserved in honey.

Salammbô turned away from this unclean food, and fell asleep on the horses' caparisons which were spread in a corner of the hall.

He awoke her before daylight.

The dog was howling. The slave went up to it quietly, and struck off its head with a single blow of his dagger. Then he rubbed the horses' nostrils with blood to revive them. The old woman cast a malediction at him from behind. Salammbô perceived this, and pressed the amulet which she wore above her heart.

They resumed their journey.

From time to time she asked whether they would not arrive soon. The road undulated over little hills. Nothing was to be heard but the grating of the grasshoppers. The sun heated the yellowed grass; the ground was all chinked with crevices which in dividing formed, as it were, monstrous paving-stones. Sometimes a viper passed, or eagles flew by; the slave still continued running. Salammbô mused beneath her veils, and in spite of the heat did not lay them aside through fear of soiling her beautiful garments.

At regular distances stood towers built by the Carthaginians for the purpose of keeping watch upon the tribes. They entered these for the sake of the shade, and then set out again.

For prudence sake they had made a wide détour the day before. But they met with no one just now; the region being a sterile one, the Barbarians had not passed that way.

Gradually the devastation began again. Sometimes a piece of mosaic would be displayed in the centre of a field, the sole remnant of a vanished mansion; and the leafless olive trees looked at a distance like large bushes of thorns. They passed through a town in which the houses were burnt to the ground. Human skeletons might be seen along the walls. There were some, too, of dromedaries and mules. Half-gnawed carrion blocked the streets.

Night fell. The sky was lowering and cloudy.

They ascended again for two hours in a westerly direction, when suddenly they perceived a quantity of little flames before them.

These were shining at the bottom of an amphitheatre. Gold plates, as they displaced one another, glanced here and there. These were the cuirasses of the Clinabarians in the Punic camp; then in the neighbourhood they distinguished other and more numerous lights, for the armies of the Mercenaries, now blended together, extended over a great space.

Salammbô made a movement as though to advance. But Schahabarim's man took her further away, and they passed along by the terrace which enclosed the camp of the Barbarians. A breach became visible in it, and the slave disappeared.

A sentry was walking upon the top of the entrenchment with a bow in his hand and a pike on his shoulder.

Salammbô drew still nearer; the Barbarian knelt and a long arrow pierced the hem of her cloak. Then as she stood motionless and shrieking, he asked her what she wanted.

"To speak to Matho," she replied. "I am a fugitive from Carthage."

He gave a whistle, which was repeated at intervals further away.

Salammbô waited; her frightened horse moved round and round, sniffing.

When Matho arrived the moon was rising behind her. But she had a yellow veil with black flowers over her face, and so many draperies about her person, that it was impossible to make any guess about her. From the top of the terrace he gazed upon this vague form standing up like a phantom in the penumbræ of the evening.

At last she said to him:

"Lead me to your tent! I wish it!"

A recollection which he could not define passed through his memory. He felt his heart beating. This air of command intimidated him.

"Follow me!" he said.

The barrier was lowered, and immediately she was in the camp of the Barbarians.

It was filled with a great tumult and a great throng. Bright fires were burning beneath hanging pots; and their purpled reflections illuminating some places left others completely in the dark. There was shouting and calling; shackled horses formed long straight lines amid the tents; the latter were round and square, of leather or of canvas; there were huts of reeds, and holes in the sand such as are made by dogs. Soldiers were carting faggots, resting on their elbows on the ground, or wrapping themselves up in mats and preparing to sleep; and Salammbô's horse sometimes stretched out a leg and jumped in order to pass over them.

She remembered that she had seen them before; but their beards were longer now, their faces still blacker, and their voices hoarser. Matho, who walked before her, waved them off with a gesture of his arm which raised his red mantle. Some kissed his hands; others bending their spines approached him to ask for orders, for he was now veritable and sole chief of the Barbarians; Spendius, Autaritus, and Narr' Havas had become disheartened, and he had displayed so much audacity and obstinacy that all obeyed him.

Salammbô followed him through the entire camp. His tent was at the end, three hundred feet from Hamilcar's entrenchments.

She noticed a wide pit on the right, and it seemed to her that faces were resting against the edge of it on a level with the ground, as decapitated heads might have done. However, their eyes moved, and from these half-opened mouths groanings escaped in the Punic tongue.

Two Negroes holding resin lights stood on both sides of the door. Matho drew the canvas abruptly aside. She followed him.

It was a deep tent with a pole standing up in the centre. It was lighted by a large lamp-holder shaped like a lotus and full of a yellow oil wherein floated handfuls of burning tow, and military things might be distinguished gleaming in the shade. A naked sword leaned against a stool by the side of a shield; whips of hippopotamus leather, cymbals, bells, and necklaces were displayed pell-mell on baskets of esparto-grass; a felt rug lay soiled with crumbs of black bread; some copper money was carelessly heaped upon a round stone in a corner, and through the rents in the canvas the wind brought the dust from without, together with the smell of the elephants, which might be heard eating and shaking their chains.

"Who are you?" said Matho.

She looked slowly around her without replying; then her eyes were arrested in the background, where something bluish and sparkling fell upon a bed of palm-branches.

She advanced quickly. A cry escaped her. Matho stamped his foot behind her.

"Who brings you here? why do you come?"

"To take it!" she replied, pointing to the zaïmph, and with the other hand she tore the veils from her head. He drew back with his elbows behind him, gaping, almost terrified.

She felt as if she were leaning upon the might of the gods; and looking at him face to face she asked him for the zaïmph; she demanded it in words abundant and superb.

Matho did not hear; he was gazing at her, and in his eyes her garments were blended with her body. The clouding of the stuffs, like the splendour of her skin, was something special and belonging to her alone. Her eyes and her diamonds sparkled; the polish of her nails continued the delicacy of the stones which loaded her fingers; the two clasps of her tunic raised her breasts somewhat and brought them closer together, and he in thought lost himself in the narrow interval between them whence there fell a thread holding a plate of emeralds which could be seen lower down beneath the violet gauze. She had as earrings two little sapphire scales, each supporting a hollow pearl filled with liquid scent. A little drop would fall every moment through the holes in the pearl and moisten her naked shoulder. Matho watched it fall.

He was carried away by ungovernable curiosity; and, like a child laying his hand upon a strange fruit, he tremblingly and lightly touched the top of her chest with the tip of his finger: the flesh, which was somewhat cold, yielded with an elastic resistance.

This contact, though scarcely a sensible one, shook Matho to the very depths of his nature. An uprising of his whole being urged him towards her. He would fain have enveloped her, absorbed her, drunk her. His bosom was panting, his teeth were chattering.

Taking her by the wrists he drew her gently to him, and then sat down upon a cuirass beside the palm-tree bed which was covered with a lion's skin. She was standing. He looked up at her, holding her thus between his knees, and repeating:

"How beautiful you are! how beautiful you are!"

His eyes, which were continually fixed upon hers, pained her; and the uncomfortableness, the repugnance increased in so acute a fashion that Salammbô put a constraint upon herself not to cry out. The thought of Schahabarim came back to her, and she resigned herself.

Matho still kept her little hands in his own; and from time to time, in spite of the priest's command, she turned away her face and tried to thrust him off by jerking her arms. He opened his nostrils the better to breathe in the perfume which exhaled from her person. It was a fresh, indefinable emanation, which nevertheless made him dizzy, like the smoke from a perfuming-pan. She smelt of honey, pepper, incense, roses, with another odour still.

But how was she thus with him in his tent, and at his disposal? Some one no doubt had urged her. She had not come for the zaïmph. His arms fell, and he bent his head whelmed in sudden reverie.

To soften him Salammbô said to him in a plaintive voice:

"What have I done to you that you should desire my death?"

"Your death!"

She resumed:

"I saw you one evening by the light of my burning gardens amid fuming cups and my slaughtered slaves, and your anger was so strong that you bounded towards me and I was obliged to fly! Then terror entered into Carthage. There were cries of the devastation of the towns, the burning of the country-seats, the massacre of the soldiery; it was you who had ruined them, it was you who had murdered them! I hate you! Your very name gnaws me like re-

morse! You are execrated more than the plague, and
the Roman war! The provinces shudder at your fury,
the furrows are full of corpses! I have followed the
traces of your fires as though I were travelling behind
Moloch!"

Matho leaped up; his heart was swelling with
colossal pride; he was raised to the stature of a
god.

With quivering nostrils and clenched teeth she
went on:

"As if your sacrilege were not enough, you came
to me in my sleep covered with the zaïmph! Your
words I did not understand; but I could see that you
wished to drag me to some terrible thing at the bottom of an abyss."

Matho, writhing his arms, exclaimed:

"No! no! it was to give it to you! to restore it to
you! It seemed to me that the goddess had left her
garment for you, and that it belonged to you! In her
temple or in your house, what does it matter? are
you not all-powerful, immaculate, radiant and beautiful even as Tanith?" And with a look of boundless
adoration he added:

"Unless perhaps you are Tanith?"

"I, Tanith!" said Salammbô to herself.

They left off speaking. The thunder rolled in the
distance. Some sheep bleated, frightened by the
storm.

"Oh! come near!" he went on, "come near!
fear nothing!

"Formerly I was only a soldier mingled with the
common herd of the Mercenaries, ay, and so meek
that I used to carry wood on my back for the others.
Do I trouble myself about Carthage! The crowd of

4—3

its people move as though lost in the dust of your
sandals, and all its treasures, with the provinces,
fleets, and islands, do not raise my envy like the
freshness of your lips and the turn of your shoulders.
But I wanted to throw down its walls that I might
reach you to possess you! Moreover, I was revenging
myself in the meantime! At present I crush men
like shells, and I throw myself upon phalanxes; I put
aside the sarissæ with my hands, I check the stallions
by the nostrils; a catapult would not kill me! Oh!
if you knew how I think of you in the midst of war!
Sometimes the memory of a gesture or of a fold of
your garment suddenly seizes me and entwines me
like a net! I perceive your eyes in the flames of the
phalaricas and on the gilding of the shields! I hear
your voice in the sounding of the cymbals. I turn
aside, but you are not there! and I plunge again into
the battle!"

He raised his arms whereon his veins crossed one
another like ivy on the branches of a tree. Sweat
flowed down his breast between his square muscles;
and his breathing shook his sides with his bronze
girdle all garnished with thongs hanging down to his
knees, which were firmer than marble. Salammbô,
who was accustomed to eunuchs, yielded to amazement at the strength of this man. It was the
chastisement of the goddess or the influence of
Moloch in motion around her in the five armies.
She was overwhelmed with lassitude; and she listened in a state of stupor to the intermittent shouts
of the sentinels as they answered one another.

The flames of the lamp flickered in the squalls of
hot air. There came at times broad lightning flashes;
then the darkness increased; and she could only see

Matho's eyeballs like two coals in the night. However, she felt that a fatality was surrounding her, that she had reached a supreme and irrevocable moment, and making an effort she went up again towards the zaïmph and raised her hands to seize it.

"What are you doing?" exclaimed Matho.

"I am going back to Carthage," she placidly replied.

He advanced folding his arms and with so terrible a look that her heels were immediately nailed, as it were, to the spot.

"Going back to Carthage!" He stammered, and, grinding his teeth, repeated:

"Going back to Carthage! Ah! you came to take the zaïmph, to conquer me, and then disappear! No, no! you belong to me! and no one now shall tear you from here! Oh! I have not forgotten the insolence of your large tranquil eyes, and how you crushed me with the haughtiness of your beauty! 'Tis my turn now! You are my captive, my slave, my servant! Call, if you like, on your father and his army, the Ancients, the rich, and your whole accursed people! I am the master of three hundred thousand soldiers! I will go and seek them in Lusitania, in the Gauls, and in the depths of the desert, and I will overthrow your town and burn all its temples; the triremes shall float on the waves of blood! I will not have a house, a stone, or a palm tree remaining! And if men fail me I will draw the bears from the mountains and urge on the lions! Seek not to fly or I kill you!"

Pale and with clenched fists he quivered like a harp whose strings are about to burst. Suddenly sobs stifled him, and he sank down upon his hams.

"Ah! forgive me! I am a scoundrel, and viler than scorpions, than mire and dust! Just now while you were speaking your breath passed across my face, and I rejoiced like a dying man who drinks lying flat on the edge of a stream. Crush me, if only I feel your feet! curse me, if only I hear your voice! Do not go! have pity! I love you! I love you!"

He was on his knees on the ground before her; and he encircled her form with both his arms, his head thrown back, and his hands wandering; the gold discs hanging from his ears gleamed upon his bronzed neck; big tears rolled in his eyes like silver globes; he sighed caressingly, and murmured vague words lighter than a breeze and sweet as a kiss.

Salammbô was invaded by a weakness in which she lost all consciousness of herself. Something at once inward and lofty, a command from the gods, obliged her to yield herself; clouds uplifted her, and she fell back swooning upon the bed amid the lion's hair. The zaïmph fell, and enveloped her; she could see Matho's face bending down above her breast.

"Moloch, thou burnest me!" and the soldier's kisses, more devouring than flames, covered her; she was as though swept away in a hurricane, taken in the might of the sun.

He kissed all her fingers, her arms, her feet, and the long tresses of her hair from one end to the other.

"Carry it off," he said, "what do I care? take me away with it! I abandon the army! I renounce everything! Beyond Gades, twenty days' journey into the sea, you come to an island covered with gold dust, verdure, and birds. On the mountains large flowers filled with smoking perfumes rock like

eternal censers; in the citron trees, which are higher
than cedars, milk-coloured serpents cause the fruit to
fall upon the turf with the diamonds in their jaws;
the air is so mild that it keeps you from dying. Oh!
I shall find it, you will see. We shall live in crystal
grottoes cut out at the foot of the hills. No one
dwells in it yet, or I shall become the king of the
country."

He brushed the dust off her cothurni; he wanted
her to put a quarter of a pomegranate between her
lips; he heaped up garments behind her head to make
a cushion for her. He sought for means to serve
her, and to humble himself, and he even spread the
zaïmph over her feet as if it were a mere rug.

"Have you still," he said, "those little gazelle's
horns on which your necklaces hang? You will give
them to me! I love them!" For he spoke as if
the war were finished, and joyful laughs broke from
him. The Mercenaries, Hamilcar, every obstacle had
now disappeared. The moon was gliding between
two clouds. They could see it through an opening
in the tent. "Ah, what nights have I spent gazing
at her! she seemed to me like a veil that hid your
face; you would look at me through her; the memory
of you was mingled with her beams; then I could no
longer distinguish you!" And with his head between
her breasts he wept copiously.

"And this," she thought, "is the formidable man
who makes Carthage tremble!"

He fell asleep. Then disengaging herself from his
arm she put one foot to the ground, and she perceived that her chainlet was broken.

The maidens of the great families were accustomed
to respect these shackles as something that was al-

most religious, and Salammbô, blushing, rolled the two pieces of the golden chain around her ankles.

Carthage, Megara, her house, her room, and the country that she had passed through, whirled in tumultuous yet distinct images through her memory. But an abyss had yawned and thrown them far back to an infinite distance from her.

The storm was departing; drops of water splashing rarely, one by one, made the tent-roof shake.

Matho slept like a drunken man, stretched on his side, and with one arm over the edge of the couch. His band of pearls was raised somewhat, and uncovered his brow; his teeth were parted in a smile; they shone through his black beard, and there was a silent and almost outrageous gaiety in his half-closed eyelids.

Salammbô looked at him motionless, her head bent and her hands crossed.

A dagger was displayed on a table of cypress-wood at the head of the bed; the sight of the gleaming blade fired her with a sanguinary desire. Mournful voices lingered at a distance in the shade, and like a chorus of geniuses urged her on. She approached it; she seized the steel by the handle. At the rustling of her dress Matho half opened his eyes, putting forth his mouth upon her hands, and the dagger fell.

Shouts arose; a terrible light flashed behind the canvas. Matho raised the latter; they perceived the camp of the Libyans enveloped in great flames.

Their reed huts were burning, and the twisting stems burst in the smoke and flew off like arrows; black shadows ran about distractedly on the red horizon. They could hear the shrieks of those who were in the huts; the elephants, oxen, and horses

plunged in the midst of the crowd crushing it together with the stores and baggage that were being
rescued from the fire. Trumpets sounded. There
were calls of "Matho! Matho!" Some people at the
door tried to get in.

"Come along! Hamilcar is burning the camp of
Autaritus!"

He made a spring. She found herself quite alone.

Then she examined the zaïmph; and when she
had viewed it well she was surprised that she had
not the happiness which she had once imagined to
herself. She stood with melancholy before her accomplished dream.

But the lower part of the tent was raised, and a
monstrous form appeared. Salammbô could at first
distinguish only the two eyes and a long white
beard which hung down to the ground; for the rest
of the body, which was cumbered with the rags of
a tawny garment, trailed along the earth; and with
every forward movement the hands passed into
the beard and then fell again. Crawling in this way
it reached her feet, and Salammbô recognised the
aged Gisco.

In fact, the Mercenaries had broken the legs of
the captive Ancients with a brass bar to prevent
them from taking to flight; and they were all rotting
pell-mell in a pit in the midst of filth. But the
sturdiest of them raised themselves and shouted when
they heard the noise of platters, and it was in this
way that Gisco had seen Salammbô. He had guessed
that she was a Carthaginian woman by the little balls
of sandastrum flapping against her cothurni; and
having a presentiment of an important mystery he
had succeeded, with the assistance of his companions,

in getting out of the pit; then with elbows and hands he had dragged himself twenty paces further on as far as Matho's tent. Two voices were speaking within it. He had listened outside and had heard everything.

"It is you!" she said at last, almost terrified.

"Yes, it is I!" he replied, raising himself on his wrists. "They think me dead, do they not?"

She bent her head. He resumed:

"Ah! why have the Baals not granted me this mercy!" He approached so close that he was touching her. "They would have spared me the pain of cursing you!"

Salammbô sprang quickly back, so much afraid was she of this unclean being, who was as hideous as a larva and as terrible as a phantom.

"I am nearly one hundred years old," he said. "I have seen Agathocles; I have seen Regulus and the eagles of the Romans passing over the harvests of the Punic fields! I have seen all the terrors of battles and the sea encumbered with the wrecks of our fleets! Barbarians whom I used to command have chained my four limbs like a slave that has committed murder. My companions are dying around me, one after the other; the odour of their corpses awakes me in the night; I drive away the birds that come to peck out their eyes; and yet not for a single day have I despaired of Carthage! Though I had seen all the armies of the earth against her, and the flames of the siege overtop the height of the temples, I should have still believed in her eternity! But now all is over! all is lost! The gods execrate her! A curse upon you who have quickened her ruin by your disgrace!"

She opened her lips.

"Ah! I was there!" he cried. "I heard you gur-
gling with love like a prostitute; then he told you of
his desire and you allowed him to kiss your hands!
But if the frenzy of your unchastity urged you to it,
you should at least have done as do the fallow deer,
which hide themselves in their copulations, and not
have displayed your shame beneath your father's very
eyes!"

"What?" she said.

"Ah! you did not know that the two entrenchments are sixty cubits from each other and that your
Matho, in the excess of his pride, has posted himself
just in front of Hamilcar. Your father is there behind
you; and could I climb the path which leads to the
platform, I should cry to him: 'Come and see your
daughter in the Barbarian's arms! She has put on the
garment of the goddess to please him; and in yielding her body to him she surrenders with the glory of
your name the majesty of the gods, the vengeance of
her country, even the safety of Carthage!" The motion of his toothless mouth moved his beard throughout its length; his eyes were riveted upon her and
devoured her; panting in the dust he repeated:

"Ah! sacrilegious one! May you be accursed! accursed! accursed!"

Salammbô had drawn back the canvas; she held it
raised at arm's length, and without answering him she
looked in the direction of Hamilcar.

"It is this way, is it not?" she said.

"What matters it to you? Turn away! Begone!
Rather crush your face against the earth! It is a holy
spot which would be polluted by your gaze!"

She threw the zaïmph about her waist, and quickly
picked up her veils, mantle, and scarf. "I hasten

thither!" she cried; and making her escape Salammbô disappeared.

At first she walked through the darkness without meeting any one, for all were betaking themselves to the fire; the uproar was increasing and great flames purpled the sky behind; a long terrace stopped her.

She turned round to right and left at random, seeking for a ladder, a rope, a stone, something in short to assist her. She was afraid of Gisco, and it seemed to her that shouts and footsteps were pursuing her. Day was beginning to break. She perceived a path in the thickness of the entrenchment. She took the hem of her robe, which impeded her, in her teeth, and in three bounds she was on the platform.

A sonorous shout burst forth beneath her in the shade, the same which she had heard at the foot of the galley staircase, and leaning over she recognised Schahabarim's man with his coupled horses.

He had wandered all night between the two entrenchments; then disquieted by the fire, he had gone back again trying to see what was passing in Matho's camp; and, knowing that this spot was nearest to his tent, he had not stirred from it, in obedience to the priest's command.

He stood up on one of the horses. Salammbô let herself slide down to him; and they fled at full gallop, circling the Punic camp in search of a gate.

Matho had re-entered his tent. The smoky lamp gave but little light, and he also believed that Salammbô was asleep. Then he delicately touched the lion's skin on the palm-tree bed. He called but she did not answer; he quickly tore away a strip of the canvas to let in some light; the zaïmph was gone.

The earth trembled beneath thronging feet. Shouts, neighings, and clashing of armour rose in the air, and clarion flourishes sounded the charge. It was as though a hurricane were whirling around him. Immoderate frenzy made him leap upon his arms, and he dashed outside.

The long files of the Barbarians were descending the mountain at a run, and the Punic squares were advancing against them with a heavy and regular oscillation. The mist, rent by the rays of the sun, formed little rocking clouds which as they rose gradually discovered standards, helmets, and points of pikes. Beneath the rapid evolutions portions of the earth which were still in the shadow seemed to be displaced bodily; in other places it looked as if huge torrents were crossing one another, while thorny masses stood motionless between them. Matho could distinguish the captains, soldiers, heralds, and even the serving-men, who were mounted on asses in the rear. But instead of maintaining his position in order to cover the foot-soldiers, Narr' Havas turned abruptly to the right, as though he wished himself to be crushed by Hamilcar.

His horsemen outstripped the elephants, which were slackening their speed; and all the horses, stretching out their unbridled heads, galloped at so furious a rate that their bellies seemed to graze the earth. Then suddenly Narr' Havas went resolutely up to a sentry. He threw away his sword, lance and javelins, and disappeared among the Carthaginians.

The king of the Numidians reached Hamilcar's tent, and pointing to his men, who were standing still at a distance, he said:

"Barca! I bring them to you. They are yours."

Then he prostrated himself in token of bondage, and to prove his fidelity recalled all his conduct from the beginning of the war.

First, he had prevented the siege of Carthage and the massacre of the captives; then he had taken no advantage of the victory over Hanno after the defeat at Utica. As to the Tyrian towns, they were on the frontiers of his kingdom. Finally he had not taken part in the battle of the Macaras; and he had even expressly absented himself in order to evade the obligation of fighting against the Suffet.

Narr' Havas had in fact wished to aggrandise himself by encroachments upon the Punic provinces, and had alternately assisted and forsaken the Mercenaries according to the chances of victory. But seeing that Hamilcar would ultimately prove the stronger, he had gone over to him; and in his desertion there was perhaps something of a grudge against Matho, whether on account of the command or of his former love.

The Suffet listened without interrupting him. The man who thus presented himself in an army where vengeance was his due was not an auxiliary to be despised; Hamilcar at once divined the utility of such an alliance in his great projects. With the Numidians he would get rid of the Libyans. Then he would draw off the West to the conquest of Iberia; and, without asking Narr' Havas why he had not come sooner, or noticing any of his lies, he kissed him, striking his breast thrice against his own.

It was to bring matters to an end and in despair that he had fired the camp of the Libyans. This army came to him like a relief from the gods; dissembling his joy he replied:

"May the Baals favour you! I do not know what

the Republic will do for you, but Hamilcar is not ungrateful."

The tumult increased; some captains entered. He was arming himself as he spoke.

"Come, return! You will use your horsemen to beat down their infantry between your elephants and mine. Courage! exterminate them!"

And Narr' Havas was rushing away when Salammbô appeared.

She leaped down quickly from her horse. She opened her ample cloak and spreading out her arms displayed the zaïmph.

The leathern tent, which was raised at the corners, left visible the entire circuit of the mountain with its thronging soldiers, and as it was in the centre Salammbô could be seen on all sides. An immense shouting burst forth, a long cry of triumph and hope. Those who were marching stopped; the dying leaned on their elbows and turned round to bless her. All the Barbarians knew now that she had recovered the zaïmph; they saw her or believed that they saw her from a distance; and other cries, but those of rage and vengeance, resounded in spite of the plaudits of the Carthaginians. Thus did the five armies in tiers upon the mountain stamp and shriek around Salammbô.

Hamilcar, who was unable to speak, nodded her his thanks. His eyes were directed alternately upon the zaïmph and upon her, and he noticed that her chainlet was broken. Then he shivered, being seized with a terrible suspicion. But soon recovering his impassibility he looked sideways at Narr' Havas without turning his face.

The king of the Numidians held himself apart in a discreet attitude; on his forehead he bore a little of the dust which he had touched when prostrating himself. At last the Suffet advanced towards him with a look full of gravity.

"As a reward for the services which you have rendered me, Narr' Havas, I give you my daughter. Be my son," he added, "and defend your father!"

Narr' Havas gave a great gesture of surprise; then he threw himself upon Hamilcar's hands and covered them with kisses.

Salammbô, calm as a statue, did not seem to understand. She blushed a little as she cast down her eyelids, and her long curved lashes made shadows upon her cheeks.

Hamilcar wished to unite them immediately in indissoluble betrothal. A lance was placed in Salammbô's hands and by her offered to Narr' Havas; their thumbs were tied together with a thong of ox-leather; then corn was poured upon their heads, and the grains that fell around them rang like rebounding hail.

XII.

The Aqueduct.

TWELVE hours afterwards all that remained of the Mercenaries was a heap of wounded, dead, and dying. Hamilcar had suddenly emerged from the bottom of the gorge, and again descended the western slope that looked towards Hippo-Zarytus, and the space being broader at this spot he had taken care to draw the Barbarians into it. Narr' Havas had encompassed them with his horse; the Suffet meanwhile drove them back and crushed them. Then, too, they were conquered beforehand by the loss of the zaïmph; even those who cared nothing about it had experienced anguish and something akin to enfeeblement. Hamilcar, not indulging his pride by holding the field of battle, had retired a little further off on the left to some heights, from which he commanded them.

The shape of the camps could be recognised by their sloping palisades. A long heap of black cinders was smoking on the site of the Libyans; the devastated soil showed undulations like the sea, and the tents with their tattered canvas looked like dim ships half lost in the breakers. Cuirasses, forks,

(41)

clarions, pieces of wood, iron and brass, corn, straw, and garments were scattered about among the corpses; here and there a phalarica on the point of extinction burned against a heap of baggage; in some places the earth was hidden with shields; horses' carcasses succeeded one another like a series of hillocks; legs, sandals, arms, and coats of mail were to be seen, with heads held in their helmets by the chin-pieces and rolling about like balls; heads of hair were hanging on the thorns; elephants were lying with their towers in pools of blood, with entrails exposed, and gasping. The foot trod on slimy things, and there were swamps of mud although no rain had fallen.

This confusion of dead bodies covered the whole mountain from top to bottom.

Those who survived stirred as little as the dead. Squatting in unequal groups they looked at one another scared and without speaking.

The lake of Hippo-Zarytus shone at the end of a long meadow beneath the setting sun. To the right an agglomeration of white houses extended beyond a girdle of walls; then the sea spread out indefinitely; and the Barbarians, with their chins in their hands, sighed as they thought of their native lands. A cloud of grey dust was falling.

The evening wind blew; then every breast dilated, and as the freshness increased, the vermin might be seen to forsake the dead, who were colder now, and to run over the hot sand. Crows, looking towards the dying, rested motionless on the tops of the big stones.

When night had fallen yellow-haired dogs, those unclean beasts which followed the armies, came quite softly into the midst of the Barbarians. At first they

licked the clots of blood on the still tepid stumps; and soon they began to devour the corpses, biting into the stomachs first of all.

The fugitives reappeared one by one like shadows; the women also ventured to return, for there were still some of them left, especially among the Libyans, in spite of the dreadful massacre of them by the Numidians.

Some took ropes' ends and lighted them to use as torches. Others held crossed pikes. The corpses were placed upon these and were conveyed apart.

They were found lying stretched in long lines, on their backs, with their mouths open, and their lances beside them; or else they were piled up pell-mell so that it was often necessary to dig out a whole heap in order to discover those that were wanting. Then the torch would be passed slowly over their faces. They had received complicated wounds from hideous weapons. Greenish strips hung from their foreheads; they were cut in pieces, crushed to the marrow, blue from strangulation, or broadly cleft by the elephants' ivory. Although they had died at almost the same time there existed differences between their various states of corruption. The men of the North were puffed up with livid swellings, while the more nervous Africans looked as though they had been smoked, and were already drying up. The Mercenaries might be recognised by the tattooing on their hands: the old soldiers of Antiochus displayed a sparrow-hawk; those who had served in Egypt, the head of the cynocephalus; those who had served with the princes of Asia, a hatchet, a pomegranate, or a hammer; those who had served in the Greek republics, the side-view of a citadel or the name of an archon; and some were

4—4

to be seen whose arms were entirely covered with these multiplied symbols, which mingled with their scars and their recent wounds.

Four great funeral piles were erected for the men of Latin race, the Samnites, Etruscans, Campanians, and Bruttians.

The Greeks dug pits with the points of their swords. The Spartans removed their red cloaks and wrapped them round the dead; the Athenians laid them out with their faces towards the rising sun; the Cantabrians buried them beneath a heap of pebbles; the Nasamonians bent them double with ox-leather thongs, and the Garamantians went and interred them on the shore so that they might be perpetually washed by the waves. But the Latins were grieved that they could not collect the ashes in urns; the Nomads regretted the heat of the sands in which bodies were mummified, and the Celts, the three rude stones beneath a rainy sky at the end of an islet-covered gulf.

Vociferations arose, followed by a lengthened silence. This was to oblige the souls to return. Then the shouting was resumed persistently at regular intervals.

They made excuses to the dead for their inability to honour them as the rites prescribed: for, owing to this deprivation, they would pass for infinite periods through all kinds of chances and metamorphoses; they questioned them and asked them what they desired; others loaded them with abuse for having allowed themselves to be conquered.

The bloodless faces lying back here and there on wrecks of armour showed pale in the light of the great funeral-pile; tears provoked tears, the sobs became shriller, the recognitions and embracings more their eyes with the bodkins of their hair. The men came next and tortured them from their feet, which they cut off at the ankles, to their foreheads, from which they took crowns of skin to put upon their own heads. The Eaters of Uncleanness were atrocious in their devices. They envenomed the wounds by pouring into them dust, vinegar, and fragments of pottery; others waited behind; blood flowed, and they rejoiced like vintagers round fuming vats.

Matho, however, was seated on the ground, at the very place where he had happened to be when the battle ended, his elbows on his knees, and his temples in his hands; he saw nothing, heard nothing, and had ceased to think.

At the shrieks of joy uttered by the crowd he raised his head. Before him a strip of canvas caught on a pole, and trailing on the ground, sheltered in confused fashion baskets, carpets, and a lion's skin. He recognised his tent; and he riveted his eyes upon the ground as though Hamilcar's daughter, when she disappeared, had sunk into the earth.

The torn canvas flapped in the wind; the long rags of it sometimes passed across his mouth, and he perceived a red mark like the print of a hand. It was the hand of Narr' Havas, the token of their alliance. Then Matho rose. He took a firebrand which was still smoking, and threw it disdainfully upon the wrecks of his tent. Then with the toe of his cothurn he pushed the things which fell out back towards the flame so that nothing might be left.

Suddenly, without any one being able to guess from what point he had sprung up, Spendius appeared.

The former slave had fastened two fragments of a

lance against his thigh; he limped with a piteous look, breathing forth complaints the while.

"Remove that," said Matho to him. "I know that you are a brave fellow!" For he was so crushed by the injustice of the gods that he had not strength enough to be indignant with men.

Spendius beckoned to him and led him to a hollow of the mountain, where Zarxas and Autaritus were lying concealed.

They had fled like the slave, the one although he was cruel, and the other in spite of his bravery. But who, said they, could have expected the treachery of Narr' Havas, the burning of the camp of the Libyans, the loss of the zaïmph, the sudden attack by Hamilcar, and, above all, his manœuvres which forced them to return to the bottom of the mountain beneath the instant blows of the Carthaginians? Spendius made no acknowledgment of his terror, and persisted in maintaining that his leg was broken.

At last the three chiefs and the schalischim asked one another what decision should now be adopted.

Hamilcar closed the road to Carthage against them; they were caught between his soldiers and the provinces belonging to Narr' Havas; the Tyrian towns would join the conquerors; the Barbarians would find themselves driven to the edge of the sea, and all these united forces would crush them. This would infallibly happen.

Thus no means presented themselves of avoiding the war. Accordingly they must prosecute it to the bitter end. But how were they to make the necessity of an interminable battle understood by all these disheartened people, who were still bleeding from their wounds.

"I will undertake that!" said Spendius.

Two hours afterwards a man who came from the direction of Hippo-Zarytus climbed the mountain at a run. He waved some tablets at arm's length, and as he shouted very loudly the Barbarians surrounded him.

The tablets had been despatched by the Greek soldiers in Sardinia. They recommended their African comrades to watch over Gisco and the other captives. A Samian trader, one Hipponax, coming from Carthage, had informed them that a plot was being organised to promote their escape, and the Barbarians were urged to take every precaution; the Republic was powerful.

Spendius's stratagem did not succeed at first as he had hoped. This assurance of the new peril, so far from exciting frenzy, raised fears; and remembering Hamilcar's warning, lately thrown into their midst, they expected something unlooked for and terrible. The night was spent in great distress; several even got rid of their weapons, so as to soften the Suffet when he presented himself.

But on the following day, at the third watch, a second runner appeared, still more breathless and blackened with dust. The Greek snatched from his hand a roll of papyrus covered with Phœnician writing. The Mercenaries were entreated not to be disheartened; the brave men of Tunis were coming with large reinforcements.

Spendius first read the letter three times in succession; and held up by two Cappadocians, who bore him seated on their shoulders, he had himself conveyed from place to place and re-read it. For seven hours he harangued.

He reminded the Mercenaries of the promises of the Great Council; the Africans of the cruelties of the stewards, and all the Barbarians of the injustice of Carthage. The Suffet's mildness was only a bait to capture them; those who surrendered would be sold as slaves, and the vanquished would perish under torture. As to flight, what routes could they follow? Not a nation would receive them. Whereas by continuing their efforts they would obtain at once freedom, vengeance, and money! And they would not have long to wait, since the people of Tunis, the whole of Libya, was rushing to relieve them. He showed the unrolled papyrus: "Look at it! read! see their promises! I do not lie."

Dogs were straying about with their black muzzles all plastered with red. The men's uncovered heads were growing hot in the burning sun. A nauseous smell exhaled from the badly buried corpses. Some even projected from the earth as far as the waist. Spendius called them to witness what he was saying; then he raised his fists in the direction of Hamilcar.

Matho, moreover, was watching him, and to cover his cowardice he displayed an anger by which he gradually found himself carried away. Devoting himself to the gods he heaped curses upon the Carthaginians. The torture of the captives was child's play. Why spare them, and be ever dragging this useless cattle after one? "No! we must put an end to it! their designs are known! a single one might ruin us! no pity! Those who are worthy will be known by the speed of their legs and the force of their blows."

Then they turned again upon the captives. Several were still in the last throes; they were finished by a thrust of a heel in the mouth or a stab with the point of a javelin.

Then they thought of Gisco. Nowhere could he be seen; they were disturbed with anxiety. They wished at once to convince themselves of his death and to participate in it. At last three Samnite shepherds discovered him at a distance of fifteen paces from the spot where Matho's tent lately stood. They recognized him by his long beard and they called the rest.

Stretched on his back, his arms against his hips, and his knees close together, he looked like a dead man laid out for the tomb. Nevertheless his wasted sides rose and fell, and his eyes, wide-opened in his pallid face, gazed in a continuous and intolerable fashion.

The Barbarians looked at him at first with great astonishment. Since he had been living in the pit he had been almost forgotten; rendered uneasy by old memories they stood at a distance and did not venture to raise their hands against him.

But those who were behind were murmuring and pressing forward when a Garamantian passed through the crowd; he was brandishing a sickle; all understood his thought; their faces purpled, and smitten with shame they shrieked:

"Yes! yes!"

The man with the curved steel approached Gisco. He took his head, and, resting it upon his knee, sawed it off with rapid strokes; it fell; two great jets of blood made a hole in the dust. Zarxas leaped upon it, and lighter than a leopard ran towards the Carthaginians.

Then when he had covered two thirds of the mountain he drew Gisco's head from his breast by the beard, whirled his arm rapidly several times,— and the mass, when thrown at last, described a long parabola and disappeared behind the Punic entrenchments.

Soon at the edge of the palisades there rose two crossed standards, the customary sign for claiming a corpse.

Then four heralds, chosen for their width of chest, went out with great clarions, and speaking through the brass tubes declared that henceforth there would be between Carthaginians and Barbarians neither faith, pity, nor gods, that they refused all overtures beforehand, and that envoys would be sent back with their hands cut off.

Immediately afterwards, Spendius was sent to Hippo-Zarytus to procure provisions; the Tyrian city sent them some the same evening. They ate greedily. Then when they were strengthened they speedily collected the remains of their baggage and their broken arms; the women massed themselves in the centre, and heedless of the wounded left weeping behind them, they set out along the edge of the shore like a herd of wolves taking its departure.

They were marching upon Hippo-Zarytus, resolved to take it, for they had need of a town.

Hamilcar, as he perceived them at a distance, had a feeling of despair in spite of the pride which he experienced in seeing them fly before him. He ought to have attacked them immediately with fresh troops. Another similar day and the war was over! If matters were protracted they would return with greater strength; the Tyrian towns would join them; his clemency towards the vanquished had been of no avail. He resolved to be pitiless.

The same evening he sent the Great Council a dromedary laden with bracelets collected from the dead, and with horrible threats ordered another army to be despatched.

All had for a long time believed him lost; so that on learning his victory they felt a stupefaction which was almost terror. The vaguely announced return of the zaïmph completed the wonder. Thus the gods and the might of Carthage seemed now to belong to him.

None of his enemies ventured upon complaint or recrimination. Owing to the enthusiasm of some and the pusillanimity of the rest, an army of five thousand men was ready before the interval prescribed had elapsed.

This army promptly made its way to Utica in order to support the Suffet's rear, while three thousand of the most notable citizens embarked in vessels which were to land them at Hippo-Zarytus, whence they were to drive back the Barbarians.

Hanno had accepted the command; but he intrusted the army to his lieutenant, Magdassin, so as to lead the troops which were to be disembarked himself, for he could no longer endure the shaking of the litter. His disease had eaten away his lips and nostrils, and had hollowed out a large hole in his face; the back of his throat could be seen at a distance of ten paces, and he knew himself to be so hideous that he wore a veil over his head like a woman.

Hippo-Zarytus paid no attention to his summonings nor yet to those of the Barbarians; but every morning the inhabitants lowered provisions to the latter in baskets, and shouting from the tops of the towers pleaded the exigencies of the Republic and conjured them to withdraw. By means of signs they addressed the same protestations to the Carthaginians who were stationed on the sea.

Hanno contented himself with blockading the harbour without risking an attack. However, he persuaded the judges of Hippo-Zarytus to admit three hundred soldiers. Then he departed to the Cape Grapes, and made a long circuit so as to hem in the Barbarians, an inopportune and even dangerous operation. His jealousy prevented him from relieving the Suffet; he arrested his spies, impeded him in all his plans, and compromised the success of the enterprise. At last Hamilcar wrote to the Great Council to rid him of Hanno, and the latter returned to Carthage furious at the baseness of the Ancients and the madness of his colleague. Hence, after so many hopes, the situation was now still more deplorable; but there was an effort not to reflect upon it and even not to talk about it.

As if all this were not sufficient misfortune at one time, news came that the Sardinian Mercenaries had crucified their general, seized the strongholds, and everywhere slaughtered those of Chanaanitish race. The Roman people threatened the Republic with immediate hostilities unless she gave twelve hundred talents with the whole of the island of Sardinia. They had accepted the alliance of the Barbarians, and they despatched to them flat-bottomed boats laden with meal and dried meat. The Carthaginians pursued these, and captured five hundred men; but three days afterwards a fleet coming from Byzacena, and conveying provisions to Carthage, foundered in a storm. The gods were evidently declaring against her.

Upon this the citizens of Hippo-Zarytus, under
pretence of an alarm, made Hanno's three hundred
men ascend their walls; then coming behind them
they took them by the legs, and suddenly threw them
over the ramparts. Some who were not killed were
pursued, and went and drowned themselves in the
sea.

Utica was enduring the presence of soldiers, for
Magdassin had acted like Hanno, and in accordance
with his orders and deaf to Hamilcar's prayers,
was surrounding the town. As for these, they were
given wine mixed with mandrake, and were then
slaughtered in their sleep. At the same time the
Barbarians arrived; Magdassin fled; the gates were
opened; and thenceforward the two Tyrian towns displayed an obstinate devotion to their new friends and
an inconceivable hatred to their former allies.

This abandonment of the Punic cause was a
counsel and a precedent. Hopes of deliverance revived. Populations hitherto uncertain hesitated no
longer. Everywhere there was a stir. The Suffet
learnt this, and he had no assistance to look for! He
was now irrevocably lost.

He immediately dismissed Narr' Havas, who was
to guard the borders of his kingdom. As for himself,
he resolved to re-enter Carthage in order to obtain
soldiers and begin the war again.

The Barbarians posted at Hippo-Zarytus perceived
his army as it descended the mountain.

Where could the Carthaginians be going? Hunger,
no doubt, was urging them on; and, distracted by
their sufferings, they were coming in spite of their
weakness to give battle. But they turned to the
right: they were fleeing. They might be overtaken

and all be crushed. The Barbarians dashed in pursuit of them.

The Carthaginians were checked by the river. It was wide this time and the west wind had not been blowing. Some crossed by swimming, and the rest on their shields. They resumed their march. Night fell. They were out of sight.

The Barbarians did not stop; they went higher to find a narrower place. The people of Tunis hastened thither, bringing those of Utica along with them. Their numbers increased at every bush; and the Carthaginians, as they lay on the ground, could hear the tramping of their feet in the darkness. From time to time Barca had a volley of arrows discharged behind him in order to check them, and several were killed. When day broke they were in the Ariana Mountains, at the spot where the road makes a bend.

Then Matho, who was marching at the head, thought that he could distinguish something green on the horizon on the summit of an eminence. Then the ground sank, and obelisks, domes, and houses appeared! It was Carthage. He leaned against a tree to keep himself from falling, so rapidly did his heart beat.

He thought of all that had come to pass in his existence since the last time that he had passed that way! It was an infinite surprise, it stunned him. Then he was transported with joy at the thought of seeing Salammbô again. The reasons which he had for execrating her returned to his recollection, but he very quickly rejected them. Quivering and with straining eyeballs he gazed at the lofty terrace of a palace above the palm trees beyond Eschmoun; a

smile of ecstasy lighted his face as if some great
light had reached him; he opened his arms, and sent
kisses on the breeze, and murmured: "Come! come!"
A sigh swelled his breast, and two long tears like
pearls fell upon his beard.

"What stays you?" cried Spendius. "Make
haste! Forward! The Suffet is going to escape us!
But your knees are tottering, and you are looking at
me like a drunken man!"

He stamped with impatience and urged Matho,
his eyes twinkling as at the approach of an object
long aimed at.

"Ah! we have reached it! We are there! I
have them!"

He had so convinced and triumphant an air that
Matho was surprised from his torpor, and felt himself
carried away by it. These words, coming when his
distress was at its height, drove his despair to vengeance, and pointed to food for his wrath. He bounded
upon one of the camels that were among the baggage, snatched up its halter, and with the long rope,
struck the stragglers with all his might, running right
and left alternately, in the rear of the army, like a
dog driving a flock.

At his thundering voice the lines of men closed
up; even the lame hurried their steps; the intervening space lessened in the middle of the isthmus.
The foremost of the Barbarians were marching in the
dust raised by the Carthaginians. The two armies
were coming close, and were on the point of touching. But the Malqua gate, the Tagaste gate, and the
great gate of Khamon threw wide their leaves. The
Punic square divided; three columns were swallowed
up, and eddied beneath the porches. Soon the mass,

being too tightly packed, could advance no further; pikes clashed in the air, and the arrows of the Barbarians were shivering against the walls.

Hamilcar was to be seen on the threshold of Khamon. He turned round and shouted to his men to move aside. He dismounted from his horse; and pricking it on the croup with the sword which he held, sent it against the Barbarians.

It was a black stallion, which was fed on balls of meal, and would bend its knees to allow its master to mount. Why was he sending it away? Was this a sacrifice?

The noble horse galloped into the midst of the lances, knocked down men, and, entangling its feet in its entrails, fell down, then rose again with furious leaps; and while they were moving aside, trying to stop it, or looking at it in surprise, the Carthaginians had united again; they entered, and the enormous gate shut echoing behind them.

It would not yield. The Barbarians came crushing against it; — and for some minutes there was an oscillation throughout the army, which became weaker and weaker, and at last ceased.

The Carthaginians had placed soldiers on the aqueduct, they began to hurl stones, balls, and beams. Spendius represented that it would be best not to persist. The Barbarians went and posted themselves further off, all being quite resolved to lay siege to Carthage.

The rumour of the war, however, had passed beyond the confines of the Punic empire; and from the pillars of Hercules to beyond Cyrene shepherds mused on it as they kept their flocks, and caravans

talked about it at night in the light of the stars.
This great Carthage, mistress of the seas, splendid as
the sun, and terrible as a god, actually found men
who were daring enough to attack her! Her fall
even had been asserted several times; and all had
believed it for all wished it: the subject populations, the tributary villages, the allied provinces, the
independent hordes, those who execrated her for her
tyranny or were jealous of her power, or coveted
her wealth. The bravest had very speedily joined the
Mercenaries. The defeat at the Macaras had checked
all the rest. At last they had recovered confidence,
had gradually advanced and approached; and now
the men of the eastern regions were lying on the
sandhills of Clypea on the other side of the gulf. As
soon as they perceived the Barbarians they showed
themselves.

They were not Libyans from the neighbourhood
of Carthage, who had long composed the third army,
but nomads from the tableland of Barca, bandits from
Cape Phiscus and the promontory of Dernah, from
Phazzana and Marmarica. They had crossed the
desert, drinking at the brackish wells walled in with
camels' bones; the Zuaeces, with their covering of
ostrich feathers, had come on quadrigæ; the Garamantians, masked with black veils, rode behind on their
painted mares; others were mounted on asses, onagers,
zebras, and buffaloes; while some dragged after
them the roofs of their sloop-shaped huts together
with their families and idols. There were Ammo-
nians with limbs wrinkled by the hot water of the
springs; Atarantians, who curse the sun; Troglodytes,
who bury their dead with laughter beneath branches
of trees; and the hideous Auseans, who eat grass-

4—5

hoppers; the Achyrmachidæ, who eat lice; and the vermilion-painted Gysantians, who eat apes.

All were ranged along the edge of the sea in a great straight line. Afterwards they advanced like tornadoes of sand raised by the wind. In the centre of the isthmus the throng stopped, the Mercenaries, who were posted in front of them, close to the walls, being unwilling to move.

Then from the direction of Ariana appeared the men of the West, the people of the Numidians. In fact, Narr' Havas governed only the Massylians; and, moreover, as they were permitted by custom to abandon their king when reverses were sustained, they had assembled on the Zainus, and then had crossed it at Hamilcar's first movement. First were seen running up all the hunters from Malethut-Baal and Gáraphos, clad in lions' skins, and with the staves of their pikes driving small lean horses with long manes; then marched the Gætulians in cuirasses of serpents' skin; then the Pharusians, wearing lofty crowns made of wax and resin; and the Caunians, Macarians, and Tillabarians, each holding two javelins and a round shield of hippopotamus leather. They stopped at the foot of the Catacombs among the first pools of the Lagoon.

But when the Libyans had moved away, the multitude of the Negroes appeared like a cloud on a level with the ground, in the place which the others had occupied. They were there from the White Harousch, the Black Harousch, the desert of Augila, and even from the great country of Agazymba, which is four months' journey south of the Garamantians, and from regions further still! In spite of their red

wooden jewels, the filth of their black skin made
them look like mulberries that had been long rolling
in the dust. They had bark-thread drawers, dried-
grass tunics, fallow-deer muzzles on their heads; they
shook rods furnished with rings, and brandished cows'
tails at the end of sticks, after the fashion of standards, howling the while like wolves.

Then behind the Numidians, Marusians, and Gætu
lians pressed the yellowish men, who are spread
through the cedar forests beyond Taggir. They
had cat-skin quivers flapping against their shoulders,
and they led in leashes enormous dogs, which were
as high as asses, and did not bark.

Finally, as though Africa had not been sufficiently
emptied, and it had been necessary to seek further
fury in the very dregs of the races, men might be
seen behind the rest, with beast-like profiles and
grinning with idiotic laughter — wretches ravaged
by hideous diseases, deformed pigmies, mulattoes of
doubtful sex, albinos whose red eyes blinked in the
sun; stammering out unintelligible sounds, they put a
finger into their mouths to show that they were
hungry.

The confusion of weapons was as great as that of
garments and peoples. There was not a deadly invention that was not present — from wooden daggers,
stone hatchets and ivory tridents, to long sabres
toothed like saws, slender, and formed of a yielding
copper blade. They handled cutlasses which were
forked into several branches like antelopes' horns,
bills fastened to the ends of ropes, iron triangles,
clubs and bodkins. The Ethiopians from the Bam-
botus had little poisoned darts hidden in their nair.

Many had brought pebbles in bags. Others, empty handed, chattered with their teeth.

This multitude was stirred with a ceaseless swell. Dromedaries, smeared all over with tar-like streaks, knocked down the women, who carried their children on their hips. The provisions in the baskets were pouring out; in walking, pieces of salt, parcels of gum, rotten dates, and gourou nuts were crushed under foot; and sometimes on vermin-covered bosoms there would hang a slender cord supporting a diamond that the Satraps had sought, an almost fabulous stone, sufficient to purchase an empire. Most of them did not even know what they desired. They were impelled by fascination or curiosity; and nomads who had never seen a town were frightened by the shadows of the walls.

The isthmus was now hidden by men; and this long surface, whereon the tents were like huts amid an inundation, stretched as far as the first lines of the other Barbarians, which were streaming with steel and were posted symmetrically upon both sides of the aqueduct.

The Carthaginians had not recovered from the terror caused by their arrival when they perceived the siege-engines sent by the Tyrian towns coming straight towards them like monsters and like buildings — with their masts, arms, ropes, articulations, capitals and carapaces, sixty carroballistas, eighty onagers, thirty scorpions, fifty tollenos, twelve rams, and three gigantic catapults which hurled pieces of rock of the weight of fifteen talents. Masses of men clinging to their bases pushed them on; at every step a quivering shook them, and in this way they arrived in front of the walls.

But several days were still needed to finish the preparations for the siege. The Mercenaries, taught by their defeats, would not risk themselves in useless engagements; and on both sides there was no haste, for it was well known that a terrible action was about to open, and that the result of it would be complete victory or complete extermination.

Carthage might hold out for a long time; her broad walls presented a series of re-entrant and projecting angles, an advantageous arrangement for repelling assaults.

Nevertheless a portion had fallen down in the direction of the Catacombs, and on dark nights lights could be seen in the dens of Malqua through the disjointed blocks. These in some places overlooked the top of the ramparts. It was here that the Mercenaries' wives, who had been driven away by Matho, were living with their new husbands. On seeing the men again their hearts could stand it no longer. They waved their scarfs at a distance; then they came and chatted in the darkness with the soldiers through the cleft in the wall, and one morning the Great Council learned that they had all fled. Some had passed through between the stones; others with greater intrepidity had let themselves down with ropes.

At last Spendius resolved to accomplish his design.

The war, by keeping him at a distance, had hitherto prevented him; and since the return to before Carthage, it seemed to him that the inhabitants suspected his enterprise. But soon they diminished the sentries on the aqueduct. There were not too many people for the defence of the walls.

The former slave practised himself for some days in shooting arrows at the flamingoes on the lake. Then one moonlight evening he begged Matho to light a great fire of straw in the middle of the night, while all his men were to shout at the same time; and taking Zarxas with him, he went away along the edge of the gulf in the direction of Tunis.

When on a level with the last arches they returned straight towards the aqueduct; the place was unprotected: they crawled to the base of the pillars.

The sentries on the platform were walking quietly up and down.

Towering flames appeared; clarions rang; and the soldiers on vedette, believing that there was an assault, rushed away in the direction of Carthage.

One man had remained. He showed black against the background of the sky. The moon was shining behind him, and his shadow, which was of extravagant size, looked in the distance like an obelisk proceeding across the plain.

They waited until he was in position just before them. Zarxas seized his sling, but whether from prudence or from ferocity Spendius stopped him. "No, the whiz of the bullet would make a noise! Let me!"

Then he bent his bow with all his strength, resting the lower end of it against the great toe of his left foot; he took aim, and the arrow went off.

The man did not fall. He disappeared.

"If he were wounded we should hear him!" said Spendius; and he mounted quickly from story to story as he had done the first time, with the assisttance of a rope and a harpoon. Then when he had reached the top and was beside the corpse, he let it fall again. The Balearian fastened a pick and a mallet to it and turned back.

The trumpets sounded no longer. All was now quiet. Spendius had raised one of the flag-stones and, entering the water, had closed it behind him.

Calculating the distance by the number of his steps, he arrived at the exact spot where he had noticed an oblique fissure; and for three hours until morning he worked in continuous and furious fashion, breathing with difficulty through the interstices in the upper flag-stones, assailed with anguish, and twenty times believing that he was going to die. At last a crack was heard, and a huge stone ricocheting on the lower arches rolled to the ground,— and suddenly a cataract, an entire river, fell from the skies into the plain. The aqueduct, being cut through in the centre, was emptying itself. It was death to Carthage and victory for the Barbarians.

In an instant the awakened Carthaginians appeared on the walls, the houses, and the temples. The Barbarians pressed forward with shouts. They danced in delirium around the great waterfall, and came up and wet their heads in it in the extravagance of their joy.

A man in a torn, brown tunic was perceived on the summit of the aqueduct. He stood leaning over the very edge with both hands on his hips, and was looking down below him as though astonished at his work.

Then he drew himself up. He surveyed the horizon with a haughty air which seemed to say: "All that is now mine!" The applause of the Barbarians burst forth, while the Carthaginians, comprehending their disaster at last, shrieked with despair. Then he began to run about the platform from one end to the other, — and like a chariot-driver triumphant at the Olympic Games, Spendius, distraught with pride, raised his arms aloft.

XIII.

THE Barbarians had no need of a circumvallation on the side of Africa, for it was theirs. But to facilitate the approach to the walls, the entrenchments bordering the ditch were thrown down. Matho next divided the army into great semicircles so as to encompass Carthage the better. The hoplites of the Mercenaries were placed in the first rank, and behind them the slingers and horsemen; quite at the back were the baggage, chariots, and horses; and the engines bristled in front of this throng at a distance of three hundred paces from the towers.

Amid the infinite variety of their nomenclature (which changed several times in the course of the centuries) these machines might be reduced to two systems: some acted like slings, and the rest like bows.

The first, which were the catapults, was composed of a square frame with two vertical uprights and a horizontal bar. In its anterior portion was a cylinder, furnished with cables, which held back a great beam bearing a spoon for the reception of projectiles; its base was caught in a skein of twisted thread, and when the ropes were let go it sprang up and struck against the bar, which, checking it with a shock, multiplied its power.

The second presented a more complicated mechanism. A cross-bar had its centre fixed on a little pillar, and from this point of juncti n there branched off at right angles a sort of channel; two caps containing twists of horse-hair stood at the extremities of the cross-bar; two small beams were fastened to them to hold the extremities of a rope which was brought to the bottom of the channel upon a tablet of bronze. This metal plate was released by a spring, and sliding in grooves impelled the arrows.

The catapults were likewise called onagers, after the wild asses which fling up stones with their feet, and the ballistas scorpions, on account of a hook which stood upon the tablet, and being lowered by a blow of the fist, released the spring.

Their construction required learned calculations; the wood selected had to be of the hardest substance, and their gearing all of brass; they were stretched with levers, tackle-blocks, capstans or tympanums; the direction of the shooting was changed by means of strong pivots; they were moved forward on cylinders, and the most considerable of them, which were brought piece by piece, were set up in front of the enemy.

Spendius arranged three great catapults opposite the three principal angles; he placed a ram before every gate, a ballista before every tower, while carroballistas were to move about in the rear. But it was necessary to protect them against the fire thrown by the besieged, and first of all to fill up the trench which separated them from the walls.

They pushed forward galleries formed of hurdles of green reeds, and oaken semicircles like enormous shields gliding on three wheels; the workers were sheltered in little huts covered with raw hides and stuffed with wrack; the catapults and ballistas were protected by rope curtains which had been steeped in vinegar to render them incombustible. The women and children went to procure stones on the strand, and gathered earth with their hands and brought it to the soldiers.

The Carthaginians also made preparations.

Hamilcar had speedily reassured them by declaring that there was enough water left in the cisterns for one hundred and twenty-three days. This assertion, together with his presence, and above all that of the zaïmph among them, gave them good hopes. Carthage recovered from its dejection; those who were not of Chanaanitish origin were carried away by the passion of the rest.

The slaves were armed, the arsenals were emptied, and every citizen had his own post and his own employment. Twelve hundred of the fugitives had survived, and the Suffet made them all captains; and carpenters, armourers, blacksmiths, and goldsmiths were intrusted with the engines. The Carthaginians had kept a few in spite of the conditions of the peace with Rome. These were repaired. They understood such work.

The two northern and eastern sides, being protected by the sea and the gulf, remained inaccessible. On the wall fronting the Barbarians they collected tree-trunks, mill-stones, vases filled with sulphur, and vats filled with oil, and built furnaces. Stones were heaped up on the platforms of the towers, and the houses bordering immediately on the rampart were crammed with sand in order to strengthen it and increase its thickness.

The Barbarians grew angry at the sight of these preparations. They wished to fight at once. The weights which they put into the catapults were so extravagantly heavy that the beams broke, and the attack was delayed.

At last on the thirteenth day of the month of Schabar,— at sunrise,— a great blow was heard at the gate of Khamon.

Seventy-five soldiers were pulling at ropes arranged at the base of a gigantic beam which was suspended horizontally by chains hanging from a framework, and which terminated in a ram's head of pure brass. It had been swathed in ox-hides; it was bound at intervals with iron bracelets; it was thrice as thick as a man's body, one hundred and twenty cubits long, and under the crowd of naked arms pushing it forward and drawing it back, it moved to and fro with a regular oscillation.

The other rams before the other gates began to be in motion. Men might be seen mounting from step to step in the hollow wheels of the tympanums. The pulleys and caps grated, the rope curtains were lowered, and showers of stones and showers of arrows burst forth simultaneously; all the scattered slingers ran up. Some approached the rampart hiding pots of resin under their shields; then they would hurl these with all their might. This hail of bullets, darts, and flames passed above the first ranks in the form of a curve which fell behind the walls. But long cranes, used for masting vessels, were reared on the summit of the ramparts; and from them there descended some of those enormous pincers which terminated in two semicircles toothed on the inside. They bit the rams. The soldiers clung to the beam and drew it back. The Carthaginians hauled in order to pull it up; and the action was prolonged until the evening.

When the Mercenaries resumed their task on the following day, the tops of the walls were completely carpeted with bales of cotton, sails, and cushions; the battlements were stopped up with mats; and a line of forks and blades, fixed upon sticks, might be distinguished among the cranes on the rampart. A furious resistance immediately began.

Trunks of trees fastened to cables fell and rose alternately and battered the rams; cramps hurled by the ballistas tore away the roofs of the huts; and streams of flints and pebbles poured from the platforms of the towers.

At last the rams broke the gates of Khamon and Tagaste. But the Carthaginians had piled up such an abundance of materials on the inside that the leaves did not open. They remained standing.

Then they drove augers against the walls; these were applied to the joints of the blocks, so as to detach the latter. The engines were better managed, the men serving them were divided into squads, and they were worked from morning till evening without interruption and with the monotonous precision of a weaver's loom.

Spendius attended to them untiringly. It was he who stretched the skeins of the ballistas. In order that the twin tensions might completely correspond, the ropes as they were tightened were struck on the right and left alternately until both sides gave out an equal sound. Spendius would mount upon the timbers. He would strike the ropes softly with the extremity of his foot, and strain his ears like a musician tuning a lyre. Then when the beam of the catapult rose, when the pillar of the ballista trembled with the shock of the spring, when the stones were shooting in rays, and the darts pouring in streams, he would incline his whole body and fling his arms into the air as though to follow them.

The soldiers admired his skill and executed his commands. In the gaiety of their work they gave utterance to jests on the names of the machines. Thus the plyers for seizing the rams were called "wolves," and the galleries were covered with "vines;" they were lambs, or they were going to gather the grapes; and as they loaded their pieces they would say to the onagers: "Come, pick well!" and to the scorpions: "Pierce them to the heart!" These jokes, which were ever the same, kept up their courage.

Nevertheless the machines did not demolish the rampart. It was formed of two walls and was completely filled with earth. The upper portions were beaten down, but each time the besieged raised them again. Matho ordered the construction of wooden towers which should be as high as the towers of stone. They cast turf, stakes, pebbles and chariots with their wheels into the trench so as to fill it up the more quickly; but before this was accomplished the immense throng of Barbarians undulated over the plain with a single movement and came beating against the foot of the walls like an overflowing sea.

They moved forward the rope ladders, straight ladders, and sambucas, the latter consisting of two

poles from which a series of bamboos terminating in
a movable bridge were lowered by means of tackling.
They formed numerous straight lines resting against
the wall, and the Mercenaries mounted them in files,
holding their weapons in their hands. Not a Carthaginian showed himself; already two thirds of the
rampart had been covered. Then the battlements
opened, vomiting flames and smoke like dragon
jaws; the sand scattered and entered the joints of
their armour; the petroleum fastened on their garments; the liquid lead hopped on their helmets and
made holes in their flesh; a rain of sparks splashed
against their faces, and eyeless orbits seemed to
weep tears as big as almonds. There were men all
yellow with oil, with their hair in flames. They began to run and set fire to the rest. They were extinguished with mantles steeped in blood, which
were thrown from a distance over their faces. Some
who had no wounds remained motionless, stiffer
than stakes, their mouths open and their arms outspread.

The assault was renewed for several days in succession, the Mercenaries hoping to triumph by extraordinary energy and audacity.

Sometimes a man raised on the shoulders of
another would drive a pin between the stones, and then
making use of it as a step to reach further, would
place a second and a third; and, protected by the
edge of the battlements, which stood out from the
wall, they would gradually raise themselves in this
way; but on reaching a certain height they always
fell back again. The great trench was full to overflowing; the wounded were massed pell-mell with
the dead and dying beneath the footsteps of the liv-

ing. Calcined trunks formed black spots amid opened entrails, scattered brains, and pools of blood; and arms and legs projecting half way out of a heap, would stand straight up like props in a burning vineyard.

The ladders proving insufficient the tollenos were brought into requisition, —instruments consisting of a long beam set transversely upon another, and bearing at its extremity a quadrangular basket which would hold thirty foot-soldiers with their weapons.

Matho wished to ascend in the first that was ready. Spendius stopped him.

Some men bent over a capstan; the great beam rose, became horizontal, reared itself almost vertically, and being overweighted at the end, bent like a huge reed. The soldiers, who were crowded together, were hidden up to their chins; only their helmet-plumes could be seen. At last when it was twenty cubits high in the air it turned several times to the right and to the left, and then was depressed; and like a giant arm holding a cohort of pigmies in its hand, it laid the basketful of men upon the edge of the wall. They leaped into the crowd and never returned.

All the other tollenos were speedily made ready. But a hundred times as many would have been needed for the capture of the town. They were utilised in a murderous fashion: Ethiopian archers were placed in the baskets; then, the cables having been fastened, they remained suspended and shot poisoned arrows. The fifty tollenos commanding the battlements thus surrounded Carthage like monstrous vultures; and the Negroes laughed to see the guards on the rampart dying in grievous convulsions.

Hamilcar sent hoplites to these posts, and every morning made them drink the juice of certain herbs which protected them against the poison.

One evening when it was dark he embarked the best of his soldiers on lighters and planks, and turning to the right of the harbour, disembarked on the Taenia. Then he advanced to the first lines of the Barbarians, and taking them in flank, made a great slaughter. Men hanging to ropes would descend at night from the top of the wall with torches in their hands, burn the works of the Mercenaries, and then mount up again.

Matho was exasperated; every obstacle strengthened his wrath, which led him into terrible extravagances. He mentally summoned Salammbô to an interview; then he waited. She did not come; this seemed to him a fresh piece of treachery,—and henceforth he execrated her. If he had seen her corpse he would perhaps have gone away. He doubled the outposts, he planted forks at the foot of the rampart, he drove caltrops into the ground, and he commanded the Libyans to bring him a whole forest that he might set it on fire and burn Carthage like a den of foxes.

Spendius went on obstinately with the siege. He sought to invent terrible machines such as had never before been constructed.

The other Barbarians, encamped at a distance on the isthmus, were amazed at these delays; they murmured, and they were let loose.

Then they rushed with their cutlasses and javelins, and beat against the gates with them. But the nakedness of their bodies facilitating the infliction of wounds, the Carthaginians massacred them freely; and the
4—6

Mercenaries rejoiced at it, no doubt through jealousy about the plunder. Hence there resulted quarrels and combats between them. Then, the country having been ravaged, provisions were soon scarce. They grew disheartened. Numerous hordes went away, but the crowd was so great that the loss was not apparent.

The best of them tried to dig mines, but the earth, being badly supported, fell in. They began again in other places, but Hamilcar always guessed the direction that they were taking by holding his ear against a bronze shield. He bored counter-mines beneath the path along which the wooden towers were to move, and when they were pushed forward they sank into the holes.

At last all recognised that the town was impregnable, unless a long terrace were raised to the same height as the walls, so as to enable them to fight on the same level. The top of it should be paved so that the machines might be rolled along. Then Carthage would find it quite impossible to resist.

The town was beginning to suffer from thirst. The water which was worth two kesitahs the bath at the opening of the siege was now sold for a shekel of silver; the stores of meat and corn were also becoming exhausted; there was a dread of famine, and some even began to speak of useless mouths, which terrified every one.

From the square of Khamon to the temple of Melkarth the streets were cumbered with corpses; and, as it was the end of the summer, the combatants were annoyed by great black flies. Old men carried off the wounded, and the devout continued

the fictitious funerals of their relatives and friends
who had died far away during the war. Waxen
statues with clothes and hair were displayed across
the gates. They melted in the heat of the tapers
burning beside them; the paint flowed down upon
their shoulders, and tears streamed over the faces of
the living, as they chanted mournful songs beside
them. The crowd meanwhile ran to and fro; armed
bands passed; captains shouted orders, while the
shock of the rams beating against the rampart was
constantly heard.

The temperature became so heavy that the bodies
swelled and would no longer fit into the coffins.
They were burned in the centre of the courts. But
the fires, being too much confined, kindled the
neighbouring walls, and long flames suddenly burst
from the houses like blood spirting from an artery.
Thus Moloch was in possession of Carthage; he
clasped the ramparts, he rolled through the streets,
he devoured the very corpses.

Men wearing cloaks made of collected rags in
token of despair, stationed themselves at the corners
of the cross-ways. They declaimed against the Ancients and against Hamilcar, predicted complete ruin
to the people, and invited them to universal destruction and license. The most dangerous were the henbane-drinkers; in their crisis they believed themselves
wild beasts, and leaped upon the passers-by to rend
them. Mobs formed around them, and the defence
of Carthage was forgotten. The Suffet devised the
payment of others to support his policy.

In order to retain the genius of the gods within
the town their images had been covered with chains.
Black veils were placed upon the Pataec gods, and

hair-cloths around the altars; and attempts were made
to excite the pride and jealousy of the Baals by singing in their ears: "Thou art about to suffer thyself
to be vanquished! Are the others perchance more
strong? Show thyself! aid us! that the peoples may
not say: 'Where are now their gods?'"

The colleges of the pontiffs were agitated by un-
ceasing anxiety. Those of Rabbetna were especially
afraid — the restoration of the zaïmph having been of
no avail. They kept themselves shut up in the third
enclosure which was as impregnable as a fortress.
Only one among them, the high priest Schahabarim,
ventured to go out.

He used to visit Salammbô. But he would either
remain perfectly silent, gazing at her with fixed eyeballs, or else would be lavish of words, and the re-
proaches that he uttered were harder than ever.

With inconceivable inconsistency he could not
forgive the young girl for having followed his commands; Schahabarim had guessed all, and this haunting thought revived the jealousies of his impotence.
He accused her of being the cause of the war.
Matho, according to him, was besieging Carthage to
recover the zaïmph; and he poured out imprecations
and sarcasms upon this Barbarian who pretended to
the possession of holy things. Yet it was not this
that the priest wished to say.

But just now Salammbô felt no terror of him.
The anguish which she used formerly to suffer had
left her. A strange peacefulness possessed her. Her
gaze was less wandering, and shone with limpid fire.

Meanwhile the python had become ill again; and
as Salammbô, on the contrary, appeared to be recovering, old Taanach rejoiced in the conviction that by

its decline it was taking away the languor of her mistress.

One morning she found it coiled up behind the bed of ox-hides, colder than marble, and with its head hidden by a heap of worms. Her cries brought Salammbô to the spot. She turned it over for a while with the tip of her sandal, and the slave was amazed at her insensibility.

Hamilcar's daughter no longer prolonged her fasts with so much fervour. She passed whole days on the top of her terrace, leaning her elbows against the balustrade, and amusing herself by looking out before her. The summits of the walls at the end of the town cut uneven zigzags upon the sky, and the lances of the sentries formed what was like a border of corn-ears throughout their length. Further away she could see the manœuvres of the Barbarians between the towers; on days when the siege was interrupted she could even distinguish their occupations. They mended their weapons, greased their hair, and washed their bloodstained arms in the sea; the tents were closed; the beasts of burden were feeding; and in the distance the scythes of the chariots, which were all ranged in a semicircle, looked like a silver scimitar lying at the base of the mountains. Schahabarim's talk recurred to her memory. She was waiting for Narr' Havas, her betrothed. In spite of her hatred she would have liked to see Matho again. Of all the Carthaginians she was perhaps the only one who would have spoken to him without fear.

Her father often came into her room. He would sit down panting on the cushions, and gaze at her with an almost tender look, as if he found some rest from his fatigues in the sight of her. He sometimes questioned her about her journey to the camp of the Mercenaries. He even asked her whether any one had urged her to it; and with a shake of the head she answered, No,—so proud was Salammbô of having saved the zaïmph.

But the Suffet always came back to Matho under pretence of making military inquiries. He could not understand how the hours which she had spent in the tent had been employed. Salammbô, in fact, said nothing about Gisco; for as words had an effective power in themselves, curses, if reported to any one, might be turned against him; and she was silent about her wish to assassinate, lest she should be blamed for not having yielded to it. She said that the schalischim appeared furious, that he had shouted a great deal, and that he had then fallen asleep. Salammbô told no more, through shame perhaps, or else because she was led by her extreme ingenuousness to attach but little importance to the soldier's kisses. Moreover, it all floated through her head in a melancholy and misty fashion, like the recollection of a depressing dream; and she would not have known in what way or in what words to express it.

One evening when they were thus face to face with each other, Taanach came in looking quite scared. An old man with a child was yonder in the courts, and wished to see the Suffet.

Hamilcar turned pale, and then quickly replied:

"Let him come up!"

Iddibal entered without prostrating himself. He held a young boy, covered with a goat's-hair cloak, by the hand, and at once raised the hood which screened his face.

"Here he is, Master! Take him!"

The Suffet and the slave went into a corner of the room.

The child remained in the centre standing upright, and with a gaze of attention rather than of astonishment he surveyed the ceiling, the furniture, the pearl necklaces trailing on the purple draperies, and the majestic maiden who was bending over towards him.

He was perhaps ten years old, and was not taller than a Roman sword. His curly hair shaded his swelling forehead. His eyeballs looked as if they were seeking for space. The nostrils of his delicate nose were broad and palpitating, and upon his whole person was displayed the indefinable splendour of those who are destined to great enterprises. When he had cast aside his extremely heavy cloak, he remained clad in a lynx skin, which was fastened about his waist, and he rested his little naked feet, which were all white with dust, resolutely upon the pavement. But he no doubt divined that important matters were under discussion, for he stood motionless, with one hand behind his back, his chin lowered, and a finger in his mouth.

At last Hamilcar attracted Salammbô with a sign and said to her in a low voice:

"You will keep him with you, you understand! No one, even though belonging to the house, must know of his existence!"

Then, behind the door, he again asked Iddibal whether he was quite sure that they had not been noticed.

"No!" said the slave, "the streets were empty."

As the war filled all the provinces he had feared for his master's son. Then, not knowing where to hide him, he had come along the coasts in a sloop, and for three days Iddibal had been tacking about in the gulf and watching the ramparts. At last, that evening, as the environs of Khamon seemed to be deserted, he had passed briskly through the channel and landed near the arsenal, the entrance to the harbour being free.

But soon the Barbarians posted an immense raft in front of it in order to prevent the Carthaginians from coming out. They were again rearing the wooden towers, and the terrace was rising at the same time.

Outside communications were cut off and an intolerable famine set in.

The besieged killed all the dogs, all the mules, all the asses, and then the fifteen elephants which the Suffet had brought back. The lions of the temple of Moloch had become ferocious, and the hierodules no longer durst approach them. They were fed at first with the wounded Barbarians; then they were thrown corpses that were still warm; they refused them, and they all died. People wandered in the twilight along the old enclosures, and gathered grass and flowers among the stones to boil them in wine, wine being cheaper than water. Others crept as far as the enemy's outposts, and entered the tents to steal food, and the stupefied Barbarians sometimes allowed them to return. At last a day arrived when the Ancients resolved to slaughter the horses of Eschmoun privately. They were holy animals whose manes were plaited by the pontiffs with gold ribbons, and whose existence denoted the motion of the sun — the idea of fire in its most exalted form. Their flesh was cut into equal portions and buried behind the altar. Then

every evening the Ancients, alleging some act of devotion, would go up to the temple and regale themselves in secret, and each would take away a piece
beneath his tunic for his children. In the deserted
quarters remote from the walls, the inhabitants, whose
misery was not so great, had barricaded themselves
through fear of the rest.

The stones from the catapults, and the demolitions
commanded for purposes of defence, had accumulated
heaps of ruins in the middle of the streets. At the
quietest times masses of people would suddenly rush
along with shouts; and from the top of the Acropolis
the conflagrations were like purple rags scattered
upon the terraces and twisted by the wind.

The three great catapults did not stop in spite of
all these works. Their ravages were extraordinary:
thus a man's head rebounded from the pediment of
the Syssitia; a woman who was being confined in the
street of Kinisdo was crushed by a block of marble,
and her child was carried with the bed as far as the
crossways of Cinasyn, where the coverlet was found.

The most annoying were the bullets of the slingers.
They fell upon the roofs, and in the gardens, and in
the middle of the courts, while people were at table
before a slender meal with their hearts big with
sighs. These cruel projectiles bore engraved letters
which stamped themselves upon the flesh; — and in-
sults might be read on corpses such as "pig,"
"jackal," "vermin," and sometimes jests: "Catch it!"
or "I have well deserved it!"

The portion of the rampart which extended from
the corner of the harbours to the height of the cisterns was broken down. Then the people of Malqua
found themselves caught between the old enclosure

of Byrsa behind, and the Barbarians in front. But there was enough to be done in thickening the wall and making it as high as possible without troubling about them; they were abandoned; all perished; and although they were generally hated, Hamilcar came to be greatly abhorred.

On the morrow he opened the pits in which he kept stores of corn, and his stewards gave it to the people. For three days they gorged themselves.

Their thirst, however, only became the more intolerable, and they could constantly see before them the long cascade formed by the clear falling water of the aqueduct. A thin vapor, with a rainbow beside it, went up from its base, beneath the rays of the sun, and a little stream curving through the plain fell into the gulf.

Hamilcar did not give way. He was reckoning upon an event, upon something decisive and extraordinary.

His own slaves tore off the silver plates from the temple of Melkarth; four long boats were drawn out of the harbour, they were brought by means of capstans to the foot of the Mappalian quarter, the wall facing the shore was bored, and they set out for the Gauls to buy Mercenaries there at no matter what price. Nevertheless, Hamilcar was distressed at his inability to communicate with the king of the Numidians, for he knew that he was behind the Barbarians, and ready to fall upon them. But Narr' Havas, being too weak, was not going to make any venture alone; and the Suffet had the rampart raised twelve palms higher, all the material in the arsenals piled up in the Acropolis, and the machines repaired once more.

Sinews taken from bulls' necks, or else stags'

hamstrings, were commonly employed for the twists of the catapults. However, neither stags nor bulls were in existence in Carthage. Hamilcar asked the Ancients for the hair of their wives; all sacrificed it, but the quantity was not sufficient. In the buildings of the Syssitia there were twelve hundred marriageable slaves destined for prostitution in Greece and Italy, and their hair, having been rendered elastic by the use of unguents, was wonderfully well adapted for engines of war. But the subsequent loss would be too great. Accordingly it was decided that a choice should be made of the finest heads of hair among the wives of the plebeians. Careless of their country's needs, they shrieked in despair when the servants of the Hundred came with scissors to lay hands upon them.

The Barbarians were animated with increased fury. They could be seen in the distance taking fat from the dead to grease their machines, while others pulled out the nails and stitched them end to end to make cuirasses. They devised a plan of putting into the catapults vessels filled with serpents which had been brought by the Negroes; the clay pots broke on the flag-stones, the serpents ran about, seemed to multiply, and, so numerous were they, to issue naturally from the walls. Then the Barbarians, not satisfied with their invention, improved upon it; they hurled all kinds of filth, human excrements, pieces of carrion, corpses. The plague reappeared. The teeth of the Carthaginians fell out of their mouths, and their gums were discoloured like those of camels after too long a journey.

The machines were set up on the terrace, although the latter did not as yet reach everywhere to the height of the rampart. Before the twenty-three towers on the fortifications stood twenty-three others of wood. All the tollenos were mounted again, and in the centre, a little further back, appeared the formidable helepolis of Demetrius Poliorcetes, which Spendius had at last reconstructed. Of pyramidal shape, like the pharos of Alexandria, it was one hundred and thirty cubits high and twenty-three wide, with nine stories, diminishing as they approached the summit, and protected by scales of brass; they were pierced with numerous doors and were filled with soldiers, and on the upper platform there stood a catapult flanked by two ballistas.

Then Hamilcar planted crosses for those who should speak of surrender, and even the women were brigaded. The people lay in the streets and waited full of distress.

Then one morning before sunrise (it was the seventh day of the month of Nyssan) they heard a great shout uttered by all the Barbarians simultaneously; the leaden-tubed trumpets pealed, and the great Paphlagonian horns bellowed like bulls. All rose and ran to the rampart.

A forest of lances, pikes, and swords bristled at its base. It leaped against the walls, the ladders grappled them; and Barbarians' heads appeared in the intervals of the battlements.

Beams supported by long files of men were battering at the gates; and, in order to demolish the wall at places where the terrace was wanting, the Mercenaries came up in serried cohorts, the first line crawling, the second bending their hams, and the others rising in succession to the last who stood upright; while elsewhere, in order to climb up, the tallest advanced in front and the lowest in the rear, and all rested their shields upon their helmets with their left arms, joining them together at the edges so tightly that they might have been taken for an assemblage of large tortoises. The projectiles slid over these oblique masses.

The Carthaginians threw down mill-stones, pestles, vats, casks, beds, everything that could serve as a weight and could knock down. Some watched at the embrasures with fishermen's nets, and when the Barbarian arrived he found himself caught in the meshes, and struggled like a fish. They demolished their own battlements; portions of wall fell down raising a great dust; and as the catapults on the terrace were shooting over against one another, the stones would strike together and shiver into a thousand pieces, making a copious shower upon the combatants.

Soon the two crowds formed but one great chain of human bodies; it overflowed into the intervals in the terrace, and, somewhat looser at the two extremities, swayed perpetually without advancing. They clasped one another, lying flat on the ground like wrestlers. They crushed one another. The women leaned over the battlements and shrieked. They were dragged away by their veils, and the whiteness of their suddenly uncovered sides shone in the arms of the Negroes as the latter buried their daggers in them. Some corpses did not fall, being too much pressed by the crowd, and, supported by the shoulders of their companions, advanced for some minutes quite upright and with staring eyes. Some who had both temples pierced by a javelin swayed their heads about like bears. Mouths, opened to shout, remained gaping; severed hands flew through the air. Mighty blows were dealt, which were long talked of by the survivors.

Meanwhile arrows darted from the towers of wood and stone. The tollenos moved their long yards rapidly; and as the Barbarians had sacked the old cemetery of the aborigines beneath the Catacombs, they hurled the tombstones against the Carthaginians. Sometimes the cables broke under the weight of too heavy baskets, and masses of men, all with uplifted arms, would fall from the sky.

Up to the middle of the day the veterans had attacked the Taenia fiercely in order to penetrate into the harbour and destroy the fleet. Hamilcar had a fire of damp straw lit upon the roofing of Khamon, and as the smoke blinded them they fell back to the left, and came to swell the horrible rout which was pressing forward in Malqua. Some syntagmata composed of sturdy men, chosen expressly for the purpose, had broken in three gates. They were checked by lofty barriers made of planks studded with nails, but a fourth yielded easily; they dashed over it at a run and rolled into a pit in which there were hidden snares. At the south-west angle Autaritus and his men broke down the rampart, the fissure in which had been stopped up with bricks. The ground behind rose, and they climbed it nimbly. But on the top they found a second wall composed of stones and long beams lying quite flat and alternating like the squares on a chess-board. It was a Gaulish fashion, and had been adapted by the Suffet to the requirements of the situation; the Gauls imagined themselves before a town in their own country. Their attack was weak, and they were repulsed.

All the roundway, from the street of Khamon as

far as the Green Market, now belonged to the Barbarians, and the Samnites were finishing off the dying with blows of stakes; or else with one foot on the wall were gazing down at the smoking ruins beneath them, and the battle which was beginning again in the distance.

The slingers, who were distributed through the rear, were still shooting. But the springs of the Acarnanian slings had broken from use, and many were throwing stones with the hand like shepherds; the rest hurled leaden bullets with the handle of a whip. Zarxas, his shoulders covered with his long black hair, went about everywhere, and led on the Barbarians. Two pouches hung at his hips; he thrust his left hand into them continually, while his right arm whirled round like a chariot-wheel.

Matho had at first refrained from fighting, the better to command all the Barbarians at once. He had been seen along the gulf with the Mercenaries, near the lagoon with the Numidians, and on the shores of the lake among the Negroes, and from the back part of the plain he urged forward masses of soldiers who came ceaselessly against the ramparts. By degrees he had drawn near; the smell of blood, the sight of carnage, and the tumult of clarions had at last made his heart leap. Then he had gone back into his tent, and throwing off his cuirass had taken his lion's skin as being more convenient for battle. The snout fitted upon his head, bordering his face with a circle of fangs; the two fore-paws were crossed upon his breast, and the claws of the hinder ones fell beneath his knees.

He had kept on his strong waist-belt, wherein gleamed a two-edged axe, and with his great sword in both hands he had dashed impetuously through the breach. Like a pruner cutting willow-branches and trying to strike off as much as possible so as to make the more money, he marched along mowing down the Carthaginians around him. Those who tried to seize him in flank he knocked down with blows of the pommel; when they attacked him in front he ran them through; if they fled he clove them. Two men leaped together upon his back; he bounded backwards against a gate and crushed them. His sword fell and rose. It shivered on the angle of a wall. Then he took his heavy axe, and front and rear he ripped up the Carthaginians like a flock of sheep. They scattered more and more, and he was quite alone when he reached the second enclosure at the foot of the Acropolis. The materials which had been flung from the summit cumbered the steps and were heaped up higher than the wall. Matho turned back amid the ruins to summons his companions.

He perceived their crests scattered over the multitude; they were sinking and their wearers were about to perish; he dashed towards them; then the vast wreath of red plumes closed in, and they soon rejoined him and surrounded him. But an enormous crowd was discharging from the side streets. He was caught by the hips, lifted up and carried away outside the rampart to a spot where the terrace was high.

Matho shouted a command and all the shields sank upon the helmets; he leaped upon them in order to catch hold somewhere so as to re-enter Carthage; and, flourishing his terrible axe, ran over the shields, which resembled waves of bronze, like a marine god, with brandished trident, over his billows.

However, a man in a white robe was walking along the edge of the rampart, impassible, and indifferent to the death which surrounded him. Sometimes he would spread out his right hand above his eyes in order to find out some one. Matho happened to pass beneath him. Suddenly his eyeballs flamed, his livid face contracted; and raising both his lean arms he shouted out abuse at him.

Matho did not hear it; but he felt so furious and cruel a look entering his heart that he uttered a roar. He hurled his long axe at him; some people threw themselves upon Schahabarim; and Matho seeing him no more fell back exhausted.

A terrible creaking drew near, mingled with the rhythm of hoarse voices singing together.

It was the great helepolis surrounded by a crowd of soldiers. They were dragging it with both hands, hauling it with ropes, and pushing it with their shoulders,—for the slope rising from the plain to the terrace, though extremely gentle, was found impracticable for machines of such prodigious weight. However, it had eight wheels banded with iron, and it had been advancing slowly in this way since the morning, like a mountain raised upon another. Then there appeared an immense ram issuing from its base. The doors along the three fronts which faced the town fell down, and cuirassed soldiers appeared in the interior like pillars of iron. Some might be seen climbing and descending the two staircases which crossed the stories. Some were waiting to dart out as soon as the cramps of the doors touched the walls; in the middle of the upper platform the skeins of the ballistas were turning, and the great beam of the catapult was being lowered.

4—7

Hamilcar was at that moment standing upright on the roof of Melkarth. He had calculated that it would come directly towards him, against what was the most invulnerable place in the wall, which was for that very reason denuded of sentries. His slaves had for a long time been bringing leathern bottles along the roundway, where they had raised with clay two transverse partitions forming a sort of basin. The water was flowing insensibly along the terrace, and strange to say, it seemed to cause Hamilcar no anxiety.

But when the helepolis was thirty paces off, he commanded planks to be placed over the streets between the houses from the cisterns to the rampart; and a file of people passed from hand to hand helmets and amphoras, which were emptied continually. The Carthaginians, however, grew indignant at this waste of water. The ram was demolishing the wall, when suddenly a fountain sprang forth from the disjointed stones. Then the lofty brazen mass, nine stories high, which contained and engaged more than three thousand soldiers, began to rock gently like a ship. In fact, the water, which had penetrated the terrace, had broken up the path before it; its wheels stuck in the mire; the head of Spendius, with distended cheeks blowing an ivory cornet, appeared between leathern curtains on the first story. The great machine, as though convulsively upheaved, advanced perhaps ten paces; but the ground softened more and more, the mire reached to the axles, and the helepolis stopped, leaning over frightfully to one side. The catapult rolled to the edge of the platform, and carried away by the weight of its beam, fell, shattering the lower stories beneath it. The soldiers who were standing on the doors slipped into the abyss, or else held on to the extremities of the long beams, and by their weight increased the inclination of the helepolis, which was going to pieces with creakings in all its joints.

The other Barbarians rushed up to help them, massing themselves into a compact crowd. The Carthaginians descended from the rampart, and, assailing them in the rear, killed them at leisure. But the chariots furnished with the sickles hastened up, and galloped round the outskirts of the multitude. The latter ascended the wall again; night came on; and the Barbarians gradually retired.

Nothing could now be seen on the plain but a sort of perfectly black, swarming mass, which extended from the bluish gulf to the purely white lagoon; and the lake, which had received streams of blood, stretched further away like a great purple pool.

The terrace was now so laden with corpses that it looked as though it had been constructed of human bodies. In the centre stood the helepolis covered with armour; and from time to time huge fragments broke off from it, like stones from a crumbling pyramid. Broad tracks made by the streams of lead might be distinguished on the walls. A broken-down wooden tower burned here and there, and the houses showed dimly like the stages of a ruined amphitheatre. Heavy fumes of smoke were rising, and rolling with them sparks which were lost in the dark sky.

The Carthaginians, however, who were consumed by thirst, had rushed to the cisterns. They broke open the doors. A miry swamp stretched at the bottom.

What was to be done now? Moreover, the Barbarians were countless, and when their fatigue was over they would begin again.

The people deliberated all night in groups at the corners of the streets. Some said that they ought to send away the women, the sick, and the old men; others proposed to abandon the town, and found a colony far away. But vessels were lacking, and when the sun appeared no decision had been made.

There was no fighting that day, all being too much exhausted. The sleepers looked like corpses.

Then the Carthaginians, reflecting upon the cause of their disasters, remembered that they had not dispatched to Phœnicia the annual offering due to Tyrian Melkarth, and a great terror came upon them. The gods were indignant with the Republic, and were, no doubt, about to prosecute their vengeance.

They were considered as cruel masters, who were appeased with supplications and allowed themselves to be bribed with presents. All were feeble in comparison with Moloch the Devourer. The existence, the very flesh of men, belonged to him; and hence in order to preserve it, the Carthaginians used to offer up a portion of it to him, which calmed his fury. Children were burned on the forehead, or on the nape of the neck, with woollen wicks; and as this mode of satisfying Baal brought in much money to the priests, they failed not to recommend it as being easier and more pleasant.

This time, however, the Republic itself was at stake. But as every profit must be purchased by some loss, and as every transaction was regulated

according to the needs of the weaker and the demands of the stronger, there was no pain great
enough for the god, since he delighted in such as
was of the most horrible description, and all were
now at his mercy. He must accordingly be fully
gratified. Precedents showed that in this way the
scourge would be made to disappear. Moreover, it
was believed that an immolation by fire would purify
Carthage. The ferocity of the people was predis-
posed towards it. The choice, too, must fall exclusively upon the families of the great.

The Ancients assembled. The sitting was a long
one. Hanno had come to it. As he was now unable
to sit he remained lying down near the door, half hidden among the fringes of the lofty tapestry; and
when the pontiff of Moloch asked them whether they
would consent to surrender their children, his voice
suddenly broke forth from the shadow like the roaring of a genius in the depths of a cavern. He regretted, he said, that he had none of his own blood
to give; and he gazed at Hamilcar, who faced him at
the other end of the hall. The Suffet was so much
disconcerted by this look that it made him lower his
eyes. All successively bent their heads in approval;
and in accordance with the rites he had to reply to
the high priest: "Yes; be it so." Then the Ancients
decreed the sacrifice in traditional circumlocution,—
because there are things more troublesome to say than
to perform.

The decision was almost immediately known in
Carthage, and lamentations resounded. The cries of
women might everywhere be heard; their husbands
consoled them, or railed at them with remonstrances.

But three hours afterwards extraordinary tidings

were spread abroad: the Suffet had discovered springs at the foot of the cliff. There was a rush to the place. Water might be seen in holes dug in the sand, and some were already lying flat on the ground and drinking.

Hamilcar did not himself know whether it was by the determination of the gods or through the vague recollection of a revelation which his father had once made to him; but on leaving the Ancients he had gone down to the shore and had begun to dig the gravel with his slaves.

He gave clothing, boots, and wine. He gave all the rest of the corn that he was keeping by him. He even let the crowd enter his palace, and he opened kitchens, stores, and all the rooms,—Salammbô's alone excepted. He announced that six thousand Gaulish Mercenaries were coming, and that the king of Macedonia was sending soldiers.

But on the second day the springs diminished, and on the evening of the third they were completely dried up. Then the decree of the Ancients passed everywhere from lip to lip, and the priests of Moloch began their task.

Men in black robes presented themselves in the houses. In many instances the owners had deserted them under pretence of some business, or of some dainty that they were going to buy; and the servants of Moloch came and took the children away. Others themselves surrendered them stupidly. Then they were brought to the temple of Tanith, where the priestesses were charged with their amusement and support until the solemn day.

They visit Hamilcar suddenly and found him in his gardens.

"Barca! we come for that that you know of—your son!" They added that some people had met him one evening during the previous moon in the centre of the Mappalian district being led by an old man.

He was as though suffocated at first. But speedily understanding that any denial would be vain, Hamilcar bowed; and he brought them into the commercial house. Some slaves who had run up at a sign kept watch round about it.

He entered Salammbô's room in a state of distraction. He seized Hannibal with one hand, snatched up the cord of a trailing garment with the other, tied his feet and hands with it, thrust the end into his mouth to form a gag, and hid him under the bed of ox-hides by letting an ample drapery fall to the ground.

Afterwards he walked about from right to left, raised his arms, wheeled round, bit his lips. Then he stood still with staring eyeballs, and panted as though he were about to die.

But he clapped his hands three times. Giddenem appeared.

"Listen!" he said, "go and take from among the slaves a male child from eight to nine years of age, with black hair and swelling forehead! Bring him here! make haste!"

Giddenem soon entered again, bringing forward a young boy.

He was a miserable child, at once lean and bloated; his skin looked greyish, like the infected rag hanging to his sides; his head was sunk between his shoulders, and with the back of his hand he was rubbing his eyes, which were filled with flies.

How could he ever be confounded with Hannibal! and there was no time to choose another. Hamilcar looked at Giddenem; he felt inclined to strangle him.

"Begone!" he cried; and the master of the slaves fled.

The misfortune which he had so long dreaded was therefore come, and with extravagant efforts he strove to discover whether there was not some mode, some means to escape it.

Abdalonim suddenly spoke from behind the door. The Suffet was being asked for. The servants of Moloch were growing impatient.

Hamilcar repressed a cry as though a red hot iron had burnt him; and he began anew to pace the room like one distraught. Then he sank down beside the balustrade, and, with his elbows on his knees, pressed his forehead into his shut fists.

The porphyry basin still contained a little clear water for Salammbô's ablutions. In spite of his repugnance and all his pride, the Suffet dipped the child into it, and, like a slave merchant, began to wash him and rub him with strigils and red earth. Then he took two purple squares from the receptacles round the wall, placed one on his breast and the other on his back, and joined them together on the collar bones with two diamond clasps. He poured perfume upon his head, passed an electrum necklace around his neck, and put on him sandals with heels of pearl,—sandals belonging to his own daughter! But he stamped with shame and vexation; Salammbô, who busied herself in helping him, was as pale as he. The child, dazzled by such splendour, smiled and, growing bold even, was beginning to clap his hands and jump, when Hamilcar took him away.

He held him firmly by the arm as though he were afraid of losing him, and the child, who was hurt, wept a little as he ran beside him.

When on a level with the ergastulum, under a palm tree, a voice was raised, a mournful and supplicant voice. It murmured: "Master! oh! master!"

Hamilcar turned and beside him perceived a man of abject appearance, one of the wretches who led a haphazard existence in the household.

"What do you want?" said the Suffet.

The slave, who trembled horribly, stammered:

"I am his father!"

Hamilcar walked on; the other followed him with stooping loins, bent hams, and head thrust forward. His face was convulsed with unspeakable anguish, and he was choking with suppressed sobs, so eager was he at once to question him, and to cry: "Mercy!"

At last he ventured to touch him lightly with one finger on the elbow.

"Are you going to ——?" He had not strength to finish, and Hamilcar stopped quite amazed at such grief.

He had never thought — so immense was the abyss separating them from each other — that there could be anything in common between them. It even appeared to him a sort of outrage, an encroachment upon his own privileges. He replied with a look colder and heavier than an executioner's axe; the slave swooned and fell in the dust at his feet. Hamilcar strode across him.

The three black-robed men were waiting in the great hall, and standing against the stone disc. Immediately he tore his garments, and rolled upon the pavement uttering piercing cries.

"Ah! poor little Hannibal! Oh! my son! my con-
solation! my hope! my life! Kill me also! take me
away! Woe! Woe!" He ploughed his face with
his nails, tore out his hair, and shrieked like the
women who lament at funerals. "Take him away
then! my suffering is too great! begone! kill me like
him!" The servants of Moloch were astonished that
the great Hamilcar was so weak-spirited. They were
almost moved by it.

A noise of naked feet became audible, with a
broken throat-rattling like the breathing of a wild
beast speeding along, and a man, pale, terrible, and
with outspread arms appeared on the threshold of the
third gallery, between the ivory pots; he exclaimed:

"My child!"

Hamilcar threw himself with a bound upon the
slave, and covering the man's mouth with his hand
exclaimed still more loudly:

"It is the old man who reared him! he calls him
'my child!' it will make him mad! enough! enough!"
And hustling away the three priests and their victim
he went out with them and with a great kick shut
the door behind him.

Hamilcar strained his ears for some minutes in
constant fear of seeing them return. He then thought
of getting rid of the slave in order to be quite sure
that he would see nothing; but the peril had not
wholly disappeared, and, if the gods were provoked
at the man's death, it might be turned against his
son. Then, changing his intention, he sent him by
Taanach the best from his kitchens—a quarter of a
goat, beans, and preserved pomegranates. The slave,
who had eaten nothing for a long time, rushed upon
them; his tears fell into the dishes.

Hamilcar at last returned to Salammbô, and unfastened Hannibal's cords. The child in exasperation bit his hand until the blood came. He repelled him with a caress.

To make him remain quiet Salammbô tried to frighten him with Lamia, a Cyrenian ogress.

"But where is she?" he asked.

He was told that brigands were coming to put him into prison. "Let them come," he rejoined, "and I will kill them!"

Then Hamilcar told him the frightful truth. But he fell into a passion with his father, contending that he was quite able to annihilate the whole people, since he was the master of Carthage.

At last, exhausted by his exertions and anger, he fell into a wild sleep. He spoke in his dreams, his back leaning against a scarlet cushion; his head was thrown back somewhat, and his little arm, outstretched from his body, lay quite straight in an attitude of command.

When the night had grown dark Hamilcar lifted him up gently, and, without a torch, went down the galley staircase. As he passed through the mercantile house he took up a basket of grapes and a flagon of pure water; the child awoke before the statue of Aletes in the vault of gems, and he smiled—like the other—on his father's arm at the brilliant lights which surrounded him.

Hamilcar felt quite sure that his son could not be taken from him. It was an impenetrable spot communicating with the beach by a subterranean passage which he alone knew, and casting his eyes around he inhaled a great draught of air. Then he set him down upon a stool beside some golden shields.

No one at present could see him; he had no further need for watching; and he relieved his feelings. Like a mother finding again her first-born that was lost, he threw himself upon his son; he clasped him to his breast, he laughed and wept at the same time, he called him by the fondest names and covered him with kisses; little Hannibal was frightened by this terrible tenderness and was silent now.

Hamilcar returned with silent steps, feeling the walls around him, and came into the great hall where the moonlight entered through one of the apertures in the dome; in the centre the slave lay sleeping after his repast, stretched at full length upon the marble pavement. He looked at him and was moved with a sort of pity. With the tip of his cothurn he pushed forward a carpet beneath his head. Then he raised his eyes and gazed at Tanith, whose slender crescent was shining in the sky, and felt himself stronger than the Baals and full of contempt for them.

The arrangements for the sacrifice were already begun.

Part of a wall in the temple of Moloch was thrown down in order to draw out the brazen god without touching the ashes of the altar. Then as soon as the sun appeared the hierodules pushed it towards the square of Khamon.

It moved backwards sliding upon cylinders; its shoulders overlapped the walls. No sooner did the Carthaginians perceive it in the distance than they speedily took to flight, for the Baal could be looked upon with impunity only when exercising his wrath.

A smell of aromatics spread through the streets. All the temples had just been opened simultaneously, and from them there came forth tabernacles borne upon chariots, or upon litters carried by the pontiffs. Great plumes swayed at the corners of them, and rays were emitted from their slender pinnacles which terminated in balls of crystal, gold, silver or copper.

These were the Chanaanitish Baalim, offshoots of the supreme Baal, who were returning to their first cause to humble themselves before his might and annihilate themselves in his splendour.

Melkarth's pavilion, which was of fine purple, sheltered a petroleum flame; on Khamon's, which was of hyacinth colour, there rose an ivory phallus bordered with a circle of gems; between Eschmoun's curtains, which were blue as the ether, a sleeping python formed a circle with his tail, and the Patæc gods, held in the arms of their priests, looked like great infants in swaddling clothes with their heels touching the ground.

Then came all the inferior forms of the Divinity: Baal-Samin, god of celestial space; Baal-Peor, god of the sacred mountains; Baal-Zeboub, god of corruption, with those of the neighbouring countries and congenerous races: the Iarbal of Libya, the Adrammelech of Chaldæa, the Kijun of the Syrians; Derceto, with her virgin's face, crept on her fins, and the corpse of Tammouz was drawn along in the midst of a catafalque among torches and heads of hair. In order to subdue the kings of the firmament to the Sun, and prevent their particular influences from disturbing his, diversely coloured metal stars were brandished at the end of long poles; and all were there, from the dark Nebo, the genius of Mercury, to the hideous Rahab, which is the constellation of the

Crocodile. The Abaddirs, stones which had fallen from the moon, were whirling in slings of silver thread; little loaves, representing the female form, were borne on baskets by the priests of Ceres; others brought their fetishes and amulets; forgotten idols reappeared, while the mystic symbols had been taken from the very ships as though Carthage wished to concentrate herself wholly upon a single thought of death and desolation.

Before each tabernacle a man balanced a large vase of smoking incense on his head. Clouds hovered here and there, and the hangings, pendants, and embroideries of the sacred pavilions might be distinguished amid the thick vapours. These advanced slowly owing to their enormous weight. Sometimes the axles became fast in the streets; then the pious took advantage of the opportunity to touch the Baalim with their garments, which they preserved afterwards as holy things.

The brazen statue continued to advance towards the square of Khamon. The rich, carrying sceptres with emerald balls, set out from the bottom of Megara; the Ancients, with diadems on their heads, had assembled in Kinisdo, and masters of the finances, governors of provinces, sailors, and the numerous horde employed at funerals, all with the insignia of their magistracies or the instruments of their calling, were making their way towards the tabernacles which were descending from the Acropolis between the colleges of the pontiffs.

Out of deference to Moloch they had adorned themselves with the most splendid jewels. Diamonds sparkled on their black garments; but their rings were too large and fell from their wasted hands,—

nor could there have been anything so mournful as this silent crowd where earrings tapped against pale faces, and gold tiaras clasped brows contracted with stern despair.

At last the Baal arrived exactly in the centre of the square. His pontiffs arranged an enclosure with trellis-work to keep off the multitude, and remained around him at his feet.

The priests of Khamon, in tawny woollen robes, formed a line before their temple beneath the columns of the portico; those of Eschmoun, in linen mantles with necklaces of koukouphas' heads and pointed tiaras, posted themselves on the steps of the Acropolis; the priests of Melkarth, in violet tunics, took the western side; the priests of the Abaddirs, clasped with bands of Phrygian stuffs, placed themselves on the east, while towards the south, with the necromancers all covered with tattooings, and the shriekers in patched cloaks, were ranged the curates of the Patæc gods, and the Yidonim, who put the bone of a dead man into their mouths to learn the future. The priests of Ceres, who were dressed in blue robes, had prudently stopped in the street of Satheb, and in low tones were chanting a thesmophorion in the Megarian dialect.

From time to time files of men arrived, completely naked, their arms outstretched, and all holding one another by the shoulders. From the depths of their breasts they drew forth a hoarse and cavernous intonation; their eyes, which were fastened upon the colossus, shone through the dust, and they swayed their bodies simultaneously, and at equal distances, as though they were all affected by a single movement. They were so frenzied that to restore order the hierodules compelled them, with blows of the stick, to lie flat upon the ground, with their faces resting against the brass trellis-work.

Then it was that a man in a white robe advanced from the back of the square. He penetrated the crowd slowly, and people recognised a priest of Tanith — the high-priest Schahabarim. Hootings were raised, for the tyranny of the male principle prevailed that day in all consciences, and the goddess was actually so completely forgotten that the absence of her pontiffs had not been noticed. But the amazement increased when he was seen to open one of the doors in the trellis-work intended for those who entered to offer up victims. It was an outrage to their god, thought the priests of Moloch, that he had just committed, and they sought with eager gestures to repel him. Fed on the meat of the holocausts, clad in purple like kings, and wearing triple-storied crowns, they despised the pale eunuch, weakened with his macerations, and angry laughter shook their black beards, which were displayed on their breasts in the sun.

Schahabarim walked on, giving no reply, and, traversing the whole enclosure with deliberation, reached the legs of the colossus; then, spreading out both arms, he touched it on both sides, which was a solemn form of adoration. For a long time Rabbet had been torturing him, and in despair, or perhaps for lack of a god that completely satisfied his ideas, he had at last decided for this one.

The crowd, terrified by this act of apostasy, uttered a lengthened murmur. It was felt that the last tie which bound their souls to a merciful divinity was breaking.

But owing to his mutilation Schahabarim could take no part in the cult of the Baal. The men in the red cloaks shut him out from the enclosure; then, when he was outside, he went round all the colleges in succession, and the priest, henceforth without a god, disappeared in the crowd. It scattered at his approach.

Meanwhile a fire of aloes, cedar, and laurel was burning between the legs of the colossus. The tips of its long wings dipped into the flame; the unguents with which it had been rubbed flowed like sweat over its brazen limbs. Around the circular flagstone on which its feet rested, the children, wrapped in black veils, formed a motionless circle; and its extravagantly long arms reached down their palms to them as though to seize the crown that they formed and carry it to the sky.

The rich, the Ancients, the women, the whole multitude, thronged behind the priests and on the terraces of the houses. The large painted stars revolved no longer; the tabernacles were set upon the ground; and the fumes from the censers ascended perpendicularly, spreading their bluish branches through the azure like gigantic trees.

Many fainted; others became inert and petrified in their ecstasy. Infinite anguish weighed upon the breasts of the beholders. The last shouts died out one by one,—and the people of Carthage stood breathless, and absorbed in the longing of their terror.

At last the high priest of Moloch passed his left hand beneath the children's veils, plucked a lock of hair from their foreheads, and threw it upon the flames. Then the men in the red cloaks chanted the sacred hymn:

4—8

"Homage to thee, Sun! king of the two zones, self-generating Creator, Father and Mother, Father and Son, God and Goddess, Goddess and God!" And their voices were lost in the outburst of instruments sounding simultaneously to drown the cries of the victims. The eight-stringed scheminiths, the kinnors which had ten strings, and the nebals which had twelve, grated, whistled, and thundered. Enormous leathern bags, bristling with pipes, made a shrill clashing noise; the tabourines, beaten with all the players' might, resounded with heavy, rapid blows; and, in spite of the fury of the clarions, the salsalim snapped like grasshoppers' wings.

The hierodules, with a long hook, opened the seven-storied compartments on the body of the Baal. They put meal into the highest, two turtle-doves into the second, an ape into the third, a ram into the fourth, a sheep into the fifth, and as no ox was to be had for the sixth, a tawny hide taken from the sanctuary was thrown into it. The seventh compartment yawned empty still.

Before undertaking anything it was well to make trial of the arms of the god. Slender chainlets stretched from his fingers up to his shoulders and fell behind, where men by pulling them made the two hands rise to a level with the elbows, and come close together against the belly; they were moved several times in succession with little abrupt jerks. Then the instruments were still. The fire roared.

The pontiffs of Moloch walked about on the great flagstone scanning the multitude.

An individual sacrifice was necessary, a perfectly voluntary oblation, which was considered as carrying the others along with it. But no one had appeared

at the beginning wished to count them, to see whether their number corresponded with the days of the solar year; but others were brought, and it was impossible to distinguish them in the giddy motion of the horrible arms. This lasted for a long, indefinite time until the evening. Then the partitions inside assumed a darker glow, and burning flesh might be seen. Some even believed that they could descry hair, limbs, and whole bodies.

Night fell; clouds accumulated above the Baal. The funeral-pile, which was flameless now, formed a pyramid of coals up to his knees; completely red like a giant covered with blood, he looked, with his head thrown back, as though he were staggering beneath the weight of his intoxication.

In proportion as the priests made haste, the frenzy of the people increased; as the number of the victims was diminishing, some cried out to spare them, others that still more were needful. The walls, with their burden of people, seemed to be giving way beneath the howlings of terror and mystic voluptuousness. Then the faithful came into the passages, dragging their children, who clung to them; and they beat them in order to make them let go, and handed them over to the men in red. The instrument-players sometimes stopped through exhaustion; then the cries of the mothers might be heard, and the frizzling of the fat as it fell upon the coals. The henbane-drinkers crawled on all fours around the colossus, roaring like tigers; the Yidonim vaticinated, the Devotees sang with their cloven lips; the trellis-work had been broken through, all wished for a share in the sacrifice; — and fathers, whose children had died previously, cast their effigies, their playthings, their preserved bones into the fire. Some who had knives rushed upon the rest. They slaughtered one another. The hierodules took the fallen ashes at the edge of the flagstone in bronze fans, and cast them into the air that the sacrifice might be scattered over the town and even to the region of the stars.

The loud noise and great light had attracted the Barbarians to the foot of the walls; they clung to the wreck of the helepolis to have a better view, and gazed open-mouthed in horror.

XIV.

The Pass of the Hatchet.

THE Carthaginians had not re-entered their houses when the clouds accumulated more thickly; those who raised their heads towards the colossus could feel big drops on their foreheads, and the rain fell.

It fell the whole night plentifully, in floods; the thunder growled; it was the voice of Moloch; he had vanquished Tanith; and she, being now fecundated, opened up her vast bosom in heaven's heights. Sometimes she could be seen in a clear and luminous spot stretched upon cushions of cloud; and then the darkness would close in again as though she were still too weary and wished to sleep again; the Carthaginians, all believing that water is brought forth by the moon, shouted to make her travail easy.

The rain beat upon the terraces and overflowed them, forming lakes in the courts, cascades on the staircases, and eddies at the corners of the streets. It poured in warm heavy masses and urgent streams; big frothy jets leaped from the corners of all the buildings; and it seemed as though whitish cloths hung dimly upon the walls, and the washed temple-roofs shone black in the gleam of the lightning. Torrents descended from the Acropolis by a thousand paths; houses suddenly gave way, and small beams, plaster, rubbish, and furniture passed along in the streams which ran impetuously over the pavement.

Amphoras, flagons, and canvases had been placed out of doors; but the torches were extinguished; brands were taken from the funeral-pile of the Baal, and the Carthaginians bent back their necks and opened their mouths to drink. Others by the side of the miry pools, plunged their arms into them up to the arm-pits, and filled themselves so abundantly with water that they vomited it forth like buffaloes. The freshness gradually spread; they breathed in the damp air with play of limb, and in the happiness of their intoxication boundless hope soon arose. All their miseries were forgotten. Their country was born anew.

They felt the need, as it were, of directing upon others the extravagant fury which they had been unable to employ against themselves. Such a sacrifice could not be vain; although they felt no remorse they found themselves carried away by the frenzy which results from complicity in irreparable crimes.

The Barbarians had encountered the storm in their ill-closed tents; and they were still quite chilled on the morrow as they tramped through the mud in search of their stores and weapons, which were spoiled and lost.

Hamilcar went himself to see Hanno, and, in virtue of his plenary powers, intrusted the command to him. The old Suffet hesitated for a few minutes between his animosity and his appetite for authority, but he accepted nevertheless.

Hamilcar next took out a galley armed with a catapult at each end. He placed it in the gulf in front of the raft; then he embarked his stoutest troops on board such vessels as were available. He was apparently taking to flight; and running north-ward before the wind he disappeared in the mist.

But three days afterwards, when the attack was about to begin again, some people arrived tumultu-ously from the Libyan coast. Barca had come among them. He had carried off provisions every-where, and he was spreading through the country.

Then the Barbarians were indignant as though he were betraying them. Those who were most weary of the siege, and especially the Gauls, did not hesi-tate to leave the walls in order to try to rejoin him. Spendius wanted to reconstruct the helepolis; Matho had traced an imaginary line from his tent to Megara, and inwardly swore to follow it, and none of their men stirred. But the rest, under the command of Autaritus, went off, abandoning the western part of the rampart, and so profound was the careless-ness exhibited that no one even thought of replacing them.

Narr' Havas spied them from afar in the moun-tains. During the night he led all his men along the sea-shore on the outer side of the Lagoon, and en-tered Carthage.

He presented himself as a savior with six thousand men all carrying meal under their cloaks, and forty elephants laden with forage and dried meat. The people flocked quickly around them; they gave them names. The sight of these strong animals, sacred to Baal, gave the Carthaginians even more joy than the arrival of such relief; it was a token of the tender-

ness of the god, a proof that he was at last about
to interfere in the war to defend them.

Narr' Havas received the compliments of the Ancients. Then he ascended to Salammbô's palace.

He had not seen her again since the time when
in Hamilcar's tent amid the five armies he had felt
her little, cold, soft hand fastened to his own; she
had left for Carthage after the betrothal. His love,
which had been diverted by other ambitions, had
come back to him; and now he expected to enjoy
his rights, to marry her, and take her.

Salammbô did not understand how the young
man could ever become her master! Although she
asked Tanith every day for Matho's death, her horror
of the Libyan was growing less. She vaguely felt
that the hate with which he had persecuted her was
something almost religious,—and she would fain
have seen in Narr' Havas's person a reflection, as it
were, of that malice which still dazzled her. She desired to know him better, and yet his presence would
have embarrassed her. She sent him word that she
could not receive him.

Moreover, Hamilcar had forbidden his people to
admit the King of the Numidians to see her; by putting off his reward to the end of the war he hoped
to retain his devotion;—and, through dread of the
Suffet, Narr' Havas withdrew.

But he bore himself haughtily towards the Hundred. He changed their arrangements. He demanded
privileges for his men, and placed them on important posts; thus the Barbarians stared when they
perceived Numidians on the towers.

The surprise of the Carthaginians was greater still
when three hundred of their own people, who had

been made prisoners during the Sicilian war, arrived
on board an old Punic trireme. Hamilcar, in fact,
had secretly sent back to the Quirites the crews of
the Latin vessels, taken before the defection of the
Tyrian towns; and, to reciprocate the courtesy, Rome
was now sending him back her captives. She scorned
the overtures of the Mercenaries in Sardinia, and
would not even recognise the inhabitants of Utica as
subjects.

Hiero, who was ruling at Syracuse, was carried
away by this example. For the preservation of his
own States it was necessary that an equilibrium
should exist between the two peoples; he was inter-
ested, therefore, in the safety of the Chanaanites, and
he declared himself their friend, and sent them twelve
hundred oxen, with fifty-three thousand nebels of
pure wheat.

A deeper reason prompted aid to Carthage. It
was felt that if the Mercenaries triumphed, every one,
from soldier to plate-washer, would rise, and that no
government and no house could resist them.

Meanwhile Hamilcar was scouring the eastern districts. He drove back the Gauls, and all the Barbarians found that they were themselves in something
like a state of siege.

Then he set himself to harass them. He would
arrive and then retire, and by constantly renewing
this manœuvre, he gradually detached them from
their encampments. Spendius was obliged to follow
them, and in the end Matho yielded in like manner.

He did not pass beyond Tunis. He shut himself
up within its walls. This persistence was full of
wisdom, for soon Narr' Havas was to be seen issuing from the gate of Khamon with his elephants and

soldiers. Hamilcar was recalling him, but the other Barbarians were already wandering about in the provinces in pursuit of the Suffet.

The latter had received three thousand Gauls from Clypea. He had horses brought to him from Cyrenaica, and armour from Brutium, and began the war again.

Never had his genius been so impetuous and fertile. For five moons he dragged his enemies after him. He had an end to which he wished to guide them.

The Barbarians had at first tried to encompass him with small detachments, but he always escaped them. They ceased to separate. Their army amounted to about forty thousand men, and several times they enjoyed the sight of seeing the Carthaginians fall back.

The horsemen of Narr' Havas were what they found most tormenting. Often, at times of the greatest weariness, when they were advancing over the plains, and dozing beneath the weight of their arms, a great line of dust would suddenly rise on the horizon; there would be a galloping up to them, and a rain of darts would pour from the bosom of a cloud filled with flaming eyes. The Numidians in their white cloaks would utter loud shouts, raise their arms, press their rearing stallions with their knees, and, wheeling them round abruptly, would then disappear. They had always supplies of javelins and dromedaries some distance off, and they would return more terrible than before, howl like wolves, and take to flight like vultures. The Barbarians posted at the extremities of the files fell one by one; and this would continue until evening, when an attempt would be made to enter the mountains.

Although they were perilous for elephants, Hamilcar made his way in among them. He followed the long chain which extends from the promontory of Hermæum to the top of Zagouan. This, they believed, was a device for hiding the insufficiency of his troops. But the continual uncertainty in which he kept them exasperated them at last more than any defeat. They did not lose heart, and marched after him.

At last one evening they surprised a body of velites amid some big rocks at the entrance of a pass between the Silver Mountain and the Lead Mountain; the entire army was certainly in front of them, for a noise of footsteps and clarions could be heard; the Carthaginians immediately fled through the gorge. It descended into a plain, and was shaped like an iron hatchet with a surrounding of lofty cliffs. The Barbarians dashed into it in order to overtake the velites; quite at the bottom other Carthaginians were running tumultuously amid galloping oxen. A man in a red cloak was to be seen; it was the Suffet; they shouted this to one another; and they were carried away with increased fury and joy. Several, from laziness or prudence, had remained on the threshold of the pass. But some cavalry, debouching from a wood, beat them down upon the rest with blows of pike and sabre; and soon all the Barbarians were below in the plain.

Then this great human mass, after swaying to and fro for some time, stood still; they could discover no outlet.

Those who were nearest to the pass went back again, but the passage had entirely disappeared. They hailed those in front to make them go on; they were being crushed against the mountain, and from a distance they inveighed against their companions, who were unable to find the route again.

In fact the Barbarians had scarcely descended when men who had been crouching behind the rocks raised the latter with beams and overthrew them, and as the slope was steep the huge blocks had rolled down pell-mell and completely stopped up the narrow opening.

At the other extremity of the plain stretched a long passage, split in gaps here and there, and leading to a ravine which ascended to the upper plateau, where the Punic army was stationed. Ladders had been placed beforehand in this passage against the wall of cliff; and, protected by the windings of the gaps, the velites were able to seize and mount them before being overtaken. Several even made their way to the bottom of the ravine; they were drawn up with cables, for the ground at this spot was of moving sand, and so much inclined that it was impossible to climb it even on the knees. The Barbarians arrived almost immediately. But a portcullis, forty cubits high, and made to fit the intervening space exactly, suddenly sank before them like a rampart fallen from the skies.

The Suffet's combinations had therefore succeeded. None of the Mercenaries knew the mountain, and, marching as they did at the head of their columns, they had drawn on the rest. The rocks, which were somewhat narrow at the base, had been easily cast down; and, while all were running, his army had raised shouts, as of distress, on the horizon. Hamilcar, it is true, might have lost his velites, only half of whom remained, but he would have sacrificed twenty times as many for the success of such an enterprise.

The Barbarians pressed forward until morning, in compact files, from one end of the plain to the other. They felt the mountain with their hands, seeking to discover a passage.

At last day broke; and they perceived all about them a great white wall hewn with the pick. And no means of safety, no hope! The two natural outlets from this blind alley were closed by the portcullis and the heaps of rocks.

Then they all looked at one another without speaking. They sank down in collapse, feeling an icy coldness in their loins, and an overwhelming weight upon their eyelids.

They rose, and bounded against the rocks. But the lowest were weighted by the pressure of the others, and were immovable. They tried to cling to them so as to reach the top, but the bellying shape of the great masses rendered all hold impossible. They sought to cleave the ground on both sides of the gorge, but their instruments broke. They made a large fire with the tent poles, but the fire could not burn the mountain.

They returned to the portcullis; it was garnished with long nails as thick as stakes, as sharp as the spines of a porcupine, and closer than the hairs of a brush. But they were animated by such rage that they dashed themselves against it. The first were pierced to the backbone, those coming next surged over them, and all fell back, leaving human fragments and bloodstained hair on those horrible branches.

When their discouragement was somewhat abated, they made an examination of the provisions. The

Mercenaries, whose baggage was lost, possessed scarcely enough for two days; and all the rest found themselves destitute,—for they had been awaiting a convoy promised by the villages of the South.

However, some bulls were roaming about, those which the Carthaginians had loosed in the gorge to attract the Barbarians. They killed them with lance thrusts and ate them, and when their stomachs were filled their thoughts were less mournful.

The next day they slaughtered all the mules to the number of about forty; then they scraped the skins, boiled the entrails, pounded the bones, and did not yet despair; the army from Tunis had no doubt been warned, and was coming.

But on the evening of the fifth day their hunger increased; they gnawed their sword-belts, and the little sponges which bordered the bottom of their helmets.

These forty thousand men were massed into the species of hippodrome formed by the mountain about them. Some remained in front of the portcullis, or at the foot of the rocks; the rest covered the plain confusedly. The strong shunned one another, and the timid sought out the brave, who, nevertheless, were unable to save them.

To avoid infection, the corpses of the velites had been speedily buried; and the position of the graves was no longer visible.

All the Barbarians lay drooping on the ground. A veteran would pass between their lines here and there; and they would howl curses against the Carthaginians, against Hamilcar, and against Matho, although he was innocent of their disaster; but it seemed to them that their pains would have been less if he had shared them. Then they groaned, and some wept softly like little children.

They came to the captains and besought them to grant them something that would alleviate their sufferings. The others made no reply; or, seized with fury, would pick up a stone and fling it in their faces.

Several, in fact, carefully kept a reserve of food in a hole in the ground—a few handfuls of dates, or a little meal; and they ate this during the night, with their heads bent beneath their cloaks. Those who had swords kept them naked in their hands, and the most suspicious remained standing with their backs against the mountain.

They accused their chiefs and threatened them. Autaritus was not afraid of showing himself. With the Barbaric obstinacy which nothing could discourage, he would advance twenty times a day to the rocks at the bottom, hoping every time to find them perchance displaced; and swaying his heavy fur-covered shoulders, he reminded his companions of a bear coming forth from its cave in springtime to see whether the snows are melted.

Spendius, surrounded by the Greeks, hid himself in one of the gaps; as he was afraid, he caused a rumour of his death to be spread.

They were now hideously lean; their skin was overlaid with bluish marblings. On the evening of the ninth day three Iberians died.

Their frightened companions left the spot. They were stripped, and the white, naked bodies lay in the sunshine on the sand.

Then the Garamantians began to prowl slowly round about them. They were men accustomed to

4—9

existence in solitude, and they reverenced no god. At last the oldest of the band made a sign, and bending over the corpses they cut strips from them with their knives, then squatted upon their heels and ate. The rest looked on from a distance; they uttered cries of horror;—many, nevertheless, being, at the bottom of their souls, jealous of such courage.

In the middle of the night some of these approached, and, dissembling their eagerness, asked for a small mouthful, merely to try, they said. Bolder ones came up; their number increased; there was soon a crowd. But almost all of them let their hands fall on feeling the cold flesh on the edge of their lips; others, on the contrary, devoured it with delight.

That they might be led away by example, they urged one another on mutually. Such as had at first refused went to see the Garamantians, and returned no more. They cooked the pieces on coals at the point of the sword; they salted them with dust, and contended for the best morsels. When nothing was left of the three corpses, their eyes ranged over the whole plain to find others.

But were they not in possession of Carthaginians —twenty captives taken in the last encounter, whom no one had noticed up to the present? These disappeared; moreover, it was an act of vengeance. Then, as they must live, as the taste for this food had become developed, and as they were dying, they cut the throats of the water-carriers, grooms, and all the serving-men belonging to the Mercenaries. They killed some of them every day. Some ate much, recovered strength, and were sad no more.

Soon this resource failed. Then the longing was directed to the wounded and sick. Since they could not recover, it was as well to release them from their tortures; and, as soon as a man began to stagger, all exclaimed that he was now lost, and ought to be made use of for the rest. Artifices were employed to accelerate their death; the last remnant of their foul portion was stolen from them; they were trodden on as though by inadvertence; those in the last throes wishing to make believe that they were strong, strove to stretch out their arms, to rise, to laugh. Men who had swooned came to themselves at the touch of a notched blade sawing off a limb; —and they still slew, ferociously and needlessly, to sate their fury.

A mist heavy and warm, such as comes in those regions at the end of winter, sank on the fourteenth day upon the army. This change of temperature brought numerous deaths with it, and corruption was developed with frightful rapidity in the warm dampness which was kept in by the sides of the mountain. The drizzle that fell upon the corpses softened them, and soon made the plain one broad tract of rottenness. Whitish vapours floated overhead; they pricked the nostrils, penetrated the skin, and troubled the sight; and the Barbarians thought that through the exhalations of the breath they could see the souls of their companions. They were overwhelmed with immense disgust. They wished for nothing more; they preferred to die.

Two days afterwards the weather became fine again, and hunger seized them once more. It seemed to them that their stomachs were being wrenched from them with tongs. Then they rolled about in convulsions, flung handfuls of dust into their mouths, bit their arms, and burst into frantic laughter.

They were still more tormented by thirst, for they had not a drop of water, the leathern bottles having been completely dried up since the ninth day. To cheat their need they applied their tongues to the metal plates on their waist-belts, their ivory pommels, and the steel of their swords. Some former caravan-leaders tightened their waists with ropes. Others sucked a pebble. They drank urine cooled in their brazen helmets.

And they still expected the army from Tunis! The length of time which it took in coming was, according to their conjectures, an assurance of its early arrival. Besides, Matho, who was a brave fellow, would not desert them. "'Twill be to-morrow!" they would say to one another; and then to-morrow would pass.

At the beginning they had offered up prayers and vows, and practised all kinds of incantations. Just now their only feeling to their divinities was one of hatred, and they strove to revenge themselves by believing in them no more.

Men of violent disposition perished first; the Africans held out better than the Gauls. Zarxas lay stretched at full length among the Balearians, his hair over his arm, inert. Spendius found a plant with broad leaves filled abundantly with juice, and after declaring that it was poisonous, so as to keep off the rest, he fed himself upon it.

They were too weak to knock down the flying crows with stones. Sometimes when a gypaëtus was perched on a corpse, and had been mangling it for a long time, a man would set himself to crawl towards it with a javelin between his teeth. He would support himself with one hand, and after taking a good aim, throw his weapon. The white-feathered creature, disturbed by the noise, would desist and look about in a tranquil fashion like a cormorant on a rock, and would then again thrust in its hideous, yellow beak, while the man, in despair, would fall flat on his face in the dust. Some succeeded in discovering chameleons and serpents. But it was the love of life that kept them alive. They directed their souls to this idea exclusively, and clung to existence by an effort of the will that prolonged it.

The most stoical kept close to one another, seated in a circle here and there, among the dead in the middle of the plain; and wrapped in their cloaks they gave themselves up silently to their sadness.

Those who had been born in towns recalled the resounding streets, the taverns, theatres, baths, and the barbers' shops where there are tales to be heard. Others could once more see country districts at sunset, when the yellow corn waves, and the great oxen ascend the hills again with the ploughshares on their necks. Travellers dreamed of cisterns, hunters of their forests, veterans of battles; and in the somnolence that benumbed them their thoughts jostled one another with the precipitancy and clearness of dreams. Hallucinations came suddenly upon them; they sought for a door in the mountain in order to flee, and tried to pass through it. Others thought that they were sailing in a storm and gave orders for the handling of a ship, or else fell back in terror, perceiving Punic battalions in the clouds. There were some who imagined themselves at a feast, and sang.

Many through a strange mania would repeat the same word or continually make the same gesture.

Then when they happened to raise their heads and look at one another they were choked with sobs on discovering the horrible ravages made in their faces. Some had ceased to suffer, and to while away the hours told of the perils which they had escaped.

Death was certain and imminent to all. How many times had they not tried to open up a passage! As to implore terms from the conqueror, by what means could they do so? They did not even know where Hamilcar was.

The wind was blowing from the direction of the ravine. It made the sand flow perpetually in cascades over the portcullis; and the cloaks and hair of the Barbarians were being covered with it as though the earth were rising upon them and desirous of burying them. Nothing stirred; the eternal mountain seemed still higher to them every morning.

Sometimes flights of birds darted past beneath the blue sky in the freedom of the air. The men closed their eyes that they might not see them.

At first they felt a buzzing in their ears, their nails grew black, the cold reached to their breasts; they lay upon their sides and expired without a cry.

On the nineteenth day two thousand Asiatics were dead, with fifteen hundred from the Archipelago, eight thousand from Libya, the youngest of the Mercenaries and whole tribes—in all twenty thousand soldiers, or half of the army.

Autaritus, who had only fifty Gauls left, was going to kill himself in order to put an end to this state of things, when he thought he saw a man on the top of the mountain in front of him.

Owing to his elevation this man did not appear taller than a dwarf. However, Autaritus recognised a shield shaped like a trefoil on his left arm. "A Carthaginian!" he exclaimed, and immediately throughout the plain, before the portcullis and beneath the rocks, all rose. The soldier was walking along the edge of the precipice; the Barbarians gazed at him from below.

Spendius picked up the head of an ox; then having formed a diadem with two belts, he fixed it on the horns at the end of a pole in token of pacific intentions. The Carthaginian disappeared. They waited.

At last in the evening a sword-belt suddenly fell from above like a stone loosened from the cliff. It was made of red leather covered with embroidery, with three diamond stars, and stamped in the centre, it bore the mark of the Great Council: a horse beneath a palm-tree. This was Hamilcar's reply, the safe-conduct that he sent them.

They had nothing to fear; any change of fortune brought with it the end of their woes. They were moved with extravagant joy, they embraced one another, they wept. Spendius, Autaritus, and Zarxas, four Italiotes, a Negro and two Spartans offered themselves as envoys. They were immediately accepted. They did not know, however, by what means they should get away.

But a cracking sound in the direction of the rocks; and the most elevated of them, after rocking to and fro, rebounded to the bottom. In fact, if they were immovable on the side of the Barbarians — for it would have been necessary to urge them up an incline plane, and they were, moreover, heaped together owing to the narrowness of the gorge — on the others, on the contrary, it was sufficient to drive against them with violence to make them descend. The Carthaginians pushed them, and at daybreak they projected into the plain like the steps of an immense ruined staircase.

The Barbarians were still unable to climb them. Ladders were held out for their assistance; all rushed upon them. The discharge of a catapult drove the crowd back; only the Ten were taken away.

They walked amid the Clinabarians, leaning their hands on the horses' croups for support.

Now that their first joy was over they began to harbour anxieties. Hamilcar's demands would be cruel. But Spendius reassured them.

"*I* will speak!" And he boasted that he knew excellent things to say for the safety of the army.

Behind all the bushes they met with ambushed sentries, who prostrated themselves before the sword-belt which Spendius had placed over his shoulder.

When they reached the Punic camp the crowd flocked around them, and they thought that they could hear whisperings and laughter. The door of a tent opened.

Hamilcar was at the very back of it seated on a stool beside a table on which there shone a naked sword. He was surrounded by captains, who were standing.

He started back on perceiving these men, and then bent over to examine them.

Their pupils were strangely dilated, and there was a great black circle round their eyes, which extended to the lower parts of their ears; their bluish noses stood out between their hollow cheeks, which were chinked with deep wrinkles; the skin of their bodies was too large for their muscles, and was hidden be-

neath a slate-coloured dust; their lips were glued to
their yellow teeth; they exhaled an infectious odour;
they might have been taken for half-opened tombs,
for living sepulchres.

In the centre of the tent, on a mat on which the
captains were about to sit down, there was a dish of
smoking gourds. The Barbarians fastened their eyes
upon it with a shivering in all their limbs, and tears
came to their eyelids; nevertheless they restrained
themselves.

Hamilcar turned away to speak to some one. Then
they all flung themselves upon it, flat on the ground.
Their faces were soaked in the fat, and the noise of
their deglutition was mingled with the sobs of joy
which they uttered. Through astonishment, doubtless,
rather than pity, they were allowed to finish the mess.
Then when they had risen Hamilcar with a sign commanded the man who bore the sword-belt to speak.
Spendius was afraid; he stammered.

Hamilcar, while listening to him, kept turning
round on his finger a big gold ring, the same which
had stamped the seal of Carthage upon the sword-
belt. He let it fall to the ground; Spendius immediately picked it up; his servile habits came back to him
in the presence of his master. The others quivered
with indignation at such baseness.

But the Greek raised his voice and spoke for a
long time in a rapid, insidious, and even violent fashion, setting forth the crimes of Hanno, whom he knew
to be Barca's enemy, and striving to move Hamilcar's
pity by the details of their miseries and the recollection
of their devotion; in the end he became forgetful of
himself, being carried away by the warmth of his tem-
per.

Hamilcar replied that he accepted their excuses. Peace, then, was about to be concluded, and now it would be a definitive one! But he required that ten Mercenaries, chosen by himself, should be delivered up to him without weapons or tunics.

They had not expected such clemency; Spendius exclaimed: "Ah! twenty if you wish, master!"

"No! ten will suffice," replied Hamilcar quietly.

They were sent out of the tent to deliberate. As soon as they were alone, Autaritus protested against the sacrifice of their companions, and Zarxas said to Spendius:

"Why did you not kill him? his sword was there beside you!"

"Him!" said Spendius. "Him! him!" he repeated several times, as though the thing had been impossible, and Hamilcar were an immortal.

They were so overwhelmed with weariness that they stretched themselves on their backs on the ground, not knowing at what resolution to arrive.

Spendius urged them to yield. At last they consented, and went in again.

Then the Suffet put his hand into the hands of the ten Barbarians in turn, and pressed their thumbs; then he rubbed it on his garment, for their viscous skin gave a rude, soft impression to the touch, a greasy tingling which induced horripilation. Afterwards he said to them:

"You are really all the chiefs of the Barbarians, and you have sworn for them?"

"Yes!" they replied.

"Without constraint, from the bottom of your souls, with the intention of fulfilling your promises?"

They assured him that they were returning to the rest in order to fulfil them.

"Well!" rejoined the Suffet, "in accordance with the convention concluded between myself, Barca, and the ambassadors of the Mercenaries, it is you whom I choose and shall keep!"

Spendius fell swooning upon the mat. The Barbarians, as though abandoning him, pressed close together; and there was not a word, not a complaint.

Their companions, who were waiting for them, not seeing them return, believed themselves betrayed. The envoys had no doubt given themselves up to the Suffet.

They waited for two days longer; then on the morning of the third, their resolution was taken. With ropes, picks, and arrows, arranged like rungs between strips of canvas, they succeeded in scaling the rocks; and leaving the weakest, about three thousand in number, behind them, they began their march to rejoin the army at Tunis.

Above the gorge there stretched a meadow thinly sown with shrubs; the Barbarians devoured the buds. Afterwards they found a field of beans; and everything disappeared as though a cloud of grasshoppers had passed that way. Three hours later they reached a second plateau bordered by a belt of green hills.

Among the undulations of these hillocks, silvery sheaves shone at intervals from one another; the Barbarians, who were dazzled by the sun, could perceive confusedly below great black masses supporting them; these rose, as though they were expanding. They were lances in towers on elephants terribly armed.

Besides the spears on their breasts, the bodkin

tusks, the brass plates which covered their sides, and the daggers fastened to their knee-caps, they had at the extremity of their trunks a leathern bracelet, in which the handle of a broad cutlass was inserted; they had set out simultaneously from the back part of the plain, and were advancing on both sides in parallel lines.

The Barbarians were frozen with a nameless terror. They did not even try to flee. They already found themselves surrounded.

The elephants entered into this mass of men; and the spurs on their breasts divided it, the lances on their tusks upturned it like ploughshares; they cut, hewed, and hacked with the scythes on their trunks; the towers, which were full of phalaricas, looked like volcanoes on the march; nothing could be distinguished but a large heap, whereon human flesh, pieces of brass and blood made white spots, grey sheets and red fuses. The horrible animals dug out black furrows as they passed through the midst of it all.

The fiercest was driven by a Numidian who was crowned with a diadem of plumes. He hurled javelins with frightful quickness, giving at intervals a long shrill whistle. The great beasts, docile as dogs, kept an eye on him during the carnage.

The circle of them narrowed by degrees; the weakened Barbarians offered no resistance; the elephants were soon in the centre of the plain. They lacked space; they thronged half-rearing together, and their tusks clashed against one another. Suddenly Narr' Harvas quieted them, and wheeling round they trotted back to the hills.

Two syntagmata, however, had taken refuge on the right in a bend of the ground, had thrown away their arms, and were all kneeling with their faces towards the Punic tents imploring mercy with uplifted arms.

Their legs and hands were tied; then when they were stretched on the ground beside one another the elephants were brought back.

Their breasts cracked like boxes being forced; two were crushed at every step; the big feet sank into the bodies with a motion of the haunches which made the elephants appear lame. They went on to the very end.

The level surface of the plain again became motionless. Night fell. Hamilcar was delighting himself with the spectacle of his vengeance, but suddenly he started.

He saw, and all saw, some more Barbarians six hundred paces to the left on the summit of a peak! In fact four hundred of the stoutest Mercenaries, Etruscans, Libyans, and Spartans had gained the heights at the beginning, and had remained there in uncertainty until now. After the massacre of their companions they resolved to make their way through the Carthaginians; they were already descending in serried columns, in a marvellous and formidable fashion.

A herald was immediately dispatched to them. The Suffet needed soldiers; he received them unconditionally, so greatly did he admire their bravery. They could even, said the man of Carthage, come a little nearer, to a place, which he pointed out to them, where they would find provisions.

The Barbarians ran thither and spent the night in eating. Then the Carthaginians broke into clamours against the Suffet's partiality for the Mercenaries.

Did he yield to these outbursts of insatiable hatred or was it a refinement of treachery? The next day he came himself, without a sword and bare-headed, with an escort of Clinabarians, and announced to them that having too many to feed he did not intend to keep them. Nevertheless, as he wanted men and he knew of no means of selecting the good ones, they were to fight together to the death; he would then admit the conquerors into his own body-guard. This death was quite as good as another;—and then moving his soldiers aside (for the Punic standards hid the horizon from the Mercenaries) he showed them the one hundred and ninety-two elephants under Narr' Havas, forming a single straight line, their trunks brandishing broad steel blades like giant arms holding axes above their heads.

The Barbarians looked at one another silently. It was not death that made them turn pale, but the horrible compulsion to which they found themselves reduced.

The community of their lives had brought about profound friendship among these men. The camp, with most, took the place of their country; living without a family they transferred the needful tenderness to a companion, and they would fall asleep in the starlight side by side under the same cloak. And then in their perpetual wanderings through all sorts of countries, murders, and adventures, they had contracted affections, one for the other, in which the stronger protected the younger in the midst of battles, helped him to cross precipices, sponged the sweat of fevers from his brow, and stole food for him, and the weaker, a child perhaps, who had been picked up on the roadside, and had then become a Mercenary, repaid this devotion by a thousand kindnesses.

They exchanged their necklaces and earrings, presents which they had made to one another in former
days, after great peril, or in hours of intoxication. All
asked to die, and none would strike. A young fellow
might be seen here and there, saying to another
whose beard was grey: "No! no! you are more ro-
bust! you will avenge us, kill me!" and the man
would reply: "I have fewer years to live! Strike to
the heart, and think no more about it!" Brothers
gazed on one another with clasped hands, and friend
bade friend eternal farewells, standing and weeping
upon his shoulder.

They drew off their cuirasses that the sword-
points might be thrust in the more quickly. Then
there appeared the marks of the great blows which
they had received for Carthage, and which looked
like inscriptions on columns.

They placed themselves in four equal ranks, after
the fashion of gladiators, and began with timid engagements. Some had even bandaged their eyes, and
their swords waved gently through the air like blind
men's sticks. The Carthaginians hooted, and shouted
to them that they were cowards. The Barbarians became animated, and soon the combat was general,
headlong, and terrible.

Sometimes two men all covered with blood would
stop, fall into each other's arms, and die with mutual
kisses. None drew back. They rushed upon the extended blades. Their delirium was so frenzied that the
Carthaginians in the distance were afraid.

At last they stopped. Their breasts made a great
hoarse noise, and their eyeballs could be seen through
their long hair, which hung down as though it had
come out of a purple bath. Several were turning

round rapidly, like panthers wounded in the forehead. Others stood motionless looking at a corpse at their feet; then they would suddenly tear their faces with their nails, take their swords in both hands, and plunge them into their own bodies.

There were still sixty left. They asked for drink. They were told by shouts to throw away their swords, and when they had done so water was brought to them.

While they were drinking, with their faces buried in the vases, sixty Carthaginians leaped upon them and killed them with stilettos in the back.

Hamilcar had done this to gratify the instincts of his army, and, by means of this treachery, to attach it to his own person.

The war, then, was ended; at least he believed that it was; Matho would not resist; in his impatience the Suffet commanded an immediate departure.

His scouts came to tell him that a convoy had been descried, departing towards the Lead Mountain. Hamilcar did not trouble himself about it. The Mercenaries once annihilated, the Nomads would give him no further trouble. The important matter was to take Tunis. He advanced by forced marches upon it.

He had sent Narr' Havas to Carthage with the news of his victory; and the King of the Numidians, proud of his success, visited Salammbô.

She received him in her gardens under a large sycamore tree, amid pillows of yellow leather, and with Taanach beside her. Her face was covered with a white scarf, which, passing over her mouth and forehead, allowed only her eyes to be seen; but her lips shone in the transparency of the tissue like the

gems on her fingers, for Salammbô had both her hands
wrapped up, and did not make a gesture during the
whole conversation.

Narr' Havas announced the defeat of the Barbarians
to her. She thanked him with a blessing for the services which he had rendered to her father. Then he
began to tell about the whole campaign.

The doves on the palm trees around them cooed
softly, and other birds fluttered amid the grass: ring-
necked glareolas, Tartessus quails and Punic guinea-
fowl. The garden, long uncultivated, had multiplied
its verdure; coloquintidas mounted into the branches
of cassias, the asclepias was scattered over fields of
roses, all kinds of vegetation formed entwinings and
bowers; and here and there, as in the woods, sun-
rays, descending obliquely, marked the shadow of a
leaf upon the ground. Domestic animals, grown wild
again, fled at the slightest noise. Sometimes a gazelle might be seen trailing scattered peacocks' feathers
after its little black hoofs. The clamours of the distant
town were lost in the murmuring of the waves. The
sky was quite blue, and not a sail was visible on the
sea.

Narr' Havas had ceased speaking; Salammbô was
looking at him without replying. He wore a linen
robe with flowers painted on it, and with gold fringes
at the hem; two silver arrows fastened his plaited
hair at the tips of his ears; his right hand rested on
a pike-staff adorned with circles of electrum and tufts
of hair.

As she watched him a crowd of dim thoughts
absorbed her. This young man, with his gentle
voice and feminine figure, captivated her eyes by the
grace of his person, and seemed to her like an elder

4—10

sister sent by the Baals to protect her. The recollection of Matho came upon her, nor did she resist the desire to learn what had become of him.

Narr' Havas replied that the Carthaginians were advancing towards Tunis to take it. In proportion as he set forth their chances of success and Matho's weakness, she seemed to rejoice in extraordinary hope. Her lips trembled, her breast panted. When he finally promised to kill him himself, she exclaimed: "Yes! kill him! It must be so!"

The Numidian replied that he desired this death ardently, since he would be her husband when the war was over.

Salammbô started, and bent her head.

But Narr' Havas, pursuing the subject, compared his longings to flowers languishing for rain, or to lost travellers waiting for the day. He told her, further, that she was more beautiful than the moon, better than the wind of morning or than the face of a guest. He would bring for her from the country of the Blacks things such as there were none in Carthage, and the apartments in their house should be sanded with gold dust.

Evening fell, and odours of balsam were exhaled. For a long time they looked at each other in silence, and Salammbô's eyes, in the depths of her long draperies, resembled two stars in the rift of a cloud. Before the sun set he withdrew.

The Ancients felt themselves relieved of a great anxiety, when he left Carthage. The people had received him with even more enthusiastic acclamations than on the first occasion. If Hamilcar and the King of the Numidians triumphed alone over the Mercenaries it would be impossible to resist them. To weaken Barca they therefore resolved to make the aged Hanno, him whom they loved, a sharer in the deliverance of Carthage.

He proceeded immediately towards the western provinces, to take his vengeance in the very places which had witnessed his shame. But the inhabitants and the Barbarians were dead, hidden, or fled. Then his anger was vented upon the country. He burnt the ruins of the ruins, he did not leave a single tree nor a blade of grass; the children and the infirm, that were met with, were tortured; he gave the women to his soldiers to be violated before they were slaughtered.

Often, on the crests of the hills, black tents were struck as though overturned by the wind, and broad, brilliantly bordered discs, which were recognised as being chariot-wheels, revolved with a plaintive sound as they gradually disappeared in the valleys. The tribes, which had abandoned the siege of Carthage, were wandering in this way through the provinces, waiting for an opportunity, or for some victory to be gained by the Mercenaries, in order to return. But, whether from terror or famine, they all took the roads to their native lands, and disappeared.

Hamilcar was not jealous of Hanno's successes. Nevertheless he was in a hurry to end matters; he commanded him to fall back upon Tunis; and Hanno, who loved his country, was under the walls of the town on the appointed day.

For its protection it had its aboriginal population, twelve thousand Mercenaries, and, in addition, all the Eaters of Uncleanness, for like Matho they were riveted to the horizon of Carthage, and plebs and schalischim gazed at its lofty walls from afar, looking back in thought to boundless enjoyments. With this harmony of hatred, resistance was briskly organised. Leathern bottles were taken to make helmets; all the palm-trees in the gardens were cut down for lances; cisterns were dug; while for provisions they caught on the shores of the lake big white fish, fed on corpses and filth. Their ramparts, kept in ruins now by the jealousy of Carthage, were so weak that they could be thrown down with a push of the shoulder. Matho stopped up the holes in them with the stones of the houses. It was the last struggle; he hoped for nothing, and yet he told himself that fortune was fickle.

As the Carthaginians approached they noticed a man on the rampart who towered over the battlements from his belt upwards. The arrows that flew about him seemed to frighten him no more than a swarm of swallows. Extraordinary to say, none of them touched him.

Hamilcar pitched his camp on the south side; Narr' Havas, to his right, occupied the plain of Rhades, and Hanno the shore of the lake; and the three generals were to maintain their respective positions, so as all to attack the walls simultaneously.

But Hamilcar wished first to show the Mercenaries that he would punish them like slaves. He had the ten ambassadors crucified beside one another on a hillock in front of the town.

At the sight of this the besieged forsook the rampart.

Matho had said to himself that if he could pass between the walls and Narr' Havas's tents with such rapidity that the Numidians had not time to come out, he could fall upon the rear of the Carthaginian

to his face an expression of frightful sadness, for
they seemed to take up more room than on another
human face. His royal fillet, which was half unfastened, trailed with his white hair in the dust.

They thought that they had no ropes strong
enough to haul him up to the top of the cross, and
they nailed him upon it, after the Punic fashion, before it was erected. But his pride awoke in his
pain. He began to overwhelm them with abuse.
He foamed and twisted like a marine monster being
slaughtered on the shore, and predicted that they
would all end more horribly still, and that he would
be avenged.

He was. On the other side of the town, whence
there now escaped jets of flame with columns of
smoke, the ambassadors from the Mercenaries were
in their last throes.

Some who had swooned at first had just revived
in the freshness of the wind; but their chins still
rested upon their breasts, and their bodies had fallen
somewhat, in spite of the nails in their arms, which
were fastened higher than their heads; from their
heels and hands blood fell in big, slow drops, as ripe
fruit falls from the branches of a tree,—and Carthage,
gulf, mountains, and plains all appeared to them to
be revolving like an immense wheel; sometimes a
cloud of dust, rising from the ground, enveloped
them in its eddies; they burned with horrible thirst,
their tongues curled in their mouths, and they felt
an icy sweat flowing over them with their departing souls.

Nevertheless they had glimpses, at an infinite
depth, of streets, marching soldiers, and the swinging
of swords; and the tumult of battle reached them dimly

like the noise of the sea to shipwrecked men dying on the masts of a ship. The Italiotes, who were sturdier than the rest, were still shrieking. The Lacedæmonians were silent, with eyelids closed; Zarxas, once so vigorous, was bending like a broken reed; the Ethiopian beside him had his head thrown back over the arms of the cross; Autaritus was motionless, rolling his eyes; his great head of hair, caught in a cleft in the wood, fell straight upon his forehead, and his death-rattle seemed rather to be a roar of anger. As to Spendius, a strange courage had come to him; he despised life now in the certainty which he possessed of an almost immediate and an eternal emancipation, and he awaited death with impassibility.

Amid their swooning, they sometimes started at the brushing of feathers passing across their lips. Large wings swung shadows around them, croakings sounded in the air; and as Spendius's cross was the highest, it was upon his that the first vulture alighted. Then he turned his face towards Autaritus, and said slowly to him with an unaccountable smile:

"Do you remember the lions on the road to Sicca?"

"They were our brothers!" replied the Gaul, as he expired.

The Suffet, meanwhile, had bored through the walls and reached the citadel. The smoke suddenly disappeared before a gust of wind, discovering the horizon as far as the walls of Carthage; he even thought that he could distinguish people watching on the platform of Eschmoun; then, bringing back his eyes, he perceived thirty crosses of extravagant size on the shore of the Lake, to the left.

In fact, to render them still more frightful, they had been constructed with tent-poles fastened end to end, and the thirty corpses of the Ancients appeared high up in the sky. They had what looked like white butterflies on their breasts; these were the feathers of the arrows which had been shot at them from below.

A broad gold ribbon shone on the summit of the highest; it hung down to the shoulder, there being no arm on that side, and Hamilcar had some difficulty in recognising Hanno. His spongy bones had given way under the iron pins, portions of his limbs had come off, and nothing was left on the cross but shapeless remains, like the fragments of animals that are hung up on huntsmen's doors.

The Suffet could not have known anything about it; the town in front of him masked everything that was beyond and behind; and the captains who had been successively sent to the two generals had not re-appeared. Then fugitives arrived with the tale of the rout, and the Punic army halted. This catastrophe, falling upon them as it did in the midst of their victory, stupefied them. Hamilcar's orders were no longer listened to.

Matho took advantage of this to continue his ravages among the Numidians.

Hanno's camp having been overthrown, he had returned against them. The elephants came out; but the Mercenaries advanced through the plain shaking about flaming firebrands, which they had plucked from the walls, and the great beasts, in fright, ran headlong into the gulf, where they killed one another in their struggles, or were drowned beneath the weight of their cuirasses. Narr' Havas had already launched his cavalry; all threw themselves face downwards upon the ground; then, when the horses were within three paces of them, they sprang beneath their bellies, ripped them open with dagger-strokes, and half the Numidians had perished when Barca came up.

The exhausted Mercenaries could not withstand his troops. They retired in good order to the mountain of the Hot Springs. The Suffet was prudent enough not to pursue them. He directed his course to the mouths of the Macaras.

Tunis was his; but it was now nothing but a heap of smoking rubbish. The ruins fell through the breaches in the walls to the centre of the plain; quite in the background, between the shores of the gulf, the corpses of the elephants drifting before the wind conflicted, like an archipelago of black rocks floating on the water.

Narr' Havas had drained his forests of these animals, taking young and old, male and female, to keep up the war, and the military force of his kingdom could not repair the loss. The people who had seen them perishing at a distance were grieved at it; men lamented in the streets, calling them by their names like deceased friends: "Ah! the Invincible! the Victory! the Thunderer! the Swallow!" On the first day, too, there was no talk except of the dead citizens. But on the morrow the tents of the Mercenaries were seen on the mountain of the Hot Springs. Then so deep was the despair that many people, especially women, flung themselves headlong from the top of the Acropolis.

Hamilcar's designs were not known. He lived alone in his tent with none near him but a young

boy, and no one ever ate with them, not even excepting Narr' Havas. Nevertheless he showed great
deference to the latter after Hanno's defeat; but the
king of the Numidians had too great an interest in
becoming his son not to distrust him.

This inertness veiled skilful manœuvres. Hamilcar
seduced the heads of the villages by all sorts of artifices; and the Mercenaries were hunted, repulsed, and
enclosed like wild beasts. As soon as they entered a
wood, the trees caught fire around them; when they
drank of a spring it was poisoned; the caves in which
they hid in order to sleep were walled up. Their old
accomplices, the populations who had hitherto de-
fended them, now pursued them; and they continually
recognised Carthaginian armour in these bands.

Many had their faces consumed with red tetters;
this, they thought, had come to them through touching Hanno. Others imagined that it was because they
had eaten Salammbô's fishes, and far from repenting
of it, they dreamed of even more abominable sacri-
leges, so that the abasement of the Punic Gods might
be still greater. They would fain have exterminated
them.

In this way they lingered for three months along
the eastern coast, and then behind the mountain of
Selloum, and as far as the first sands of the desert.
They sought for a place of refuge, no matter where.
Utica and Hippo-Zarytus alone had not betrayed them;
but Hamilcar was encompassing these two towns.
Then they went northwards at haphazard without
even knowing the various routes. Their many miseries had confused their understandings.

The only feeling left them was one of exasperation,
which went on developing; and one day they found

themselves again in the gorges of Cobus and once more before Carthage!

Then the actions multiplied. Fortune remained equal; but both sides were so wearied that they would willingly have exchanged these skirmishes for a great battle, provided that it were really the last.

Matho was inclined to carry this proposal himself to the Suffet. One of his Libyans devoted himself for the purpose. All were convinced as they saw him depart that he would not return.

He returned the same evening.

Hamilcar accepted their challenge. The encounter should take place the following day at sunrise, in the plain of Rhades.

The Mercenaries wished to know whether he had said anything more, and the Libyan added:

"As I remained in his presence, he asked me what I was waiting for. 'To be killed!' I replied. Then he rejoined: 'No! begone! that will be to-morrow with the rest.'"

This generosity astonished the Barbarians; some were terrified by it, and Matho regretted that the emissary had not been killed.

He had still remaining three thousand Africans, twelve hundred Greeks, fifteen hundred Campanians, two hundred Iberians, four hundred Etruscans, five hundred Samnites, forty Gauls, and a troop of Naffurs, nomad bandits met with in the date region—in all seven thousand two hundred and nineteen soldiers, but not one complete syntagma. They had stopped up the holes in their cuirasses with the shoulder-blades of quadrupeds, and replaced their brass cothurni with worn sandals. Their garments were weighted with copper or steel plates; their coats of mail hung in tatters about them, and scars appeared like purple threads through the hair on their arms and faces.

The wraiths of their dead companions came back to their souls and increased their energy; they felt, in a confused way, that they were the ministers of a god diffused in the hearts of the oppressed, and were the pontiffs, so to speak, of universal vengeance! Then they were enraged with grief at what was extravagant injustice, and above all by the sight of Carthage on the horizon. They swore an oath to fight for one another until death.

The beasts of burden were killed, and as much as possible was eaten so as to gain strength; afterwards they slept. Some prayed, turning towards different constellations.

The Carthaginians arrived first in the plain. They rubbed the edges of their shields with oil to make the arrows glide off them easily; the foot-soldiers who wore long hair took the precaution of cutting it on the forehead; and Hamilcar ordered all bowls to be inverted from the fifth hour, knowing that it is disadvantageous to fight with the stomach too full. His army amounted to fourteen thousand men, or about double the number of the Barbarians. Nevertheless, he had never felt such anxiety; if he succumbed it would mean the annihilation of the Republic, and he would perish on the cross; if, on the contrary, he triumphed, he would reach Italy by way of the Pyrenees, the Gauls, and the Alps, and the empire of the Barcas would become eternal. Twenty times during the night he rose to inspect everything himself, down to the most trifling details. As to the Carthaginians, they were exasperated by their lengthened terror. Narr' Havas suspected the fidelity of his Numidians. Moreover, the Barbarians might vanquish them. A strange weakness had come upon him; every moment he drank large cups of water.

But a man whom he did not know opened his tent and laid on the ground a crown of rock-salt, adorned with hieratic designs formed with sulphur, and lozenges of mother-of-pearl; a marriage crown was sometimes sent to a betrothed husband; it was a proof of love, a sort of invitation.

Nevertheless Hamilcar's daughter had no tenderness for Narr' Havas.

The recollection of Matho disturbed her in an intolerable manner; it seemed to her that the death of this man would unburden her thoughts, just as people to cure themselves of the bite of a viper crush it upon the wound. The king of the Numidians was depending upon her; he awaited the wedding with impatience, and, as it was to follow the victory, Salammbô made him this present to stimulate his courage. Then his distress vanished, and he thought only of the happiness of possessing so beautiful a woman.

The same vision had assailed Matho; but he cast it from him immediately, and his love, which he thus thrust back, was poured out upon his companions in arms. He cherished them like portions of his own person, of his hatred,—and he felt his spirit higher, and his arms stronger; everything that he was to accomplish appeared clearly before him. If sighs sometimes escaped him, it was because he was thinking of Spendius.

He drew up the Barbarians in six equal ranks. He posted the Etruscans in the centre, all being fastened to a bronze chain; the archers were behind, and on the wings he distributed the Naffurs, who were mounted on short-haired camels, covered with ostrich feathers.

The Suffet arranged the Carthaginians in similar order. He placed the Clinabarians outside the infantry next to the velites, and the Numidians beyond; when day appeared, both sides were thus in line face to face. All gazed at each other from a distance, with round fierce eyes. There was at first some hesitation; at last both armies moved.

The Barbarians advanced slowly so as not to become out of breath, beating the ground with their feet; the centre of the Punic army formed a convex curve. Then came the burst of a terrible shock, like the crash of two fleets in collision. The first rank of the Barbarians had quickly opened up, and the marksmen, hidden behind the others, discharged their bullets, arrows, and javelins. The curve of the Carthaginians, however, flattened by degrees, became quite straight, and then bent inwards; upon this, the two sections of the velites drew together in parallel lines, like the legs of a compass that is being closed. The Barbarians, who were attacking the phalanx with fury, entered the gap; they were being lost; Matho checked them,—and while the Carthaginian wings continued to advance, he drew out the three inner ranks of his line; they soon covered his flanks, and his army appeared in triple array.

But the Barbarians placed at the extremities were the weakest, especially those on the left, who had exhausted their quivers, and the troop of velites, which had at last come up against them, was cutting them up greatly.

Matho made them fall back. His right comprised Campanians, who were armed with axes; he hurled them against the Carthaginian left; the centre attacked the enemy, and those at the other extremity, who were out of peril, kept the velites at a distance.

Then Hamilcar divided his horsemen into squadrons, placed hoplites between them, and sent them against the Mercenaries.

These cone-shaped masses presented a front of horses, and their broader sides were filled and bristling with lances. The Barbarians found it impossible to resist; the Greek foot-soldiers alone had brazen armour, all the rest had cutlasses on the end of poles, scythes taken from the farms, or swords manufactured out of the fellies of wheels; the soft blades were twisted by a blow, and while they were engaged in straightening them under their heels, the Carthaginians massacred them right and left at their ease.

But the Etruscans, riveted to their chain, did not stir; those who were dead, being prevented from falling, formed an obstruction with their corpses; and the great bronze line widened and contracted in turn, as supple as a serpent, and as impregnable as a wall. The Barbarians would come to re-form behind it, pant for a minute, and then set off again with the fragments of their weapons in their hands.

Many already had none left, and they leaped upon the Carthaginians, biting their faces like dogs. The Gauls in their pride stripped themselves of the sagum; they showed their great white bodies from a distance, and they enlarged their wounds to terrify the enemy. The voice of the crier announcing the orders could no longer be heard in the midst of the Punic syntagmata; their signals were repeated by the standards, which were raised above the dust, and every one was swept away in the swaying of the great mass that surrounded him.

Hamilcar commanded the Numidians to advance. But the Naffurs rushed to meet them.

Clad in vast black robes, with a tuft of hair on the top of the skull, and a shield of rhinoceros leather, they wielded a steel which had no handle, and which they held by a rope; and their camels, which bristled all over with feathers, uttered long, hoarse cluckings. Each blade fell on the precise spot, then rose again with a smart stroke carrying off a limb with it. The fierce beasts galloped through the syntagmata. Some, whose legs were broken, went hopping along like wounded ostriches.

The Punic infantry returned in a body upon the Barbarians, and cut them off. Their maniples wheeled about at intervals from one another. The more brilliant Carthaginian weapons encircled them like golden crowns; there was a swarming movement in the centre, and the sun, striking down upon the points of the swords, made them glitter with white flickering gleams. However, files of Clinabarians lay stretched upon the plain; some Mercenaries snatched away their armour, clothed themselves in it, and then returned to the fray. The deluded Carthaginians were several times entangled in their midst. They would stand stupidly motionless, or else would back, surge again, and triumphant shouts rising in the distance seemed to drive them along like derelicts in a storm. Hamilcar was growing desperate; all was about to perish beneath the genius of Matho and the invincible courage of the Mercenaries.

4—11

But a great noise of tabourines burst forth on the horizon. It was a crowd of old men, sick persons, children of fifteen years of age, and even women, who, being unable to withstand their distress any longer, had set out from Carthage, and, for the purpose of placing themselves under the protection of something formidable, had taken from Hamilcar's palace the only elephant that the Republic now possessed,— that one, namely, whose trunk had been cut off.

Then it seemed to the Carthaginians that their country, forsaking its walls, was coming to command them to die for her. They were seized with increased fury, and the Numidians carried away all the rest.

The Barbarians had set themselves with their backs to a hillock in the centre of the plain. They had no chance of conquering, or even of surviving; but they were the best, the most intrepid, and the strongest.

The people from Carthage began to throw spits, larding-pins and hammers, over the heads of the Numidians; those whom consuls had feared died beneath sticks hurled by women; the Punic populace was exterminating the Mercenaries.

The latter had taken refuge on the top of the hill. Their circle closed up after every fresh breach; twice it descended to be immediately repulsed with a shock; and the Carthaginians stretched forth their arms pellmell, thrusting their pikes between the legs of their companions, and raking at random before them. They slipped in the blood; the steep slope of the ground made the corpses roll to the bottom. The elephant, which was trying to climb the hillock, was up to its belly; it seemed to be sprawling over them with delight; and its shortened trunk, which was broad at the extremity, rose from time to time like an enormous leech.

Then all paused. The Carthaginians ground their teeth as they gazed at the hill, where the Barbarians were standing.

At last they dashed at them abruptly, and the fight began again. The Mercenaries would often let them approach, shouting to them that they wished to surrender; then, with frightful sneers, they would kill themselves at a blow, and as the dead fell, the rest would mount upon them to defend themselves. It was a kind of pyramid, which grew larger by degrees.

Soon there were only fifty, then only twenty, only three, and lastly only two—a Samnite armed with an axe, and Matho who still had his sword.

The Samnite with bent hams swept his axe alternately to right and left, at the same time warning Matho of the blows that were being aimed at him. "Master, this way! that way! stoop down!"

Matho had lost his shoulder-pieces, his helmet, his cuirass; he was completely naked, and more livid than the dead, with his hair quite erect, and two patches of foam at the corners of his lips,—and his sword whirled so rapidly that it formed an aureola around him. A stone broke it near the guard; the Samnite was killed and the flood of Carthaginians closed in, they touched Matho. Then he raised both his empty hands towards heaven, closed his eyes, and, opening out his arms like a man throwing himself from the summit of a promontory into the sea, hurled himself among the pikes.

They moved away before him. Several times he ran against the Carthaginians. But they always drew back and turned their weapons aside.

His foot struck against a sword. Matho tried to seize it. He felt himself tied by the wrists and knees, and fell.

Narr' Havas had been following him for some time, step by step, with one of the large nets used for capturing wild beasts, and, taking advantage of the moment when he stooped down, had involved him in it.

Then he was fastened on the elephants with his four limbs forming a cross; and all those who were not wounded escorted him, and rushed with great tumult towards Carthage.

The news of the victory had arrived in some inexplicable way at the third hour of the night; the clepsydra of Khamon had just completed the fifth as they reached Malqua; then Matho opened his eyes. There were so many lights in the houses that the town appeared to be all in flames.

An immense clamour reached him dimly; and lying on his back he looked at the stars.

Then a door closed and he was wrapped in darkness.

On the morrow, at the same hour, the last of the men left in the Pass of the Hatchet expired.

On the day that their companions had set out, some Zuaeces who were returning had tumbled the rocks down, and had fed them for some time.

The Barbarians constantly expected to see Matho appear,—and from discouragement, from languor, and from the obstinancy of sick men who object to change their situation, they would not leave the mountain; at last the provisions were exhausted and the Zuaeces went away. It was known that they numbered scarcely more than thirteen hundred men, and there was no need to employ soldiers to put an end to them.

Wild beasts, especially lions, had multiplied during the three years that the war had lasted. Narr' Havas had held a great battue, and — after tying goats at intervals — had run upon them and so driven them towards the Pass of the Hatchet; — and they were now all living in it when a man arrived who had been sent by the Ancients to find out what there was left of the Barbarians.

Lions and corpses were lying over the tract of the plain, and the dead were mingled with clothes and armour. Nearly all had the face or an arm wanting; some appeared to be still intact; others were completely dried up, and their helmets were filled with powdery skulls; feet which had lost their flesh stood out straight from the knemides; skeletons still wore their cloaks; and bones, cleaned by the sun, made gleaming spots in the midst of the sand.

The lions were resting with their breasts against the ground and both paws stretched out, winking their eyelids in the bright daylight, which was heightened by the reflection from the white rocks. Others were seated on their hind-quarters and staring before them, or else were sleeping, rolled into a ball and half hidden by their great manes; they all looked well fed, tired, and dull. They were as motionless as the mountain and the dead. Night was falling; the sky was striped with broad red bands in the west.

In one of the heaps, which in an irregular fashion embossed the plain, something rose up vaguer than a spectre. Then one of the lions set himself in motion, his monstrous form cutting a black shadow on the background of the purple sky, and when he was quite close to the man, he knocked him down with a single blow of his paw.

Then, stretching himself flat upon him, he slowly drew out the entrails with the edge of his teeth.

Afterwards he opened his huge jaws, and for some minutes uttered a lengthened roar which was repeated by the echoes in the mountain, and was finally lost in the solitude.

Suddenly some small gravel rolled down from above. The rustling of rapid steps was heard, and in the direction of the portcullis and of the gorge there appeared pointed muzzles and straight ears, with gleaming, tawny eyes. These were the jackals coming to eat what was left.

The Carthaginian, who was leaning over the top of the precipice to look, went back again.

XV.

MATHO.

THERE were rejoicings at Carthage, —rejoicings deep, universal, extravagant, frantic; the holes of the ruins had been stopped up, the statues of the gods had been repainted, the streets were strewn with myrtle branches, incense smoked at the corners of the crossways, and the throng on the terraces looked, in their variegated garments, like heaps of flowers blooming in the air.

The shouts of the water-carriers watering the pavement rose above the continual screaming of voices; slaves belonging to Hamilcar offered in his name roasted barley and pieces of raw meat; people accosted one another, and embraced one another with tears; the Tyrian towns were taken, the nomads dispersed, and all the Barbarians annihilated. The Acropolis was hidden beneath coloured velaria; the beaks of the triremes, drawn up in line outside the mole, shone like a dyke of diamonds; everywhere there was a sense of the restoration of order, the beginning of a new existence, ar.d the diffusion of vast happiness: it was the day of Salammbô's marriage with the King of the Numidians.

On the terrace of the temple of Khamon there were three long tables laden with gigantic plate, at which the priests, Ancients, and the rich were to sit, and there was a fourth and higher one for Hamilcar, Narr' Havas, and Salammbô; for as she had saved her country by the restoration of the zaïmph, the people turned her wedding into a national rejoicing, and were waiting in the square below till she should appear.

But their impatience was excited by another and more acrid longing: Matho's death has been promised for the ceremony.

It had been proposed at first to flay him alive, to pour lead into his entrails, to kill him with hunger; he should be tied to a tree, and an ape behind him should strike him on the head with a stone; he had offended Tanith, and the cynocephaluses of Tanith should avenge her. Others were of opinion that he should be led about on a dromedary after linen wicks, dipped in oil, had been inserted in his body in several places;—and they took pleasure in the thought of the large animal wandering through the streets with this man writhing beneath the fires like a candelabrum blown about by the wind.

But what citizens should be charged with his torture, and why disappoint the rest? They would have liked a kind of death in which the whole town might take part, in which every hand, every weapon, everything Carthaginian, to the very paving-stones in the streets and the waves in the gulf, could rend him, and crush him, and annihilate him. Accordingly the Ancients decided that he should go from his prison to the square of Khamon without any escort, and with his arms fastened to his back; it was forbidden to strike him to the heart, in order that he might live the longer; to put out his eyes, so that he might see his torture through; to hurl anything against his person, or to lay more than three fingers upon him at a time.

Although he was not to appear until the end of the day, the people sometimes fancied that he could be seen, and the crowd would rush towards the Acropolis, and empty the streets, to return with lengthened murmurings. Some people had remained standing in the same place since the day before, and they would call on one another from a distance and show their nails which they had allowed to grow, the better to bury them in his flesh. Others walked restlessly up and down; some were as pale as though they were awaiting their own execution.

Suddenly lofty feather fans rose above the heads, behind the Mappalian district. It was Salammbô leaving her palace; a sigh of relief found vent.

But the procession was long in coming; it marched with deliberation.

First there filed past the priests of the Pataec Gods, then those of Eschmoun, of Melkarth, and all the other colleges in succession, with the same insignia, and in the same order as had been observed at the time of the sacrifice. The pontiffs of Moloch passed with heads bent, and the multitude stood aside from them in a kind of remorse. But the priests of Rabbetna advanced with a proud step, and with lyres in their hands; the priestesses followed them in transparent robes of yellow or black, uttering cries like birds and writhing like vipers, or else whirling round to the sound of flutes to imitate the dance of the stars, while their light garments wafted puffs of delicate scents through the streets.

The Kedeschim, with painted eyelids, who symbolised the hermaphrodism of the Divinity, received applause among these women, and, being perfumed and dressed like them, they resembled them in spite of their flat breasts and narrower hips. Moreover, on this day the female principle dominated and confused all things; a mystic voluptuousness moved in the heavy air; the torches were already lighted in the depths of the sacred woods; there was to be a great celebration there during the night; three vessels had brought courtesans from Sicily, and others had come from the desert.

As the colleges arrived they ranged themselves in the courts of the temples, on the outer galleries, and along double staircases which rose against the walls, and drew together at the top. Files of white robes appeared between the colonnades, and the architecture was peopled with human statues, motionless as statues of stone.

Then came the masters of the exchequer, the governors of the provinces, and all the rich. A great tumult prevailed below. Adjacent streets were discharging the crowd, hierodules were driving it back with blows of sticks; and then Salammbô appeared in a litter surmounted by a purple canopy, and surrounded by the Ancients crowned with their golden tiaras.

Thereupon an immense shout arose; the cymbals and crotala sounded more loudly, the tabourines thundered, and the great purple canopy sank between the two pylons.

It appeared again on the first landing. Salammbô was walking slowly beneath it; then she crossed the terrace to take her seat behind on a kind of throne cut out of the carapace of a tortoise. An ivory stool with three steps was pushed beneath her feet; two Negro children knelt on the edge of the first step, and sometimes she would rest both arms, which were laden with rings of excessive weight, upon their heads.

From ankle to hip she was covered with a network of narrow meshes which were in imitation of fish scales, and shone like mother-of-pearl; her waist was clasped by a blue zone, which allowed her breasts to be seen through two crescent-shaped slashings; the nipples were hidden by carbuncle pendants. She had a headdress made of peacock's feathers studded with gems; an ample cloak, as white as snow, fell behind her,—and with her elbows at her sides, her knees pressed together, and circles of diamonds on the upper part of her arms, she remained perfectly upright in a hieratic attitude.

Her father and her husband were on two lower seats, Narr' Havas dressed in a light simar and wearing his crown of rock-salt, from which there strayed two tresses of hair as twisted as the horns of Ammon; and Hamilcar in a violet tunic figured with gold vine branches, and with a battle-sword at his side.

The python of the temple of Eschmoun lay on the ground amid pools of pink oil in the space enclosed by the tables, and, biting its tail, described a large black circle. In the middle of the circle there was a copper pillar bearing a crystal egg; and, as the sun shone upon it, rays were emitted on every side.

Behind Salammbô stretched the priests of Tanith in linen robes; on her right the Ancients, in their tiaras, formed a great gold line, and on the other side the rich with their emerald sceptres a great green line,— while quite in the background, where the priests of Moloch were ranged, the cloaks looked like a wall of purple. The other colleges occupied the lower terraces. The multitude obstructed the streets. It reached to the house-tops, and extended in long files to the summit of the Acropolis. Having thus the people at her feet, the firmament above her head, and around her the immensity of the sea, the gulf, the mountains, and the distant provinces, Salammbô in her splendour was blended with Tanith, and seemed the very genius of Carthage, and its embodied soul.

The feast was to last all night, and lamps with several branches were planted like trees on the painted woollen cloths which covered the low tables. Large electrum flagons, blue glass amphoras, tortoise-shell spoons, and small round loaves were crowded between the double row of pearl-bordered plates; bunches of grapes with their leaves had been rolled round ivory vine-stocks after the fashion of the thyrsus; blocks of snow were melting on ebony trays, and lemons, pomegranates, gourds, and watermelons formed hillocks beneath the lofty silver plate; boars with open jaws were wallowing in the dust of spices; hares, covered with their fur, appeared to be bounding amid the flowers; there were shells filled with forcemeat; the pastry had symbolic shapes; when the covers of the dishes were removed doves flew out.

The slaves, meanwhile, with tunics tucked up, were going about on tiptoe; from time to time a hymn sounded on the lyres, or a choir of voices rose. The

strained, and were on the point of breaking; the people did not feel the blows of the slaves who struck at them to drive them back; some clung to the projections of the houses; all the openings in the walls were stopped up with heads; and they howled at him the mischief that they could not inflict upon him.

It was atrocious, filthy abuse mingled with ironical encouragements and imprecations; and, his present tortures not being enough for them, they foretold to him others that should be still more terrible in eternity.

This vast baying filled Carthage with stupid continuity. Frequently a single syllable—a hoarse, deep, and frantic intonation—would be repeated for several minutes by the entire people. The walls would vibrate with it from top to bottom, and both sides of the street would seem to Matho to be coming against him, and carrying him off the ground, like two immense arms stifling him in the air.

Nevertheless he remembered that he had experienced something like it before. The same crowd was on the terraces, there were the same looks and the same wrath; but then he had walked free, all had then dispersed, for a god covered him;—and the recollection of this, gaining precision by degrees, brought a crushing sadness upon him. Shadows passed before his eyes; the town whirled round in his head, his blood streamed from a wound in his hip, he felt that he was dying; his hams bent, and he sank quite gently upon the pavement.

Some one went to the peristyle of the temple of Melkarth, took thence the bar of a tripod, heated red hot in the coals, and, slipping it beneath the first chain, pressed it against his wound. The flesh was seen to smoke; the hootings of the people drowned his voice; he was standing again.

Six paces further on, and he fell a third and again a fourth time; but some new torture always made him rise. They discharged little drops of boiling oil through tubes at him; they strewed pieces of broken glass beneath his feet; still he walked on. At the corner of the street of Satheb he leaned his back against the wall beneath the pent-house of a shop, and advanced no further.

The slaves of the Council struck him with their whips of hippopotamus leather, so furiously and long that the fringes of their tunics were drenched with sweat. Matho appeared insensible; suddenly he started off and began to run at random, making a noise with his lips like one shivering with severe cold. He threaded the street of Boudes, and the street of Sœpo, crossed the Green Market, and reached the square of Khamon.

He now belonged to the priests; the slaves had just dispersed the crowd, and there was more room. Matho gazed round him and his eyes encountered Salammbô.

At the first step that he had taken she had risen; then, as he approached, she had involuntarily advanced by degrees to the edge of the terrace; and soon all external things were blotted out, and she saw only Matho. Silence fell in her soul,— one of those abysses wherein the whole world disappears beneath the pressure of a single thought, a memory, a look. This man who was walking towards her attracted her.

Excepting his eyes he had no appearance of humanity left; he was a long, perfectly red shape; his broken bonds hung down his thighs, but they could not be distinguished from the tendons of his wrists, which were laid quite bare; his mouth remained wide open; from his eye-sockets there darted flames which seemed to rise up to his hair; — and the wretch still walked on!

He reached the foot of the terrace. Salammbô was leaning over the balustrade; those frightful eyeballs were scanning her, and there rose within her a consciousness of all that he had suffered for her. Although he was in his death agony she could see him once more kneeling in his tent, encircling her waist with his arms, and stammering out gentle words; she thirsted to feel them and hear them again; she did not want him to die! At this moment Matho gave a great start; she was on the point of shrieking aloud. He fell backwards and did not stir again.

Salammbô was borne back, nearly swooning, to her throne by the priests who flocked about her. They congratulated her; it was her work. All clapped their hands and stamped their feet, howling her name.

A man darted upon the corpse. Although he had no beard he had the cloak of a priest of Moloch on his shoulder, and in his belt that species of knife which they employed for cutting up the sacred meat, and which terminated, at the end of the handle, in a golden spatula. He cleft Matho's breast with a single blow, then snatched out the heart and laid it upon the spoon; and Schahabarim, uplifting his arm, offered it to the sun.

The sun sank behind the waves; his rays fell like long arrows upon the red heart. As the beatings diminished the planet sank into the sea; and at the last palpitation it disappeared.

4—12

Then from the gulf to the lagoon, and from the isthmus to the pharos, in all the streets, on all the houses, and on all the temples, there was a single shout; sometimes it paused, to be again renewed; the buildings shook with it; Carthage was convulsed, as it were, in the spasm of Titanic joy and boundless hope.

Narr' Havas, drunk with pride, passed his left arm beneath Salammbô's waist in token of possession; and taking a gold patera in his right hand, he drank to the Genius of Carthage.

Salammbô rose like her husband, with a cup in her hand, to drink also. She fell down again with her head lying over the back of the throne,—pale, stiff, with parted lips,—and her loosened hair hung to the ground.

Thus died Hamilcar's daughter for having touched the mantle of Tanith.

APPENDIX

APPENDIX

SAINTE-BEUVE having devoted an important study to *Salammbô**
M. Flaubert refuted his criticisms in the following letter :—

"*December*, 1862.

"MY DEAR MASTER,—Your third article on *Salammbô* has 'appeased' me (I was never very furious). My most intimate friends were somewhat angry at the other two; but I myself, to whom you have frankly told what you think of my big book, am grateful to you for having blended so much clemency with your criticism. Once more, therefore, and very sincerely, I thank you for the tokens of affection that you show me, and, without lingering over courtesies, I begin my 'Apology.'

"Are you, first of all, quite sure—in your general judgment—that you have not yielded a little too much to your nervous impressions? The subject of my book—all this barbarous, Oriental, Molochistical world—displeases you 'in itself!' You begin by suspecting the reality of my reproduction, and then you say to me : 'After all, it may be true ;' and by way of conclusion : 'So much the worse, if it is true!' You are astonished every minute; and you are vexed with me because you are astonished. Nevertheless, I cannot help it! Should I have embellished, weakened, falsified, 'Gallicised!' But you yourself reproach me with having made a poem, with having been classic in the bad sense of the word, and you assail me with 'The Martyrs!'

"Now Chateaubriand's system seems to me to be diametrically the opposite of mine. He started from a perfectly ideal standpoint; he dreamed of 'typical' martyrs. I have sought to fix a mirage by applying the methods of the modern world to antiquity, and have tried to be simple. Laugh as much as you like! Yes, I say 'simple,' not sober.

---

* *Nouveaux Lundis*, vol. iv, page 31.

Nothing is more complicated than a Barbarian. But I come to your articles in order to defend myself, and fight you foot to foot.

"At the outset I impeach you respecting Hanno's 'Periplus,' which Montesquieu admired and I do not admire at all. Who could now be made to believe that this is an 'original' document? It is evidently translated, abridged, cut, and arranged by a Greek. No Oriental, whoever he may be, ever wrote in that style. I call the emphatic and redundant Eschmounazar inscription to witness! People who call themselves sons of God, the eye of God (see Hamaker inscriptions), are not simple, as you understand simplicity. Moreover, you will grant me that the Greeks had no comprehension of the barbaric world. If they had comprehended any part of it they would not have been Greeks. The East was repugnant to Hellenism. How they travestied everything foreign that fell into their hands! I will say the same of Polybius. As far as facts are concerned, I consider him an incontestable authority; but for anything that he has not seen (or that he has intentionally omitted, for he too had a method and a school) I am well satisfied to seek elsewhere. Hanno's 'Periplus,' then, is not 'a Carthaginian monument,' and is very far from being 'the only one,' as you say it is. The Marseilles inscription, written in genuine Punic, is a genuine Carthaginian monument. It is a simple one, I allow, for it is a tariff, and it is still less so than the famous 'Periplus,' in which a little corner of the marvellous makes itself seen through the Greek;—were it only those gorilla skins which were taken for human skins, and were hung up in the temple of Moloch (translate Saturn), the description of which I have spared you; and that is something for which you should thank me! I will even tell you, between ourselves, that Hanno's 'Periplus' is perfectly hateful to me, after reading and re-reading it with the four dissertations by Bougainville (in the *Mémoires de l'Académie des Inscriptions*), without counting many a thesis for the doctorate— Hanno's 'Periplus' being a subject for theses.

"As to my heroine, I do not defend her. According to you she resembles 'a sentimental Elvira,' Velléda, or Madame Bovary. But no! Velléda is active, intelligent, European. Madame Bovary is tossed by thronging passions; Salammbô, on the contrary, remains riveted by a fixed idea. She is a maniac, a species of Saint Theresa. No matter! I am not sure of her reality; for neither you nor I, nor any one ancient or modern, can know the Eastern woman, for the reason that it is impossible to associate with her.

"You accuse me of deficiency in logic, and you ask me: 'Why did the Carthaginians massacre the Barbarians?' The reason is very simple: they hate the Mercenaries; the latter fall into their power; they are the stronger and they kill them. But 'the news,' you say, 'might have reached the camp from time to time.' By what means? And who, pray, would have brought it? The Carthaginians? But to what end?

Barbarians? But there were no more left in the town! Strangers? persons unconcerned? But I was careful to point out that no communication existed between Carthage and the army!

"With respect to Hanno (the 'bitch's milk,' be it said in passing, is not a 'jest;' it was, and *still* is, a remedy against leprosy: see the article 'Leprosy' in the 'Dictionary of Medical Sciences;' a bad article, too, the data of which I have rectified in accordance with my own observations made at Damascus and in Nubia),—Hanno, I say, escapes because the Mercenaries voluntarily permit him to escape. They are not yet *exasperated* with him. Their indignation comes afterwards with reflection; for they take a long time to comprehend all the perfidy of the Ancients (see the beginning of my fourth chapter). Matho 'prowls like a madman' round Carthage. Madman is the proper word. Was not love, as the Ancients conceived it, a madness, a curse, a disease sent by the gods? Polybius would be much 'astonished,' you say, to see his Matho in such a condition. I do not think that he would, and M. de Voltaire would not have shared in this astonishment. Recollect what he says in *Candide* (in the old woman's story) of the violence of the passions in Africa: 'It is fire, vitriol, &c.'

"Regarding the aqueduct: 'We are here in improbability up to the eyes.' Yes, my dear master, you are right, and more so than you think, —but not in the way that you think. I will tell you further on my opinion of this episode, which was introduced, not for the sake of describing the aqueduct, which gave me a great deal of trouble, but in order to bring my two heroes suitably into Carthage. It is, moreover, a reminiscence of an anecdote told by Polyænus (*Stratagems of War*), the story of Theodorus, Cleon's friend, on the occasion of the capture of Sestos by the people of Abydos.

"'One feels the want of a lexicon.' This is a reproach which I deem supremely unjust. I might have overwhelmed the reader with technical words. Far from doing so, I have taken pains to translate everything into French. I have not employed one peculiar word, without following it up immediately with its explanation. I except the names of coins, measures, and months, which are indicated by the sense of the passage. But if you meet with 'kreutzer,' 'yard,' 'piastre,' or 'penny' in a page, does that prevent you from understanding it? What would you have said if I had called Moloch 'Melek,' Hannibal 'Han-Baal,' Carthage 'Kartadda,' and if, instead of saying that the slaves at the mill wore muzzles, I had written 'pausicapes'? As to the names of perfumes and precious stones, I was obliged to take the names which are in Theophrastus, Pliny, and Athenæus. For plants I employed the Latin names, the *received words*, instead of Arabic or Phœnician words. Thus I said 'Lawsonia' instead of 'Henneh,' and even had the kindness to write 'Lausonia' with a 'w,' which is an error, and not to add *inermis*, which would have been more exact. In like manner I write 'antimony' for 'Kok'heul' and spare you 'sulphurous,' ungrateful fellow! But out of regard for the French reader, I cannot write Hannibal and Hamilcar without an 'h,' since there is a rough breathing on the 'a,' and as to adhering to Rollin! come, be reasonable!

"As to the 'temple of Tanith,' I am sure of having reconstructed it as it was, from the treatise on the Syrian goddess, the medals belonging to the Duke of Luynes, the knowledge that we possess of the temple of Jerusalem, a passage by Saint Jerome quoted by Selden (*de Diis Syriis*), the plan of the temple of Gozzo, which is quite Carthaginian, and better than all, the ruins of the temple of Thugga, which I saw myself with my own eyes, and of which no traveller nor antiquary, that I know of, has spoken. No matter, you will say, it is funny! Be it so! As to the description in itself, from the literary standpoint, I myself consider it quite comprehensible, nor is the drama impeded by it, for Spendius and Matho remain in the foreground, and are not lost from sight. There is not an isolated, gratuitous description in my book; they are all *subservient* to my characters, and have an influence immediate or remote upon the action.

"I am also unable to accept the expression 'Chinese ornamentation,' as applied to Salammbô's chamber, in spite of the epithet 'exquisite' which relieves it (as 'devouring' does 'dogs' in the famous dream), because I have not inserted a single detail which is not in the Bible, and which is not still met with in the East. You repeat that the Bible is not a guide to Carthage, (which is a disputable point); but the Hebrews were more akin to the Carthaginians than the Chinese, as you will allow. Moreover, there are climatic matters which are eternal. For the furniture and costumes I refer you to the passages collected in the 21st dissertation of Abbé Mignot (*Mémoires de l'Académie des Inscriptions*, volume xl or xli, I forget which).

"As to this taste 'for operatic effect, pomp, and emphasis,' why, pray, do you hold that things were not so once—since they are so now! Ceremonial visits, prostrations, invocations, censings, and all the rest of them, were not invented by Mahomet, I suppose.

"It is the same with Hannibal. Why do you think that I have made his childhood 'fabulous'? Is it because of his killing an eagle? A great miracle in a country where eagles abound! If the scene had been laid in the Gauls, I should have made use of an owl, a wolf, or a fox. But, Frenchman that you are, you are accustomed, *in spite of yourself*, to consider the eagle as a noble bird, as a symbol rather than as a living creature. Nevertheless, eagles exist.

"You ask me where I got 'such an idea of the Council of Carthage'? But in all analogous circumstances at times of revolution, from the Convention to the American Parliament, where only lately they were exchanging blows of sticks and revolver-shots, such sticks and revolvers were carried (like my daggers) in the sleeve of a great-coat. And my Carthaginians are more decent, too, than the Americans, since the public was not present. You quote against me a big authority, Aristotle. But Aristotle, who was more than eighty years before my period, is of no weight here. Moreover, the Stagyrite is grossly mistaken when he asserts that 'neither riot nor tyrant was ever seen at Carthage.' Do you wish for dates? Here are some: the conspiracy of Carthalon had taken place, 530 B.C.; the encroachments of Mago, 460; Hanno's conspiracy, 337; Bomilcar's conspiracy, 307. But I pass by Aristotle. Let us proceed.

"You reproach me with 'the carbuncles formed of the urine of the lynx.' This is from Theophrastus, in his 'Treatise on Precious Stones,'—and so much the worse for him! I was almost forgetting Spendius. Well no, my dear master, his stratagem is neither 'odd' nor 'strange.' It is almost stereotyped. It was provided me by Ælian (*History of Animals*) and by Polyæmus (*Stratagems*). It was even so well known since the siege of Megara by Antipater (or Antigone), that pigs were reared along with elephants, expressly that the big beasts might not be frightened by the little ones. In a word, it was a usual trick, and was probably a very hackneyed one in Spendius's time. I was not obliged to go back to Samson; for I rejected, as far as possible, all details belonging to legendary epochs.

"I come to Hamilcar's riches. The description, whatever you may say, is in the background. Hamilcar predominates over it, and I believe it to be quite natural. The Suffet's anger goes on increasing in proportion as he perceives the depredations that have been committed in his house. Far from being 'beside himself the whole time,' he does not break out until the end, when he meets with a personal insult. 'That this visit does not render him prepossessing' is of no importance to me, since it was no part of my duty to panegyrise him; but I do not think that I have 'caricatured him at the expense of the rest of his character.' The man who further on slays the Mercenaries in the way that I have shown (which is a nice feature in his son Hannibal in Italy), is just the same as he who has his goods adulterated, and his slaves flogged to death.

"You cavil at the 'eleven thousand three hundred and ninety-six men' in his army, and ask me, 'How do you know this number? who told it to you?' But this you have just yourself seen, since I stated the number of men that there were in the different corps of the Punic army. It is simply the total of the addition sum, and not one thrown in at random to give an appearance of precision.

"There is neither 'malicious vice' nor 'foolery' in my serpent. The chapter is a species of oratorical precaution to tone down the scene in the tent which, but for the serpent, might have caused an outcry. I preferred an immodest effect (if immodesty there be) with a serpent rather than with a man. Before leaving her house Salammbô entwines herself with the genius of her family, with the very religion of her country under its most ancient symbol. That is all. This may possibly be 'unbecoming in an Iliad or a Pharsalia,' but I did not pretend to write the *Iliad* or the *Pharsalia*.

"Neither is it my fault if storms are frequent in Tunis at the end of summer. Chateaubriand no more invented storms than sunsets, and both, it seems to me, belong to the whole world. Note, moreover, that the soul of the tale is Moloch, Fire, Thunder. The god is acting here under one of his forms; he is subduing Salammbô. The thunder was therefore quite in its place; it is the voice of Moloch, who is waiting outside. You will further acknowledge that I have spared you 'the classic description of a storm.' And then my poor storm does not take up in all *three* lines, and those at different places! The fire which follows was suggested by an episode in the history of Massinissa, by another in the history of Agathocles, and by a passage in Hirtius,—all three in analogous circumstances. I do not leave the atmosphere, or even the country, in which my action proceeds, as you see.

"With reference to Salammbô's perfumes you credit me with more imagination than I possess. Pray smell and inhale Judith and Esther in the Bible! They were literally soaked and poisoned with perfumes. And this is what I was careful to say as soon as Salammbô's sickness was in question.

"Why, too, will you not allow that 'the disappearance of the zaïmph' counted for 'something' in the loss of the battle, since the army of the Mercenaries contained men who believed in the zaïmph? I indicate the principal causes (three military movements) of this loss; then I add the other as a secondary and ultimate cause.

"To say that I have 'invented tortures' at the funeral of the Barbarians is not accurate. Hendreich (*Carthago, seu Carth. respublica*, 1664) has collected passages to prove that the Carthaginians were accustomed to mutilate the corpses of their enemies; and you are astonished that Barbarians who are vanquished, desperate, maddened, will not do the like to them, will not do as much on one occasion and on one occasion only? Need I remind you of Madame de Lamballe, the 'Mobiles' in '48, and of what is actually going on in the United States? I have been, on the contrary, sober and mild.

"And since we are speaking our minds to each other, I will frankly acknowledge, my dear master, that 'the Sadic pungency of imagination' wounded me a little. All your words are of weight. But such an expression from you when printed becomes almost a stigma. Do you forget that I have sat on the benches of the 'Correctionnelle' attainted of outrages upon morals, and that fools and villains find weapons in everything? Do not therefore be astonished if one of these days you read in some petty, slanderous journal, such as there are in existence, something analogous to this: 'M. G. Flaubert is a disciple of De Sade. His friend, sponsor, and master has himself said so clearly enough when criticising him, though with that subtlety and good humoured raillery which, &c.' What could I reply,— or do ?

"I bow to what follows. You are right, my dear master; I have given the thumb-stroke, I have strained history, and as you well say 'I wished to make a siege.' But with a military subject where is the harm? and then I did not altogether invent this siege; I only exaggerated it a little. That is the whole of my fault.

"But as to the 'passage in Montesquieu' relating to the immolation of children, I rebel. There is not a 'doubt' in my mind as to this horror. (Just think that human sacrifices were not completely abolished in Greece at the battle of Leuctra, 370 B.C.) In spite of the condition imposed by Gelon (480), two hundred children, according to Diodorus, were burnt in the war against Agathocles (302), and for later periods I refer to Silius Italicus, Eusebius, and especially to Saint Augustine, who affirms that the thing was still sometimes done in his time.

"You regret that I did not introduce a philosopher among the Greeks, a reasoner charged with giving us a course of ethics, and performing good actions—a gentleman in short, 'feeling like ourselves.' But come! was this possible? Aratus, whom you recall to me, is the very model that I selected, when imagining Spendius; he was a man of escalades and stratagems, who killed sentries at night well enough, and found himself dazzled by the daylight. I denied myself a contrast, it is true; but it was an easy contrast, a contrast *laboured* and false.

"I have finished the analysis and come to your judgment. You are perhaps right in your speculations on the application of the historical romance to antiquity, and it is quite possible that I have failed. Nevertheless, in accordance with all the probabilities, and with my own impressions, I believe that I have made something that resembles Carthage. But that is not the question. I laugh at archæology! If the colouring is not one, if the details jar, if the morals are not derived from religion, and the deeds from passions, if the characters are not coherent, if the costumes are not appropriate for use and the architecture for the climate, if, in a word, there is not harmony, I am wrong,—not otherwise. All depends upon that.

"But the atmosphere irritates you! I know, or rather, I feel this. Why, instead of remaining at your own personal standpoint—your lettered, modern, Parisian standpoint—why did you not come over to my side? The human soul is *not* the same everywhere, whatever M. Levallois may say. * The slightest inspection of the world will prove the contrary. I even believe that I was not so hard upon humanity in *Salammbô* as in *Madame Bovary*. The curiosity, the love

---

* In one of his articles in the *Opinion Nationale* on *Salammbô*.

which impelled me towards vanished religions and peoples, has in it something moral and sympathetic, it seems to me.

"As to style, I have sacrificed less to finish of phrase and period in this book than in the other. Metaphors are rare in it, and the epithets are positive. If I put the word 'blue' before 'stones,' it is, believe me. because 'blue' is the proper word; and be equally assured that the colour of stones can be very well distinguished by starlight. Question all travellers in the East on this point, or go there yourself and see.

"And since you blame me for using certain words, 'enormous' among others, which I do not defend (although excessive silence may produce the effect of an uproar), I too have to reproach you for certain expressions.

"I did not understand the quotation from Désaugiers, nor its object. I knit my brows at Carthaginian 'trinkets,'—'deuce of a mantle,'—'ragoût' and 'all-spiced' for Salammbô who 'toys with the serpent,' —at the 'handsome Libyan rogue' who is neither handsome nor a rogue—and at Schahabarim's 'libertine' imagination.

"One last question, O master, and an improper one: why do you consider Schahabarim almost comical, and your Port-Royal worthies so serious? In my eyes, M. Singlin is dismal by the side of my elephants. I look upon tattooed Barbarians as being less anti-human, less peculiar, less funny, and less uncommon than people who live in common and call one another 'Sir,' until death! And it is just because they are so remote from myself that I admire your talent in making me understand them. For I believe in Port-Royal, and am less anxious to live there than at Carthage. It, too, was exclusive, unnatural, strained, all of a piece, and yet true. Why will you not admit the existence of two truths, two contrary extravagances, two different monstrosities?

"I am about to finish. A little patience! Are you curious to know the *enormous* faults ('enormous' is in its place here) that I find in my book. Here they are:

"1. The pedestal is too large for the statue. Now as 'too much' is never a transgression, but 'not enough' is, one hundred pages more would have been needed, relating to Salammbô alone.

"2. Some transitions are wanting. They did exist; but I cut them out or over-shortened them, fearing to be tedious.

"3. In Chapter IV. everything relating to Gisco is *of the same tonality* as the second part of Chapter II. (Hanno). The situation is the same, and there is no progression of effect.

"4. Everything extending from the battle of the Macaras as far as the serpent, and all Chapter XIII. to the numbering of the Barbarians, sinks and disappears in the recollection. These are dull, transitory passages belonging to the background, which I was unfortunately unable to avoid and which make the book heavy in spite of the efforts after agility which I have been able to put forth. They are those which have cost me most, which I like least, and for which I am most grateful to myself.

"5. The aqueduct.

"Now for a confession! My *secret* opinion is that there was no aqueduct at Carthage at all, in spite of the actual ruins of the aqueduct. Accordingly I was careful to anticipate all objections beforehand by a hypocritical phrase addressed to archæologists. I put my foot into it heavily, by recalling that it was a Roman, and at that time a novel invention, and that the present aqueduct had been reconstructed upon the old one. The remembrance of Belisarius cutting the Roman aqueduct at Carthage pursued me, and then it was a fine entrance for Spendius and Matho. No matter! my aqueduct is a piece of cowardice! *Confiteor*.

"6. Another and last piece of roguery: Hanno.
"From love of clearness I have falsified history so far as it relates to his death. He was crucified, it is true, by the Mercenaries, but in Sardinia. The general crucified at Tunis, opposite Spendius, was called Hannibal. But what confusion this would have caused to the reader!

"Such, my dear master, is what, in my opinion, is worst in my book. I do not tell you what I consider good. But be assured that I have not constructed a fanciful Carthage. The documents about Carthage are in existence, and they are not all in Movers. We must look a little further for them. Thus Ammianus Marcellinus furnished me with the *exact* form of a gate, the poem of Corippus (the *Johanneis*) with many details respecting the African colonies, &c. &c.

"And then my example will be little followed. So where is the danger? The Leconte de Lisles and Baudelaires are less to be dreaded than the —— and the —— in this gentle country, France, where superficiality is a quality, and where the commonplace, the facile, and the silly are always applauded, adopted, and adored. There is no risk of corrupting any one in aspiring to greatness. Am I forgiven?

"I conclude by once more thanking you, my dear master. While giving me scratches, you have very tenderly pressed my hands, and although you have laughed a little in my face, you have none the less made me three great bows, three very detailed and very considerable articles, which must have been more painful to yourself than to me. It is especially for this that I am grateful to you. The counsels at the close will not be thrown away, nor will you have had to do with one devoid of sense or gratitude.— Sincerely yours,

"GUSTAVE FLAUBERT."

Sainte-Beuve replied to this letter by the following note:—

"*December* 25, 1862.

"MY DEAR FRIEND,—I was waiting with impatience for your promised letter. I read it yesterday evening, and I am reading it over again this morning. I no longer regret having written the articles, since I have induced you to *bring out* all your reasons in this way. This African sun has been singular in one respect, that it has in all of us caused an eruption of all our humours, even our secret ones. *Salammbô*, independently of the lady, is just now the name of a battle,' of many battles. I intend to do this: my articles remain as they are, and when reprinting them I shall place your 'Apology,' as you call it, at the end of the volume, without any further reply from me. I had said everything; you reply; and the attentive reader must be the judge. What I especially appreciate, and what every one will be sensible of, is that loftiness of mind and character which has enabled you to support my contradictions with perfect frankness, and which gains you perforce even higher esteem. M. Lebrun (of the Academy), who is a just man, said to me the other day concerning you: 'After all he will come out of it a bigger fellow than he was before.' This will be the general and ultimate impression.

"C. A. SAINTE-BEUVE."

M. Frœhner had criticised *Salammbô* very keenly in an article published in the *Revue Contemporaine*. In reply to his article M. Gustave Flaubert addressed the following letter to the conductor of the *Revue Contemporaine*:—

To M. Frœhner, Editor of the Revue Contemporaine.

"PARIS, *January* 21, 1863.

"SIR,—I have just read your article on *Salammbô* which appeared in the *Revue Contemporaine*. of the 31st December, 1862. In spite of my custom of replying to no criticism, I cannot accept yours. It is full of pertinence, and of things extremely flattering to myself; but as it throws doubt upon the sincerity of my studies, you will, if you please, permit me to notice several of your assertions here.

"I shall first, sir, ask you why you connect me so persistently with the Campana collection, asserting that it was my resource and permanent inspiration? Now, I had finished *Salammbô* in the month of March, six weeks before the opening of this museum. Here is an error already. We shall find other more serious ones.

"I make no pretence, sir, to archæology. I issued my book as a romance without preface or notes, and I am astonished that a man rendered illustrious, as you are, by so considerable works, should waste his leisure upon such light literature! Nevertheless, sir, I know enough about it to venture to tell you that you are altogether wrong from one end of your work to the other, through the whole length of your eighteen pages, in every paragraph and every line.

"You blame me 'for having consulted neither Falbe nor Dureau de la Malle,' by whom I, might have profited.' A thousand pardons! I have read them oftener, perhaps, than yourself, and on the very ruins of Carthage. It is possible that you may know 'nothing satisfactory about the shape, or about the principal quarters,' but others who are better informed do not share your scepticism. If we do not know the situation of the suburb of Aclas, and the place called Fuscianus, or the exact position of the principal gates of which we possess the names, etc., we are fairly well acquainted with the site of the town, the architectonic conditions of the walls, the Tænia, Mole, and Cothon. We know that the houses were coated with pitch, and that the streets were flagged; we have an idea of the Anco described in my fifteenth chapter; we have heard of Malqua, Byrsa, Megara, the Mappalian district and the Catacombs, of Eschmoun's temple situated on the Acropolis, and of Tanith's, a little to the right on turning the back to the sea. All this is found (to say nothing of Appian, Pliny, and Procopius) in this same Dureau de la Malle, with whom you accuse me of being unacquainted. It is therefore, sir, to be regretted that you did not 'enter into tedious details to show' that I had no idea of the site and disposition of ancient Carthage, 'even less,' you add, 'than had Dureau de la Malle.' But what are we to believe? whom are we to trust, since up to the present you have not been kind enough to reveal your own system of the Carthaginian topography?

"I do not, it is true, possess any text to prove to you that there existed a street of Tanners, Perfumers, or Dyers. You will, at all events, acknowledge that it is a probable hypothesis. But I did not invent Kinisdo and Cynasyn, 'words,' you say, 'the structure of which is foreign to the genius of the Semitic tongues.' Not so very foreign, however, since they are in Gesenius. Almost all my Punic names, disfigured as they are in your opinion, having been taken from Gesenius (*Scripturæ Linguæque Phœniciæ*, etc.), or from Falbe, whom I have consulted, I can assure you.

"An Orientalist of your erudition, sir, ought to have shown a little more indulgence to the Numidian name Naravasse, which I write Narr' Havas, from 'Nar-el-haouah,' fire of the breath. You should have been able to guess that the two 'm's' in *Salammbô** were employed expressly to ensure the pronunciation *Salam* and not *Salan*, and to suppose charitably that Egates instead of Ægates was a typographical error, one, moreover, corrected in the second edition of my book, which appeared a fortnight before your advice. The same holds good of 'Scissitia' for 'Syssitia,' and of the word Kabiri, which, horrible to relate! had been printed without a 'k,' even in the most serious works, such as *The Reli-*

---

* So the word is given in the French original.— *Tr.*

gions of Ancient Greece, by Maury. As to Schalischim, if I did not write (as I ought to have written) Rosch-eisch-Schalischim, it was in order to shorten a word which was already too crabbed, not supposing, moreover, that I should be examined by philologists. But since you have descended to this cavilling at words, I will rebuke two others in you : (1) 'Compendiously,' which you employ in a sense quite contrary to its own, to denote copiously, with prolixity, and (2) 'Carthachinesery,' an excellent jest, although it is not your own, but was picked up by you in a petty journal at the beginning of last month. You see, sir, that if you are sometimes ignorant of my authors, I know yours. But it might have been better, perhaps, to neglect 'these minutiæ which,' as you very well say, 'do not admit of critical examination.'

"One more, however ! Why did you underline the *and* in the following (somewhat mutilated) phrase from page 148 : 'Buy me Cappadocians *and* Asiatics.' Do you wish to shine by trying to make simpletons believe that I cannot distinguish Cappadocia from Asia Minor ? But, sir, I am acquainted with it, I have seen it, I have walked in it !

"You have read me so carelessly that you nearly always *misquote* me. I have nowhere said that the priests formed a particular caste ; nor on page 104 that the Libyan soldiers were 'possessed with a desire to drink iron,' but that the Barbarians threatened the Carthaginians that they would make them drink iron ; nor on page 103 that the guards of the legion 'wore silver horns in the middle of the forehead to make them look like rhinoceroses,' but that 'their big horses had, etc. ;' nor on page 28 that the peasants amused themselves one day by crucifying two hundred lions. The same is to be observed of the unfortunate Syssitia which I have employed, according to you, 'without knowing, doubtless, that the word denoted private corporations.—' Doubtless ' is amiable. But, doubtless, I knew the nature of these corporations, and the etymology of the word, since the first time that it appears in my book on page 7, I translate in French, 'Syssitia, companies (of traders) who kept a common table.' You have even falsified a passage from Plautus, for it is not demonstrated in the *Pœnulus* that 'the Carthaginians knew all languages,' which would have been a curious privilege for an entire nation ; there is simply in the prologue, v. 112 : '*Is omnes linguas scit ;*' which is to be translated : 'He knows all languages,' *i.e.*, the Carthaginian in question, and not all the Carthaginians.

"It is not true to say that 'Hanno was not crucified in the Mercenary war, seeing that he commanded armies long afterwards,' for you will find, sir, in Polybius, that the rebels seized his person and fastened it to a cross (in Sardinia, it is true, but at the same period), Book I. chapter xvii. It is not, therefore, 'this personage' who 'would have reason to complain of M. Flaubert,' but rather Polybius, who would have reason to complain of M. Frœhner.

"Regarding the sacrifices of children, so little 'impossible' is it that they were burnt alive in the age of Hamilcar, that, if we are to believe Cicero (*Pro Balbo*) and Strabo (Book III), they were still burnt in the days of Julius Cæsar and Tiberius. However, 'the statue of Moloch has no resemblance to the infernal machine described in *Salammbô*. The figure, composed of seven compartments in stories one above another, for enclosing the victims, belongs to the Gaulish religion. M. Flaubert can make no pretext of analogy to justify his audacious transposition.'

"No! I am without a pretext, it is true, but I have a text, the text, namely, and very description of Diodorus of which you remind me, and which does not differ from my own, as you may convince yourself by condescending to read or re-read Book XX. of Diodorus, chapter iv, joining with it the Chaldaic paraphrase by Paul Fage, which you do not mention, and which is quoted by Selden, *De Diis Syriis*, pp. 164-170, together with Eusebius, *Præparatio Evangelica*, Book I.

"How comes it, too, that history says nothing of the miraculous mantle, since you yourself say 'that it used to be shown in the temple of Venus, but much later, and only in the period of the Roman emperors?' Now I find in Athenæus, xii. 58, a very minute description of this mantle, although 'history says nothing about it.' It was bought from Dionysius the elder for 120 talents, was brought to Rome by Scipio Æmilianus, was carried back to Carthage by Caius Gracchus, returned to Rome under Heliogobalus, and was then sold to Carthage. All this is to be found again in Dureau de la Malle, by whom I have decidedly profited.

"Three lines lower you assert with the same —— candour 'that most of the other gods invoked in *Salammbô* are *pure inventions*,' and you add: 'Who ever heard of an Aptoukhos?' Who? D'Avezac (*Cyrenaïca*), referring to a temple in the neighbourhood of Cyrene; 'of a Schaoul,' but this is a name which I have given to a slave (see my 86th page), 'or of a Matismann?' He is mentioned as a god by Corippus (see *Johanneis* and *Mémoires de l'Académie des Inscriptions*, vol. xii, p. 181). 'Who does not know that Micipsa was not a divinity but a man?' Now, sir, that is what I say, and very clearly too, on that same page 86, when Salammbô calls her slaves: 'Help Kroum, Ewa, Micipsa, Schaoul!'

"You accuse me of taking Astaroth and Astarte for two distinct divinities; but near the beginning, on page 45, when Salammbô invokes Tanith, she invokes her by all her names at once: 'Anaïtis, Astarte, Derceto, Astaroth, Tiratha.' And I even was careful to say, a little farther, on page 49, that she repeated 'all these names without their having any distinct signification for her.' Are you like Salammbô? I am tempted to think so, since you make Tanith the goddess of war and not of love, of the female, humid, fertile element, in spite of Tertullian and of this very name Tiratha, of which you will find a scarcely decent but very clear explanation in Movers, *Phenic.*, Book I. p. 574.

"You are next amazed at the apes sacred to the moon, and the horses sacred to the sun. 'The details,' you are sure, 'are not to be found in any ancient author, nor in any authentic monument.' Now, for the apes I shall venture, sir, to remind you that in Egypt the cynocephalus was sacred to the moon, as may still be seen from the walls of the temples, and that the Egyptian cults had made their way into Libya and to the oases. As to the horses I do not say that there were any sacred to Æsculapius, but to Eschmoun, assimilated to Æsculapius, Iolaüs, Apollo, the Sun. Now, I find horses sacred to the sun in Pausanias (Book I, chap. i.), and in the Bible (2 Kings, chap. xxiii.). But perhaps you will deny that the temples of Egypt are authentic monuments, and the Bible and Pausanias ancient authors.

"Speaking of the Bible, I will take, sir, the great liberty of drawing your attention to Cahen's translation, page 186, where you will read this: 'At their necks they wore, hanging to a gold chain, a little figure of precious stone which they called Truth. The debates were opened when the president set the image of Truth before him.' This is a passage from Diodorus. Here is another from Ælian: 'The oldest among them was chief and judge of all; he wore round his neck a sapphire image. This image was called Truth.' It is thus, sir, that 'this Truth is a pretty invention of the author's.'

"But everything astonishes you; the malobathrum, which (may it please you) is equally well written malobathrum or malabathrum, the gold dust which is gathered to-day, as it was formerly, on the Carthaginian coast, the blue-painted ears of the elephants, the men who smear themselves with vermilion and eat vermin and apes, the Lydians in women's robes, the carbuncles of the lynx, the mandrakes which are in Hippocrates, and the chainlet for the ankles which is in the 'Song of Songs' (Cahen, vol. xvi, 37), the waterings of silphium, the wrapped-up beards, the crucified lions, etc., everything!

"Well! no sir, I have not 'borrowed all these details from the negroes of Senegambia.' For the elephants I refer you to the work by Armandi, page 256, and the authorities that he indicates, such as Florus, Diodorus, Ammianus, Marcellinus, and other negroes of Senegambia.

"As to the nomads who eat apes, crunch lice, and smear themselves with vermilion, since you might be 'asked from what source the author derived these precise details,' and, according to your own confession, you would be '*greatly at a loss* to say,' I will humbly offer you some information which will facilitate your researches.

"'The Maxyes . . . paint their bodies with vermilion. The Gysantes all paint themselves with vermilion and eat apes. Their women (those of the Andrvmachidæ), if bitten by a louse, catch it, bite it, etc.' You will see all this in the 4th Book of Herodotus, chapters cxc, cxci, and clxviii. I am not at a loss to say this.

"The same Herodotus, in his description of the army of Xerxes, apprised me that the Lydians had women's robes; moreover, Athenæus, in the chapter on the Etruscans and their resemblance to the Lydians, says that they wore women's robes; finally, the Lydian Bacchus is always represented in woman's dress. Is this enough for the Lydians and their costume?

"The beards, wrapped up as a sign of mourning, are in Cahen (Ezekiel, chap. xxiv, 17), and on the chins of the Egyptian colossuses, those of Abou-Simbal among others; the carbuncles formed by the urine of the lynx, in Theophrastus (*Treatise on Precious Stones*), and in Pliny, Book VIII., chap. lvii. And as regards the crucified lions (the number of which you make two hundred, doubtless in order to ascribe to me an absurdity which is not mine), I pray you to read chapter xviii, in the same book of Pliny, where you will learn that Scipio Æmilianus and Polybius, when walking together in the Carthaginian country, saw some which had been executed in this position, '*Quia cæteri metu pænæ similis absterrentur eadem noscia.*' Are these, sir, some of those passages taken without judgment from the *Univers Pittoresque*, 'and which superior criticism has employed with success against me?' Of what superior criticism do you speak? Is it your own?

"You are considerably diverted by the pomegranates which were watered with silphium. But this detail, sir, is not my own. It is in Pliny, Book XVII., chap. xlvii. I am very sorry for it on account of your pleasantry about 'the hellebore which ought to be cultivated at Charenton;' but as you say yourself, 'the most piercing intellect cannot supply the want of acquired knowledge.'

"You are completely in error when you assert that 'more than one of the precious stones in Hamilcar's treasury belong to Christian legends and superstitions.' No, sir! they are *all* in Pliny and Theophrastus.

"The emerald stelæ, at the entrance of the temple, which make you laugh — for you are merry — are mentioned by Philostratus, (*Life of Apollonius*), and by Theophrastus (*Treatise on Precious Stones*). Heeren (vol. ii.) quotes this passage from the latter: 'The largest Bactrian emerald is in the temple of Hercules at Tyre. It is a pillar of considerable dimensions.' Another passage in Theophrastus (Hill's translation): 'In their temple of Jupiter there was an obelisk composed of four emeralds.'

"In spite of your 'acquired knowledge' you confound jade, which is a brown-green nephrite, and comes from China, with jasper, a variety of quartz which is found in Europe and Sicily. If you had happened to open the *Dictionary of the French Academy*, at the word 'jasper,' you would have learnt, without going farther, that it is black, red, and white. You must then, sir, have moderated the transports of your ungovernable raptures, and have abstained from playfully reproaching my master and friend, Théophile Gautier, for having (in his *Romance of the Mummy*) given a woman green feet when he has really given her white ones. Thus it is not he but you who have made 'a ridiculous mistake.'

"If you had less contempt for travelling, you might have seen, in the Turin Museum, the very arm of his mummy, which was brought back from Egypt by M. Passalacqua, and in the attitude described by Théophile Gautier, 'that attitude which,' according to you, 'is certainly not Egyptian.' And, without being an engineer, you would have learned what sakiehs are for bringing water into houses, while you would have been convinced that I had not misemployed black garments by making use of them in a country where they abound, and where the women of the upper class never go out without being covered with black mantles. But, as you prefer written testimony, I shall recommend to you for everything concerning women's dress, Isaiah iii:18, the Mischna under the heading Sabbatho; 2 Samuel xiii:18; Saint Clement of Alexandria, pæd. II., 13, and the dissertations of the Abbé Mignot, in the *Mémoires de l'Académie des Inscriptions*, vol. xlii. And as to the abundance of ornamentation which amazes you so greatly, I was quite within my right in being lavish of it with peoples that incrust the floor of their apartments with gems. (*Vide* Cahen, Ezekiel xxviii, 14.) But you are unfortunate in the matter of precious stones.

"I conclude, sir, by thanking you for the amenity of the forms which you have employed,—a rare thing nowadays. I have noticed only the grossest of your inaccuracies which touch on special points. As to vague criticisms, personal estimations, and the literary examination of my book, I have not even alluded to them. I have confined myself throughout to your own ground—science, and I once more repeat that here I am indifferently strong. I know neither Hebrew, nor Arabic, nor German, nor Greek, nor Latin, and I do not boast of knowing French. I have often used translations, but sometimes originals as well. When in uncertainty I have consulted men who pass for being the most competent in France, and if I have not been 'better guided' it is because I had not the honour, the advantage of your acquaintance. Pardon me! but if I had taken your advice should I have 'succeeded better?' I doubt it. In any case, I should have been deprived of the marks of kindness which you afford me here and there in your article, and I should have spared you the species of remorse with which it ends. But, sir, be reassured, and, although you seem to be yourself frightened at your vigour, and seriously think that you have 'cut my book to pieces,' do not be 'afraid,' make yourself easy! for you have not been 'cruel' but——light. I have the honour to be, etc.

"GUSTAVE FLAUBERT."

(The *Opinion Nationale*, January 24, 1863.)

M. Frœhner replied to the above letter by a second critique, dated January 27, 1863; * M. Gustave Flaubert retorted in the following letter addressed to the conductor of the *Opinion Nationale* : —

"*February* 2, 1863.

"My Dear Monsieur Guéroult,—Excuse me if I trouble you once more. But as M. Frœhner is to reproduce in the *Opinion Nationale* what he has just published in the *Revue Contemporaine,* I venture to tell him that —

"I have, indeed, committed a *very* grave error. Instead of Diodorus, Book XX., chap. iv. read chap. xix. Another error. I forgot a passage referring to the statue of Moloch, in Dr. Jacobi's mythology, Bernard's translation, page 322, where he will see once more the seven compartments which rouse his indignation.

"And, although he has not condescended to give a single word or reply touching : (1) the topography of Carthage, (2) the mantle of Tanith, (3) the Punic names that I have disguised, and (4) the gods that I have invented, — and has observed the same silence (5) respecting the horses sacred to the sun, (6) respecting the statuette of Truth, (7) respecting the odd customs of the nomads, (8) respecting the crucified lions, and (9) respecting the waterings with silphium, together with (10) the lynx carbuncles, and (11) the Christian superstitions relating to precious stones; saying nothing also about (12) the jade and (13) the jasper; without mentioning at further length all that concerns (14) Hanno, (15) the women's costumes, (16) the robes of the Lydians, (17) the fantastic attitude of the Egyptian mummy, (18) the Campana Museum, (19) the inaccurate quotations from my book, and (20) my Latin, which he conjures you to believe false, etc.

"I am nevertheless ready with this, as with all the rest, to recognise that he is right, and that antiquity is his own private property. He may, therefore, amuse himself in peace with 'destroying my edifice' and proving that I know nothing at all, as he did victoriously in the case of MM. Léon Heuzy and Léon Renier, for I shall not answer him. I am done with this gentleman.

"I withdraw a word which appears to me to have vexed him. No, M. Frœhner is not 'light,' he is just the contrary, and if I have 'selected him as a victim from among the many writers who have depreciated my book,' it is because he had seemed to me to be the most serious of them. I was greatly mistaken.

"Finally, since he meddles with my biography (as if I were troubling myself about his !) by twice asserting (and *he* knows !) that I was six

---

* See the *Opinion Nationale,* of February 4, 1863.

years writing *Salammbô*, I will confess to him that I am now not quite sure that I was ever at Carthage.

"It remains to both of us to thank you, dear sir, I for your having spontaneously opened your journal so unreservedly to me, while as to M. Frœhner, he must be infinitely grateful to you. You have given him an opportunity of apprising many people of his existence. This foreigner was anxious to be known; now he is known—to advantage.—With kindest regards,

"GUSTAVE FLAUBERT."

(The *Opinion Nationale*, February 4, 1863.)

HERODIAS

HERODIAS

I.

N THE eastern side of the Dead Sea rose the citadel of Machærus. It was built upon a conical peak of basalt, and was surrounded by four deep valleys, one on each side, another in front, and the fourth in the rear. At the base of the citadel, crowding against one another, a group of houses stood within the circle of a wall, whose outlines undulated with the unevenness of the soil. A zigzag road, cutting through the rocks, joined the city to the fortress, the walls of which were about one hundred and twenty cubits high, having numerous angles and ornamental towers that stood out like jewels in this crown of stone overhanging an abyss.

Within the high walls stood a palace, adorned with many richly carved arches, and surrounded by a terrace that on one side of the building spread out below a wide balcony made of sycamore wood, upon which tall poles had been erected to support an awning.

One morning, just before sunrise, the tetrarch, Herod-Antipas, came out alone upon the balcony. He leaned against one of the columns and looked about him.

The crests of the hill-tops in the valley below the palace were just discernible in the light of the false dawn, although their bases, extending to the abyss, were still plunged in darkness. A light mist floated in the air; presently it lifted, and the shores of the Dead Sea became visible. The sun, rising behind Machærus, spread a rosy flush over the sky, lighting up the stony shores, the hills, and the desert, and il-luming the distant mountains of Judea, rugged and grey in the early dawn. En-gedi, the central point of the group, threw a deep black shadow; Hebron, in the background, was round-topped like a dome; Eschol had her pomegranates, Sorek her vineyards, Carmel her fields of sesame; and the tower of Antonia, with its enormous cube, dominated Jerusalem. The tetrarch turned his gaze from it to contemplate the palms of Jericho on his right; and his thoughts dwelt upon other cities of his beloved Galilee,— Capernaum, Endor, Nazareth, Tiberias — whither it might be he would never return.

The Jordan wound its way through the arid plains that met his gaze; white and glittering under the clear sky, it dazzled the eye like snow in the rays of the sun.

The Dead Sea now looked like a sheet of lapis-lazuli; and at its southern extremity, on the coast of Yemen, Antipas recognised clearly what at first he had been able only dimly to perceive. Several tents could now be plainly seen; men carrying spears were moving about among a group of horses; and dying camp-fires shone faintly in the beams of the rising sun.

This was a troop belonging to the sheikh of the Arabs, the daughter of whom the tetrarch had repudiated in order to wed Herodias, already married to one of his brothers, who lived in Italy but who had no pretensions to power.

Antipas was waiting for assistance and reinforcements from the Romans, but as Vitellius, the Governor of Syria, had not yet arrived, he was consumed with impatience and anxiety. Perhaps Agrippa had ruined his cause with the emperor, he thought. Philip, his third brother, sovereign of Batania, was arming himself clandestinely. The Jews were becoming intolerant of the tetrarch's idolatries; he knew that many were weary of his rule; and he hesitated now between adopting one of two projects: to conciliate the Arabs and win back their allegiance, or to conclude an alliance with the Parthians. Under the pretext of celebrating his birthday, he had planned to bring together, at a grand banquet, the chiefs of his troops, the stewards of his domains, and the most important men from the region about Galilee.

Antipas threw a keen glance along all the roads leading to Machærus. They were deserted. Eagles were sweeping through the air high above his head; the soldiers of the guard, placed at intervals along the ramparts, slept or dozed, leaning against the walls; all was silent within the castle.

Suddenly he heard the sound of a distant voice, seeming to come from the very depths of the earth. His cheek paled. After an instant's hesitation, he leaned far over the balcony railing, listening intently, but the voice had died away. Presently it rose again upon the quiet air; Antipas clapped his hands together loudly, crying: "Mannæus! Mannæus!"

Instantly a man appeared, naked to the waist, after the fashion of a masseur at the bath. Although emaciated, and somewhat advanced in years, he was a giant in stature, and on his hip he wore a cutlass in a bronze scabbard. His bushy hair, gathered up and held in place by a kind of comb, exaggerated the apparent size of his massive head. His eyes were heavy with sleep, but his white teeth shone, his step was light on the flagstones, and his body had the suppleness of an ape, although his countenance was as impassive as that of a mummy.

"Where is he?" demanded the tetrarch of this strange being.

Mannæus made a movement over his shoulder with his thumb, saying:

"Over there—still there!"

"I thought I heard him cry out."

And Antipas, after drawing a deep breath, asked for news of Iaokanann, afterwards known as St. John the Baptist. Had he been allowed to see the two men who had asked permission to visit his dungeon a few days before, and since that time, had any one discovered for what purpose the men desired to see him?

"They exchanged some strange words with him," Mannæus replied, "with the mysterious air of robbers conspiring at the cross-roads. Then they departed towards Upper Galilee, saying that they were the bearers of great tidings."

Antipas bent his head for a moment; then raising it quickly, said in a tone full of alarm:

"Guard him! watch him well! Do not allow any one else to see him. Keep the gates shut and the entrance to the dungeon closed fast. It must not even be suspected that he still lives!"

Mannæus had already attended to all these details, because Iaokanann was a Jew, and, like all the Samaritans, Mannæus hated the Jews.

Their temple on the Mount of Gerizim, which Moses had designed to be the centre of Israel, had been destroyed since the reign of King Hyrcanus; and the temple at Jerusalem made the Samaritans furious; they regarded its presence as an outrage against themselves, and a permanent injustice. Mannæus, indeed, had forcibly entered it, for the purpose of defiling its altar with the bones of corpses. Several of his companions, less agile than he, had been caught and beheaded.

From the tetrarch's balcony, the temple was visible through an opening between two hills. The sun, now fully risen, shed a dazzling splendour on its walls of snowy marble and the plates of purest gold that formed its roof. The structure shone like a luminous mountain, and its radiant purity indicated something almost superhuman, eclipsing even its suggestion of opulence and pride.

Mannæus stretched out his powerful arm towards Zion, and, with clenched fist and his great body drawn to its full height, he launched a bitter anathema at the city, with perfect faith that eventually his curse must be effective.

Antipas listened, without appearing to be shocked at the strength of the invectives.

When the Samaritan had become somewhat calmer, he returned to the subject of the prisoner.

"Sometimes he grows excited," said he, "then he longs to escape or talks about a speedy deliverance.

At other times he is as quiet as a sick animal, although I often find him pacing to and fro in his gloomy dungeon, murmuring, 'In order that His glory may increase, mine must diminish.'"

Antipas and Mannæus looked at each other a moment in silence. But the tetrarch was weary of pondering on this troublesome matter.

The mountain peaks surrounding the palace, looking like great petrified waves, the black depths among the cliffs, the immensity of the blue sky, the rising sun, and the gloomy valley of the abyss, filled the soul of Antipas with a vague unrest; he felt an overwhelming sense of oppression at the sight of the desert, whose uneven piles of sand suggested crumbling amphitheatres or ruined palaces. The hot wind brought an odour of sulphur, as if it had rolled up from cities accursed and buried deeper than the river-bed of the slow-running Jordan.

These aspects of nature, which seemed to his troubled fancy signs of the wrath of the gods, terrified him, and he leaned heavily against the balcony railing, his eyes fixed, his head resting upon his hands.

Presently he felt a light touch upon his shoulder. He turned, and saw Herodias standing beside him. A purple robe enveloped her, falling to her sandaled feet. Having left her chamber hurriedly, she wore no jewels nor other ornaments. A thick tress of rippling black hair hung over her shoulder and hid itself in her bosom; her nostrils, a little too large for beauty, quivered with triumph, and her face was alight with joy. She gently shook the tetrarch's shoulder, and exclaimed exultantly:

"Cæsar is our friend! Agrippa has been imprisoned!"

"Who told thee that?"

"I know it!" she replied, adding: "It was because he coveted the crown of Caligula."

While living upon the charity of Antipas and Herodias, Agrippa had intrigued to become king, a title
for which the tetrarch was as eager as he. But if this
news were true, no more was to be feared from
Agrippa's scheming.

"The dungeons of Tiberias are hard to open, and
sometimes life itself is uncertain within their depths,"
said Herodias, with grim significance.

Antipas understood her; and, although she was
Agrippa's sister, her atrocious insinuation seemed entirely justifiable to the tetrarch. Murder and outrage were to be expected in the management of
political intrigues; they were a part of the fatal in-
heritance of royal houses; and in the family of Herodias nothing was more common.

Then she rapidly unfolded to the tetrarch the
secrets of her recent undertakings, telling him how
many men had been bribed, what letters had been
intercepted, and the number of spies stationed at the
city gates. She did not hesitate even to tell him of
her success in an attempt to befool and seduce Eu-
tyches the denunciator.

"And why should I not?" she said; "it cost me
nothing. For thee, my lord, have I not done more
than that? Did I not even abandon my child?"

After her divorce from Philip, she had indeed left
her daughter in Rome, hoping that, as the wife of
the tetrarch, she might bear other children. Until
that moment she had never spoken to Antipas of her
daughter. He asked himself the reason for this sudden display of tenderness.

During their brief conversation several attendants had come out upon the balcony; one slave brought a quantity of large, soft cushions, and arranged them in a kind of temporary couch upon the floor behind his mistress. Herodias sank upon them, and turning her face away from Antipas, appeared to be weeping silently. After a few moments she dried her eyes, declared that she would dream no more, and that she was, in reality, perfectly happy. She reminded Antipas of their former long delightful interviews in the atrium; their meetings at the baths; their walks along the Sacred Way, and the sweet evening rendezvous at the villa, among the flowery groves, listening to the murmur of splashing fountains, within sight of the Roman Campagna. Her glances were as tender as in former days; she drew near to him, leaned against his breast and caressed him fondly.

But he repelled her soft advances. The love she sought to rekindle had died long ago. He thought instead of all his misfortunes, and of the twelve long years during which the war had continued. Protracted anxiety had visibly aged the tetrarch. His shoulders were bent beneath his violet-bordered toga; his whitening locks were long and mingled with his beard, and the sunlight revealed many lines upon his brow, as well as upon that of Herodias. After the tetrarch's repulse of his wife's tender overtures, the pair gazed morosely upon each other.

The mountain paths began to show signs of life. Shepherds were driving their flocks to pasture; children urged heavy-laden donkeys along the roads; while grooms belonging to the palace led the horses to the river to drink. The wayfarers descending from the heights on the farther side of Machærus disappeared behind the castle; others ascended from the valleys, and after arriving at the palace deposited their burdens in the courtyard. Many of these were purveyors to the tetrarch; others were the servants of his expected guests, arriving in advance of their masters.

Suddenly, at the foot of the terrace on the left, an Essene appeared; he wore a white robe, his feet were bare, and his demeanour indicated that he was a follower of the Stoics. Mannæus instantly rushed towards the stranger, drawing the cutlass that he wore upon his hip.

"Kill him!" cried Herodias.

"Do not touch him!" the tetrarch commanded.

The two men stood motionless for an instant, then they descended the terrace, both taking a different direction, although they kept their eyes fixed upon each other.

"I know that man," said Herodias, after they had disappeared. "His name is Phanuel, and he will try to seek out Iaokanann, since thou wert so foolish as to allow him to live."

Antipas said that the man might some day be useful to them. His attacks upon Jerusalem would gain them the allegiance of the rest of the Jews.

"No," said Herodias, "the Jews will accept any master, and are incapable of feeling any true patriotism." She added that, as for the man who was trying to influence the people with hopes cherished since the days of Nehemiah, the best policy was to suppress him.

The tetrarch replied that there was no haste about the matter, and expressed his doubt that any real danger was to be feared from Iaokanann even affecting to laugh at the idea.

4—14

"Do not deceive thyself!" exclaimed Herodias. And she retold the story of her humiliation one day when she was travelling towards Gilead, in order to purchase some of the balm for which that region was famous.

"A multitude was standing on the banks of the stream, my lord; many of the people were putting on their raiment. Standing on a hillock, a strange man was speaking to the gathering. A camel's-skin was wrapped about his loins, and his head was like that of a lion. As soon as he saw me, he launched in my direction all the maledictions of the prophets. His eyes flamed, his voice shook, he raised his arms as if he would draw down lightning upon my head. I could not fly from him; the wheels of my chariot sank in the sand up to the middle; and I could only crawl along, hiding my head with my mantle, and frozen with terror at the curses that poured upon me like a storm from heaven!"

Continuing her harangue, she declared that the knowledge that this man still existed poisoned her very life. When he had been seized and bound with cords, the soldiers were prepared to stab him if he resisted, but he had been quite gentle and obedient. After he had been thrown into prison some one had put venomous serpents into his dungeon, but strange to say, after a time they had died, leaving him uninjured. The inanity of such tricks exasperated Herodias. Besides, she inquired, why did this man make war upon her? What interest moved him to such actions? His injurious words to her, uttered before a throng of listeners, had been repeated and widely circulated; she heard them whispered everywhere.

Against a legion of soldiers she would have been brave; but this mysterious influence, more pernicious and powerful than the sword, but impossible to grasp, was maddening! Herodias strode to and fro upon the terrace, white with rage, unable to find words to express the emotions that choked her.

She had a haunting fear that the tetrarch might listen to public opinion after a time, and persuade himself it was his duty to repudiate her. Then, indeed, all would be lost! Since early youth she had cherished a dream that some day she would rule over a great empire. As an important step towards attaining this ambition, she had deserted Philip, her first husband, and married the tetrarch, who now she thought had duped her.

"Ah! I found a powerful support, indeed, when I entered thy family!" she sneered.

"It is at least the equal of thine," Antipas replied.

Herodias felt the blood of the kings and priests, her ancestors, boiling in her veins.

"Thy grandfather was a servile attendant upon the temple of Ascalon!" she went on, with fury. "Thy other ancestors were shepherds, bandits, conductors of caravans, a horde of slaves offered as tribute to King David! My forefathers were the conquerors of thine! The first of the Maccabees drove thy people out of Hebron; Hyrcanus forced them to be circumcised!" Then, with all the contempt of the patrician for the plebeian, the hatred of Jacob for Esau, she reproached him for his indifference towards palpable outrages to his dignity, his weakness regarding the Phœnicians, who had been false to him, and his cowardly attitude towards the people who detested and insulted herself.

"But thou art like them!" she cried; "Dost regret the loss of the Arab girl who danced upon these very pavements? Take her back! Go and live with her — in her tent! Eat her bread, baked in the ashes! Drink curdled sheep's-milk! Kiss her dark cheeks — and forget me!"

The tetrarch had already forgotten her presence, it appeared. He paid no further heed to her anger, but looked intently at a young girl who had just stepped out upon the balcony of a house not far away. At her side stood an elderly female slave, who held over the girl's head a kind of parasol with a handle made of long, slender reeds. In the middle of the rug spread upon the floor of the balcony stood a large open travelling-hamper or basket, and girdles, veils, head-dresses, and gold and silver ornaments were scattered about in confusion. At intervals the young girl took one object or another in her hands, and held it up admiringly. She was dressed in the costume of the Roman ladies, with a flowing tunic and a peplum ornamented with tassels of emeralds; and blue silken bands confined her hair, which seemed almost too luxuriant, since from time to time she raised a small hand to push back the heavy masses. The parasol half hid the maiden from the gaze of Antipas, but now and then he caught a glimpse of her delicate neck, her large eyes, or a fleeting smile upon her small mouth. He noted that her figure swayed about with a singularly elastic grace and elegance. He leaned forward, his eyes kindled, his breath quickened. All this was not lost upon Herodias, who watched him narrowly.

"Who is that maiden?" the tetrarch asked at last.

Herodias replied that she did not know, and her fierce demeanour suddenly changed to one of gentleness and amiability.

At the entrance to the castle the tetrarch was awaited by several Galileans, the master of the scribes, the chief of the land stewards, the manager of the salt mines, and a Jew from Babylon, commanding his troops of horse. As the tetrarch approached the group, he was greeted with respectful enthusiasm. Acknowledging the acclamations with a grave salute, he entered the castle.

As he proceeded along one of the corridors, Phanuel suddenly sprang from a corner and intercepted him.

"What! Art thou still here?" said the tetrarch in displeasure. "Thou seekest Iaokanann, no doubt."

"And thyself, my lord. I have something of great importance to tell thee."

At a sign from Antipas, the Essene followed him into a somewhat dark and gloomy room.

The daylight came faintly through a grated window. The walls were of a deep shade of crimson, so dark as to look almost black. At one end of the room stood an ebony bed, ornamented with bands of leather. A shield of gold, hanging at the head of the bed, shone like a sun in the obscurity of the apartment. Antipas crossed over to the couch and threw himself upon it in a half-reclining attitude, while Phanuel remained standing before him. Suddenly he raised one hand, and striking a commanding attitude said:

"At times, my lord, the Most High sends a message to the people through one of His sons. Iaokanann is one of these. If thou oppress him, thou shalt be punished!"

"But it is he that persecutes me!" exclaimed Antipas. "He asked me to do a thing that was impossible. Since then he has done nothing but revile me. And I was not severe with him when he began his abuse of me. But he had the hardihood to send various men from Machærus to spread dissension and discontent throughout my domain. A curse upon him! Since he attacks me, I shall defend myself."

"Without doubt, he has expressed his anger with too much violence," Phanuel replied calmly. "But do not heed that further. He must be set free."

"One does not let loose a furious animal," said the tetrarch.

"Have no fear of him now," was the quick reply. "He will go straight to the Arabs, the Gauls, and the Scythians. His work must be extended to the uttermost ends of the earth."

For a moment Antipas appeared lost in thought, as one who sees a vision. Then he said:

"His power over men is indeed great. In spite of myself, I admire him!"

"Then set him free!"

But the tetrarch shook his head. He feared Herodias, Mannæus, and unknown dangers.

Phanuel tried to persuade him, promising, as a guaranty of the honesty of his projects, the submission of the Essenians to the King. These poor people, clad only in linen, untamable in spite of severe treatment, endowed with power to divine the future by reading the stars, had succeeded in commanding a certain degree of respect.

"What is the important matter thou wouldst communicate to me?" Antipas inquired, with sudden recollection.

Before Phanuel could reply, a negro entered the room in great haste. He was covered with dust, and panted so violently that he could scarcely utter the single word:

"Vitellius!"

"Has he arrived?" asked the tetrarch.

"I have seen him, my lord. Within three hours he will be here."

Throughout the palace, doors were opening and closing and portières were swaying as if in a high wind, with the coming and going of many persons; there was a murmur of voices; sounds of the moving of heavy furniture could be heard, and the rattle of silver plates and dishes. From the highest tower a loud blast upon a conch summoned from far and near all the slaves belonging to the castle.

II.

The ramparts were thronged with people when at last Vitellius entered the castle gates, leaning on the arm of his interpreter. Behind them came an imposing red litter, decorated with plumes and mirrors. The proconsul wore a toga ornamented with the lati-clave, a broad purple band extending down the front of the garment, indicating his rank; and his feet were encased in the kind of buskins worn by consuls. A guard of lictors surrounded him. Against the wall they placed their twelve fasces — a bundle of sticks with an axe in the centre. And the populace trembled before the insignia of Roman majesty.

The gorgeous litter, borne by eight men, came to a halt. From it descended a youth. He wore many pearls upon his fingers, but he had a protruding abdomen and his face was covered with pimples. A cup of aromatic wine was offered to him. He drank it, and asked for a second draught.

The tetrarch had fallen upon his knees before the proconsul, saying that he was grieved beyond words not to have known sooner of the favour of his presence within those domains; had he been aware of the approach of his distinguished guest, he would have issued a command that every person along the route should place himself at the proconsul's orders. Of a surety, the proconsul's family was descended direct from the goddess Vitellia. A highway, leading from the Janiculum to the sea, still bore their name. Questors and consuls were innumerable in that great family; and as for the noble Lucius, now his honoured guest, it was the duty of the whole people to thank him, as the conqueror of the Cliti and the father of the young Aulus, now returning to his own domain, since the East was the country of the gods. These hyperboles were expressed in Latin, and Vitellius accepted them impassively.

He replied that the great Herod was the honour and glory of the nation; that the Athenians had chosen him to direct the Olympian games; that he had built temples in the honour of Augustus; had been patient, ingenious, terrible; and was faithful to all the Cæsars.

Between two marble columns, with bronze capitals, Herodias could now be seen advancing with the air of an empress, in the midst of a group of women and eunuchs carrying perfumed torches set in sockets of silver-gilt.

The proconsul advanced three steps to meet her. She saluted him with an inclination of her head.

"How fortunate," she exclaimed, "that henceforth Agrippa, the enemy of Tiberius, can work harm no longer!"

Vitellius did not understand her allusion, but he thought her a dangerous woman. Antipas immediately declared that he was ready to do anything for the emperor.

"Even to the injury of others?" Vitellius asked, significantly.

He had taken hostages from the king of the Parthians, but the emperor had given no further thought to the matter, because Antipas, who had been present at the conference, had, in order to gain favour, sent off despatches bearing the news. From that time he had borne a profound hatred towards the emperor and had delayed in sending assistance to him.

The tetrarch stammered in attempting to reply to the query of the proconsul. But Aulus laughed and said: "Do not be disturbed. I will protect thee!"

The proconsul feigned not to hear this remark. The fortune of the father depended, in a way, on the corrupt influence of the son; and through him it was possible that Antipas might be able to procure for the proconsul very substantial benefits, although the glances that he cast about him were defiant, and even venomous.

But now a new tumult arose just within the gates. A file of white mules entered the courtyard, mounted by men in priestly garb. These were the Sadducees and the Pharisees, who were drawn to Machærus by the same ambition: the one party hoping to be appointed public sacrificers, the other determined to retain those offices. Their faces were dark, particularly those of the Pharisees, who were enemies of

Rome and of the tetrarch.   The flowing skirts of their tunics embarrassed their movements as they attempted to pass through the throng; and their tiaras sat unsteadily upon their brows, around which were bound small bands of parchment, showing lines of writing.

Almost at the same moment, the soldiers of the advance guard arrived.   Cloth coverings had been drawn over their glittering shields to protect them from the dust.   Behind them came Marcellus, the proconsul's lieutenant, followed by the publicans, carrying their tablets of wood under their arms.

Antipas named to Vitellius the principal personages surrounding them: Tolmaï, Kanthera, Schon, Ammonius of Alexandria, who bought asphalt for Antipas; Naaman, captain of his troops of skirmishers, and Jaçim, the Babylonian.

Vitellius had noticed Mannæus.

"Who is that man?" he inquired.

The tetrarch by a significant gesture indicated that Mannæus was the executioner.   He then presented the Sadducees to the proconsul's notice.

Jonathas, a man of low stature, who spoke Greek, advanced with a firm step and begged that the great lord would honor Jerusalem with a visit.   Vitellius replied that he should probably go to Jerusalem soon.

Eleazar, who had a crooked nose and a long beard, put forth a claim, in behalf of the Pharisees, for the mantle of the high priest, held in the tower of Antonia by the civil authorities.

Then the Galileans came forward and denounced Pontius Pilate.   On one occasion, they said, a madman went seeking in a cave near Samaria for the golden vases that had belonged to King David, and

Pontius Pilate had caused several inhabitants of that region to be executed. In their excitement all the Galileans spoke at once, Mannæus's voice being heard above all others. Vitellius promised that the guilty ones should be punished.

Fresh vociferations now broke out in front of the great gates, where the soldiers had hung their shields. Their coverings having now been removed, on each shield a carving of the head of Cæsar could be seen on the umbo, or central knob. To the Jews, this seemed an evidence of nothing short of idolatry. Antipas harangued them, while Vitellius, who occupied a raised seat within the shadow of the colonnade, was astonished at their fury. Tiberius had done well, he thought, to exile four hundred of these people to Sardinia. Presently the Jews became so violent that he ordered the shields to be removed.

Then the multitude surrounded the proconsul, imploring him to abolish certain unjust laws, asking for privileges, or begging for alms. They rent their clothing and jostled one another; and at last, in order to drive them back, several slaves, armed with long staves, charged upon them, striking right and left. Those nearest the gates made their escape and descended to the road; others rushed in to take their places, so that two streams of human beings flowed in and out, compressed within the limits of the gateway.

Vitellius demanded the reason for the assembling of so great a throng. Antipas explained that they had been invited to come to a feast in celebration of his birthday; and he pointed to several men who, leaning against the battlements, were hauling up immense basket-loads of food, fruits, vegetables, antelopes and storks; large fish, of a brilliant shade of blue; grapes, melons, and pyramids of pomegranates. At this sight, Aulus left the courtyard and hastened to the kitchens, led by his taste for gormandizing, which later became the amazement of the world.

As they passed the opening to a small cellar, Vitellius perceived some objects resembling breast-plates hanging on a wall. He looked at them with interest, and then demanded that the subterranean chambers of the fortress be thrown open for his inspection. These chambers were cut into the rocky foundation of the castle, and had been formed into vaults, with pillars set at regular distances. The first vault opened contained old armour; the second was full of pikes, with long points emerging from tufts of feathers. The walls of the third chamber were hung with a kind of tapestry made of slender reeds, laid in perpendicular rows. Those of the fourth were covered with scimitars. In the middle of the fifth cell, rows of helmets were seen, the crests of which looked like a battalion of fiery serpents. The sixth cell contained nothing but empty quivers; the seventh, greaves for protecting the legs in battle; the eighth vault was filled with bracelets and armlets; and an examination of the remaining vaults disclosed forks, grappling-irons, ladders, cords, even catapults, and bells for the necks of camels; and as they descended deeper into the rocky foundation, it became evident that the whole mass was a veritable honeycomb of cells, and that below those already seen were many others.

Vitellius, Phineas, his interpreter, and Sisenna, chief of the publicans, walked among these gloomy cells, attended by three eunuchs bearing torches.

In the deep shadows hideous instruments, invented by barbarians, could be seen: tomahawks studded with nails; poisoned javelins; pincers resembling the jaws of crocodiles; in short, the tetrarch possessed in his castle munitions of war sufficient for forty thousand men.

He had accumulated these weapons in anticipation of a possible alliance against him among his enemies. But he bethought him that the proconsul might believe, or assert, that he had collected this armoury in order to attack the Romans; so he hastened to offer explanations of all that Vitellius had observed.

Some of these things did not belong to him at all, he said: many of them were necessary to defend the place against brigands and marauders, especially the Arabs. Many of the objects in the vaults had been the property of his father, and he had allowed them to remain untouched. As he spoke, he managed to get in advance of the proconsul and preceded him along the corridors with rapid steps. Presently he halted and stood close against the wall as the party came up; he spoke quickly, standing with his hands on his hips, so that his voluminous mantle covered a wide space of the wall behind him. But just above his head the top of a door was visible. Vitellius remarked it instantly, and demanded to know what it concealed.

The tetrarch explained that the door was fastened, and that none could open it save the Babylonian, Jaçim.

"Summon him, then!" was the command.

A slave was sent to find Jaçim, while the group awaited his coming.

The father of Jaçim had come from the banks of the Euphrates to offer his services, as well as those of five hundred horsemen, in the defence of the eastern frontier. After the division of the kingdom, Jaçim had lived for a time with Philip, and was now in the service of Antipas.

Presently he appeared among the vaults, carrying an archer's bow on his shoulder and a whip in his hand. Cords of many colours were lashed tightly about his knotted legs; his massive arms were thrust through a sleeveless tunic, and a fur cap shaded his face. His chin was covered with a heavy, curling beard.

He appeared not to comprehend what the interpreter said to him at first. But Vitellius threw a meaning glance at Antipas, who quickly made the Babylonian understand the command of the proconsul. Jaçim immediately laid both his hands against the door, giving it a powerful shove; whereupon it quietly slid out of sight into the wall.

A wave of hot air surged from the depths of the cavern. A winding path descended and turned abruptly. The group followed it, and soon arrived at the threshold of a kind of grotto, somewhat larger than the other subterranean cells.

An arched window at the back of this chamber gave directly upon a precipice, which formed a defense for one side of the castle. A honeysuckle vine, cramped by the low-studded ceiling, blossomed bravely. The sound of a running stream could be heard distinctly. In this place was a great number of beautiful white horses, perhaps a hundred. They were eating barley from a plank placed on a level with their mouths. Their manes had been coloured a deep blue; their hoofs were wrapped in coverings of woven grass, and the hair between their ears was puffed out like a peruke. As they stood quietly eating, they switched their tails gently to and fro. The proconsul regarded them in silent admiration.

They were indeed wonderful animals; supple as serpents, light as birds. They were trained to gallop rapidly, following the arrow of the rider, and dash into the midst of a group of the enemy, overturning men and biting them savagely as they fell. They were sure-footed among rocky passes, and would jump fearlessly over yawning chasms; and, while ready to gallop across the plains a whole day without tiring, they would stop instantly at the command of the rider.

As soon as Jaçim entered their quarters, they trotted up to him, as sheep crowd around the shepherd; and, thrusting forward their sleek necks, they looked at him with a gaze like that of inquiring children. From force of habit, he emitted a raucous cry, which excited them; they pranced about, impatient at their confinement and longing to run.

Antipas, fearing that if Vitellius knew of the existence of these creatures, he would take them away, had shut them up in this place, made especially to accommodate animals in case of siege.

"This close confinement cannot be good for them," said Vitellius, "and there is a risk of losing them by keeping them here. Make an inventory of their number, Sisenna."

The publican drew a writing-tablet from the folds of his robe, counted the horses, and recorded the number carefully.

It was the habit of the agents of the fiscal companies to corrupt the governors in order to pillage the provinces. Sisenna was among the most flourishing of these agents, and was seen everywhere, with his claw-like fingers and his eyelids continually blinking.

After a time the party returned to the court. Heavy, round bronze lids, sunk in the stones of the pavement, covered the cisterns of the palace. Vitellius noticed that one of these was larger than the others, and that when struck by his foot it had not their sonority. He struck them all, one after another; then stamped upon the ground and shouted:

"I have found it! I have found the buried treasure of Herod!"

Searching for buried treasure was a veritable mania among the Romans.

The tetrarch swore that no treasure was hidden in that spot.

"What is concealed there, then?" the proconsul demanded.

"Nothing—that is, only a man—a prisoner."

"Show him to me!"

The tetrarch hesitated to obey, fearing that the Jews would discover his secret. His reluctance to lift the cover made Vitellius impatient.

"Break it in!" he cried to his lictors. Mannæus heard the command, and, seeing a lictor step forward armed with a hatchet, he feared that the man intended to behead Iaokanann. He stayed the hand of the lictor after the first blow, and then slipped between the heavy lid and the pavement a kind of hook. He braced his long, lean arms, raised the cover slowly, and in a moment it lay flat upon the stones. The bystanders admired the strength of the old man.

Under the bronze lid was a wooden trap-door of the same size. At a blow of the fist it folded back, allowing a wide hole to be seen, the mouth of an

rmmense pit, with a flight of winding steps leading down into the darkness. Those that bent over to peer into the cavern beheld a vague and terrifying shape in its depths.

This proved to be a human being, lying on the ground. His long locks hung over a camel's-hair robe that covered his shoulders. Slowly he rose to his feet. His head touched a grating embedded in the wall; and as he moved about he disappeared, from time to time, in the shadows of his dungeon.

The rich tiaras of the Romans sparkled brilliantly in the sunlight, and their glittering sword-hilts threw out glancing golden rays. The doves, flying from their cotes, circled above the heads of the multitude. It was the hour when Mannæus was accustomed to feed them. But now he crouched beside the tetrarch, who stood near Vitellius. The Galileans, the priests, and the soldiers formed a group behind them; all were silent, waiting with painful anticipation for what might happen.

A deep groan, hollow and startling, rose from the pit.

Herodias heard it from the farther end of the palace. Drawn by an irresistible though terrible fascination, she made her way through the throng, and, reaching Mannæus, she leant one hand on his shoulder and bent over to listen.

The hollow voice rose again from the depths of the earth.

"Woe to thee, Sadducees and Pharisees! Thy voices are like the tinkling of cymbals! O race of vipers, bursting with pride!"

The voice of Iaokanann was recognised. His name was whispered about. Spectators from a distance pressed closer to the open pit.

4—15

"Woe to thee, O people! Woe to the traitors of Judah, and to the drunkards of Ephraim, who dwell in the fertile valleys and stagger with the fumes of wine!

"May they disappear like running water; like the slug that sinks into the sand as it moves; like an abortion that never sees the light!

"And thou, too, Moab! hide thyself in the midst of the cypress, like the sparrow; in caverns, like the wild hare! The gates of the fortress shall be crushed more easily than nut-shells; the walls shall crumble; cities shall burn; and the scourge of God shall not cease! He shall cause your bodies to be bathed in your own blood, like wool in the dyer's vat. He shall rend you, as with a harrow; He shall scatter the remains of your bodies from the tops of the mountains!"

Of which conqueror was he speaking? Was it Vitellius? Only the Romans could bring about such an extermination. The people began to cry out: "Enough! enough! let him speak no more!"

But the prisoner continued, in louder tones:

"Beside the corpses of their mothers, thy little ones shall drag themselves over the ashes of the burned cities. At night men will creep from their hiding-places to seek a bit of food among the ruins, even at the risk of being cut down with the sword. Jackals shall pick thy bones in the public places, where at eventide the fathers were wont to gather. At the bidding of Gentiles, thy maidens shall be forced to cease their lamentations and to make music upon the zither, and the bravest of thy sons shall learn to bend their backs, chafed with heavy burdens."

The listeners remembered the days of exile, and

all the misfortunes and catastrophes of the past. These words were like the anathemas of the ancient prophets. The captive thundered them forth like bolts from heaven.

Presently his voice became almost as sweet and harmonious as if he were uttering a chant. He spoke of the world's redemption from sin and sorrow; of the glories of heaven; of gold in place of clay; of the desert blossoming like the rose. "That which is now worth sixty pieces of silver will not cost a single obol. Fountains of milk shall spring from the rocks; men shall sleep, well satisfied, among the wine-presses. The people shall prostrate themselves before Thee, and Thy reign shall be eternal, O Son of David!"

The tetrarch suddenly recoiled from the opening of the pit; the mention of the existence of a son of David seemed to him like a menace to himself.

Iaokanann then poured forth invectives against him for presuming to aspire to royalty.

"There is no other king than the Eternal God!" he cried; and he cursed Antipas for his luxurious gardens, his statues, his furniture of carved ivory and precious woods, comparing him to the impious Ahab.

Antipas broke the slender cord attached to the royal seal that he wore around his neck, and throwing the seal into the pit, he commanded his prisoner to be silent.

But Iaokanann replied: "I shall cry aloud like a savage bear, like the wild ass, like a woman in travail! The punishment of heaven has already visited itself upon thy incest! May God afflict thee with the sterility of mules!"

At these words, a sound of suppressed laughter arose here and there among the listeners.

Vitellius had remained close to the opening of the dungeon while Iaokanann was speaking. His interpreter, in impassive tones, translated into the Roman tongue all the threats and invectives that rolled up from the depths of the gloomy prison. The tetrarch and Herodias felt compelled to remain near at hand. Antipas listened, breathing heavily; while the woman, with parted lips, gazed into the darkness of the pit, her face drawn with an expression of fear and hatred.

The terrible man now turned towards her. He grasped the bars of his prison, pressed against them his bearded face, in which his eyes glowed like burning coals, and cried:

"Ah! Is it thou, Jezebel? Thou hast captured thy lord's heart with the tinkling of thy feet. Thou didst neigh to him like a mare. Thou didst prepare thy bed on the mountain top, in order to accomplish thy sacrifices!

"The Lord shall take from thee thy sparkling jewels, thy purple robes and fine linen; the bracelets from thine arms, the anklets from thy feet; the golden ornaments that dangle upon thy brow, thy mirrors of polished silver, thy fans of ostrich plumes, the shoes with their heels of mother-of-pearl, that serve to increase thy stature; thy glittering diamonds, the scent of thy hair, the tint of thy nails,—all the artifices of thy coquetry shall disappear, and missiles shall be found wherewith to stone the adulteress!"

Herodias looked around for some one to defend her. The Pharisees lowered their eyes hypocritically. The Sadducees turned away their heads, fearing to offend the proconsul should they appear to sympathise with her. Antipas was almost in a swoon.

Louder still rose the voice from the dungeon; the neighbouring hills gave back an echo with startling effect, and Machærus seemed actually surrounded and showered with curses.

"Prostrate thyself in the dust, daughter of Babylon, and scourge thyself! Remove thy girdle and thy shoes, gather up thy garments and walk through the flowing stream; thy shame shall follow thee, thy disgrace shall be known to all men, thy bosom shall be rent with sobs. God execrates the stench of thy crimes! Accursèd one! die like a dog!"

At that instant the trap-door was suddenly shut down and secured by Mannæus, who would have liked to strangle Iaokanann then and there.

Herodias glided away and disappeared within the palace. The Pharisees were scandalised at what they had heard. Antipas, standing among them, attempted to justify his past conduct and to excuse his present situation.

"Without doubt," said Eleazar, "it was necessary for him to marry his brother's wife; but Herodias was not a widow, and besides, she had a child, which she abandoned; and that was an abomination."

"You are wrong," objected Jonathas the Sadducee; "the law condemns such marriages but does not actually forbid them."

"What matters it? All the world shows me injustice," said Antipas, bitterly; "and why? Did not Absalom lie with his father's wives, Judah with his daughter-in-law, Ammon with his sister, and Lot with his daughters?"

Aulus, who had been reposing within the palace,

now reappeared in the court. After he had heard how matters stood, he approved the attitude of the tetrarch. "A man should never allow himself to be annoyed," said he, "by such foolish criticism." And he laughed at the censure of the priests and the fury of Iaokanann, saying that his words were of little importance.

Herodias, who also had reappeared, and now stood at the top of a flight of steps, called loudly:

"You are wrong, my lord! He ordered the people to refuse to pay the tax!"

"Is that true?" he demanded. The general response was affirmative, Antipas adding his word to the declaration of the others.

Vitellius had a misgiving that the prisoner might be able to escape; and, as the conduct of Antipas appeared to him rather suspicious, he established his own sentinels at the gates, at intervals along the walls, and in the courtyard itself.

At last he retired to the apartments assigned to him, accompanied by his priests. Without touching directly upon the question of the coveted offices of public sacrificers, each one laid his own grievances before the proconsul. They fairly beset him with complaints and requests, but he soon dismissed them from his presence.

As Jonathas left the proconsul's apartments he perceived Antipas standing under an arch, talking to an Essene, who wore a long white robe and flowing locks. Jonathas regretted that he had raised his voice in defense of the tetrarch.

One thought now consoled Herod-Antipas. He was no longer personally responsible for the fate of Iaokanann. The Romans had assumed that charge.

What a relief! He had noticed Phanuel pacing slowly through the court, and calling him to his side, he pointed out the guards established by Vitellius, saying:

"They are stronger than I! I cannot now set the prisoner free! It is not my fault if he remains in his dungeon."

The courtyard was empty. The slaves were sleeping. The day was drawing to a close, and the sunset spread a deep rosy glow over the horizon, against which the smallest objects stood out like silhouettes. Antipas was able to distinguish the excavations of the salt-mines at the farther end of the Dead Sea, but the tents of the Arabs were no longer visible. As the moon rose, the effect of the day's excitement passed away, and a feeling of peace entered his heart.

Phanuel, also wearied by the recent agitating scenes, remained beside the tetrarch. He sat in silence for some time, his chin resting on his breast. At last he spoke in confidence to Antipas, and revealed what he had wished to say.

From the beginning of the month, he said, he had been studying the heavens every morning before daybreak, when the constellation of Perseus was at the zenith; Agalah was scarcely visible; Algol was even less bright; Mira-Cetus had disappeared entirely; from all of which he augured the death of some man of great importance, to occur that very night in Machærus.

Who was the man? Vitellius was too closely guarded to be reached. No one would kill Iaokanann.

"It is I!" thought the tetrarch.

It might be that the Arabs would return and make a successful attack upon him. Perhaps the proconsul would discover his relations with the Parthians. Several men whom Antipas had recognized as hired assassins from Jerusalem, had escorted the priests in the train of the proconsul; they all carried daggers concealed beneath their robes. The tetrarch had no doubt whatever of the exactness of Phanuel's skill in astrology.

Suddenly he bethought him of Herodias. He would consult her. He hated her, certainly, but she might give him courage; and besides, in spite of his dislike, not all the bonds were yet broken of that sorcery which once she had woven about him.

When he entered her chamber, he was met by the pungent odor of cinnamon burning in a porphyry vase; and the perfume of powders, unguents, cloud-like gauzes and embroideries light as feathers, filled the air with fragrance.

He did not speak of Phanuel's prophecy, nor of his own fear of the Jews and the Arabs. Herodias had already accused him of cowardice. He spoke only of the Romans, and complained that Vitellius had not confided to him any of his military projects. He said he supposed the proconsul was the friend of Caligula, who often visited Agrippa; and expressed a surmise that he himself might be exiled, or that perhaps his throat would be cut.

Herodias, who now treated him with a kind of disdainful indulgence, tried to reassure him. At last she took from a small casket a curious medallion, ornamented with a profile of Tiberius. The sight of it, she said, as she gave it to Antipas, would make the lictors turn pale and silence all accusing voices.

Antipas, filled with gratitude, asked her how the medallion had come into her possession.

"It was given to me," was her only answer.

At that moment Antipas beheld a bare arm slipping through a portière hanging in front of him. It was the arm of a youthful woman, as graceful in outline as if carved from ivory by Polyclitus. With a movement a little awkward and at the same time charming, it felt about the wall an instant, as if seeking something, then took down a tunic hanging upon a hook near the doorway, and disappeared.

An elderly female attendant passed quietly through the room, lifted the portière and went out. A sudden recollection pierced the memory of the tetrarch.

''Is that woman one of thy slaves?'' he asked.

"What matters that to thee?" was the disdainful reply.

III.

The great banqueting-hall was filled with guests. This apartment had three naves, like a basilica, which were separated by columns of sandalwood, whose capitals were of sculptured bronze. On each side of the apartment was a gallery for spectators, and a third, with a façade of gold filigree, was at one end, opposite an immense arch at the other.

The candelabra burning on the tables, which were spread the whole length of the banqueting-hall, glowed like clusters of flaming flowers among the painted cups, the plates of shining copper, the cubes of snow and heaps of luscious grapes. Through the large windows the guests could see lighted torches on the terraces of the neighbouring houses; for this night Antipas was giving a feast to his friends, his own people, and to any one that presented himself at the castle.

The slaves, alert as dogs, glided about noiselessly in felt sandals, carrying dishes to and fro.

The table of the proconsul was placed beneath the gilded balcony upon a platform of sycamore wood. Rich tapestries from Babylon were hung about the pavilion, giving a certain effect of seclusion.

Upon three ivory couches, one facing the great hall, and the other two placed one on either side of the pavilion, reclined Vitellius, his son Aulus, and Antipas; the proconsul being near the door, at the left, Aulus on the right, the tetrarch occupying the middle couch.

Antipas wore a heavy black mantle, the texture of which was almost hidden by coloured embroideries and glittering decorations; his beard was spread out like a fan; blue powder had been scattered over his hair, and on his head rested a diadem covered with precious stones. Vitellius still wore the purple band, the emblem of his rank, crossed diagonally over a linen toga.

Aulus had tied behind his back the sleeves of his violet robe, embroidered with silver. His clustering curls were laid in carefully arranged rows; a necklace of sapphires gleamed against his throat, plump and white as that of a woman. Crouched upon a rug near him, with legs crossed was a pretty little boy, upon whose face shone a perpetual smile. Aulus had found him somewhere among the kitchens and had taken a violent fancy to him. He had made the child one of his suite, but as he never could remember his protégé's Chaldean name, called him simply "the

Asiatic." From time to time the little fellow sprang up and played about the dining-table, and his antics appeared to amuse the guests.

At one side of the tetrarch's pavilion were the tables at which were seated his priests and officers; also a number of persons from Jerusalem, and the more important men from the Grecian cities. At the table on the left of the proconsul sat Marcellus with the publicans, several friends of the tetrarch, and various representatives from Cana, Ptolemais, and Jericho. Seated at other tables were mountaineers from Liban and many of the old soldiers of Herod's army; a dozen Thracians, a Greek and two Germans; besides huntsmen and herdsmen, the Sultan of Palmyra, and sailors from Eziongaber. Before each guest was placed a roll of soft bread, upon which to wipe the fingers. As soon as they were seated, hands were stretched out with the eagerness of a vulture's claws, seizing upon olives, pistachios, and almonds. Every face was joyous, every head was crowned with flowers, except those of the Pharisees, who refused to wear the wreaths, regarding them as a symbol of Roman voluptuousness and vice. They shuddered when the attendants sprinkled them with galburnum and incense, the use of which the Pharisees reserved strictly for services in the Temple.

Antipas observed that Aulus rubbed himself under the arms, as if annoyed by heat or chafing; and promised to give him three flasks of the same kind of precious balm that had been used by Cleopatra.

A captain from the garrison of Tiberias who had just arrived, placed himself behind the tetrarch, as a protection in case any unexpected trouble should arise. But his attention was divided between observing the movements of the proconsul and listening to the conversation of his neighbours.

There was, naturally, much talk of Iaokanann, and other men of his stamp.

"It is said," remarked one of the guests, "that Simon of Gitta washed away his sins in fire. And a certain man called Jesus"—

"He is the worst of them all!" interrupted Eleazar. "A miserable imposter!"

At this a man sprang up from a table near the tetrarch's pavilion, and made his way towards the place where Eleazar sat. His face was almost as pale as his linen robe, but he addressed the Pharisees boldly, saying: "That is a lie! Jesus has performed miracles!"

Antipas expressed a long-cherished desire to see the man Jesus perform some of his so-called miracles. "You should have brought him with you," he said to the last speaker, who was still standing. "Tell us what you know about him," he commanded.

Then the stranger said that he himself, whose name was Jacob, having a daughter who was very ill, had gone to Capernaum to implore the Master to heal his child. The Master had answered him, saying: "Return to thy home: she is healed!" And he had found his daughter standing at the threshold of his house, having risen from her couch when the gnomon had marked the third hour, the same moment that he had made his supplication to Jesus.

The Pharisees admitted that certain mysterious arts and powerful herbs existed that would heal the sick. It was said that the marvelous plant known as *baaras* grew even in Machærus, the power of which rendered its consumer invulnerable against all attacks; but to cure disease without seeing or touching the afflicted person was clearly impossible, unless, indeed, the man Jesus called in the assistance of evil spirits.

The friends of Antipas and the men from Galilee nodded wisely, saying: "It is evident that he is aided by demons of some sort!"

Jacob, standing between their table and that of the priests, maintained a silence at once lofty and respectful.

Several voices exclaimed: "Prove his power to us!"

Jacob leaned over the priests' table, and said slowly, in a half-suppressed tone, as if awe-struck by his own words:

"Know ye not, then, that He is the Messiah?"

The priests stared at one another, and Vitellius demanded the meaning of the word. His interpreter paused a moment before translating it. Then he said that Messiah was the name to be given to one who was to come, bringing the enjoyment of all blessings, and giving them domination over all the peoples of the earth. Certain persons believed that there were to be two Messiahs; one would be vanquished by Gog and Magog, the demons of the North; but the other would exterminate the Prince of Evil; and for centuries the coming of this Saviour of mankind had been expected at any moment.

At this, the priests began to talk in low tones among themselves. Eleazar addressed Jacob, saying that it had always been understood that the Messiah would be a son of David, not of a carpenter; and that he would confirm the law, whereas this Nazarene attacked it. Furthermore, as a still stronger argument against the pretender, it had been promised that the Messiah should be preceded by Elias.

"But Elias has come!" Jacob answered.

"Elias! Elias!" was repeated from one end of the banqueting-hall to the other.

In imagination, all fancied that they could see an old man, a flight of ravens above his head, standing before an altar, which a flash of lightning illumined, revealing the idolatrous priests that were thrown into the torrent; and the women, sitting in the galleries, thought of the widow of Sarepta.

Jacob then declared that he knew Elias; that he had seen him, and that many of the guests there assembled had seen him!

"His name!" was the cry from all lips.

"Iaokanann!"

Antipas fell back in his chair as if a heavy blow had struck him on the breast. The Sadducees rose from their seats and rushed towards Jacob. Eleazar raised his voice to a shout in order to make himself heard. When order was finally restored, he draped his mantle about his shoulders, and, with the air of a judge, proceeded to put questions to Jacob.

"Since the prophet is dead"—he began.

Murmurs interrupted him. Many persons believed that Elias was not dead, but had only disappeared.

Eleazar rebuked those who had interrupted him; and continuing, asked:

"And dost thou believe that he has indeed come to life again?"

"Why should I not believe it?" Jacob replied.

The Sadducees shrugged their shoulders. Jonathas, opening wide his little eyes, gave a forced, buffoon-like laugh. Nothing could be more absurd, said he, than the idea that a human body could have eternal life; and he declaimed, for the benefit of the proconsul, this line from a contemporaneous poet:

Nec crescit, nec post mortem durare videtur.

By this time Aulus was leaning over the side cf
the pavilion, with pale face, a perspiring brow, and
both hands outspread upon his stomach.

The Sadducees pretended to be deeply moved at
the sight of his suffering, thinking that perhaps the
next day the offices of sacrificers would be theirs.
Antipas appeared to be in despair at his guest's
agony. Vitellius preserved a calm demeanour, although
he felt some anxiety, for the loss of his son would
mean the loss of his fortune.

But Aulus, quickly recovering after he had relieved
his over-burdened stomach, was as eager to eat as
before.

"Let some one bring me marble-dust," he commanded, "or clay of Naxos, sea-water — anything!
Perhaps it would do me good to bathe."

He swallowed a quantity of snow; then hesitated
between a ragoût and a dish of blackbirds; an ! finally
decided in favour of gourds served with honey. The
little Asiatic gazed at his master in astonishment and
admiration; to him this exhibition of gluttony denoted
a wonderful being belonging to a superior race.

The feast went on. Slaves served the guests with
kidneys, dormice, nightingales, mince-meat dressed
with vine-leaves. The priests discoursed among
themselves regarding the supposed resurrection. Ammonius, pupil of Philon, the Platonist, pronounced
them stupid, and told the Greeks that he laughed at
their oracles.

Marcellus and Jacob were seated side by side.
Marcellus described the happiness he had felt under
the baptism of Mithra, and Jacob made him promise
to become a follower of Jesus.

The wines of the palm and the tamarisk, those of Safed and of Byblos, ran from the amphoras into the crateras, from the crateras into the cups, and from the cups down the guests' throats. Every one talked, all hearts expanding under the good cheer. Jaçim, although a Jew, did not hesitate to express his admiration of the planets. A merchant from Aphaka amazed the nomads with his description of the marvels in the temple of Hierapolis; and they wished to know the cost of a pilgrimage to that place. Others held fast to the principles of their native religion. A German, who was nearly blind, sang a hymn celebrating that promontory in Scandinavia where the gods were wont to appear with halos around their heads. The people from Sichem declined to eat turtles, out of deference to the dove Azima.

Several groups stood talking near the middle of the banqueting-hall, and the vapour of their breath, mingled with the smoke from the candles, formed a light mist. Presently Phanuel slipped quietly into the room, keeping close to the wall. He had been out in the open courtyard, to make another survey of the heavens. He stopped when he reached the pavilion of the tetrarch, fearing he would be splashed with drops of oil if he approached the other tables, which, to an Essene, would be a great defilement.

Suddenly violent blows resounded upon the castle gates. The news of the imprisonment of Iaokanann had spread rapidly, and now it appeared that the whole surrounding population was flocking to the castle. Men with torches were hastening along the roads in all directions; a black mass of people swarmed in the ravine; and from all throats came the cry: "Iaokanann! Iaokanann!"

"That man will ruin everything," said Jonathas.

"We shall have no more money if this continues," said the Pharisees.

Accusations, recriminations, and pleadings were heard on all sides.

"Protect us!"

"Compel them to cease!"

"Thou didst abandon thy religion!"

"Impious as all the Herods!"

"Less impious than thou!" Antipas retorted. "Was it not my father that erected thy Temple?"

Then the Pharisees, children of the proscribed tribes, partisans of Mattathias, accused the tetrarch of all the crimes committed by his family.

The Pharisees had pointed skulls, bristling beards, feeble hands, snub noses, great round eyes, and their countenances bore a resemblance to that of a bull-dog. A dozen of these people, scribes and attendants upon the priests, who picked up their living from the refuse of holocausts, rushed to the foot of the pavilion and threatened Antipas with their knives. He attempted to speak to them, being only slightly protected by some of the Sadducees. Suddenly he perceived Mannæus at a distance and made him a sign to approach. The expression on the face of Vitellius indicated that he regarded all this turmoil as no concern of his.

The Pharisees, leaning against the pavilion, were now beside themselves with demoniac fury. They broke plates and dashed them upon the floor. The attendants had served them with a ragoût composed of the flesh of the wild ass, an unclean animal, and their anger knew no bounds. Aulus rallied them jeeringly apropos of the ass's head, which he declared they honoured. He flung other sarcasms at them, re-

4—16

garding their antipathy to the flesh of swine, intimating that no doubt their hatred arose from the fact that that beast had killed their beloved Bacchus, and saying it was to be feared they were too fond of wine, since a golden vine had been discovered in the Temple.

The priests did not understand his sneers, and Phineas, of Galilean origin, refused to translate them. Aulus suddenly became angry, the more so because the little Asiatic, frightened at the tumult, had disappeared. The feast no longer pleased the noble glutton; the dishes were vulgar, and not sufficiently disguised with delicate flavourings. After a time his displeasure abated, as he caught sight of a dish of Syrian lambs' tails, dressed with spices, a favourite dainty.

To Vitellius the character of the Jews seemed frightful. Their God was like Moloch, several altars to whom he had passed upon his route; and he recalled the stories he had heard of the mysterious Jew who fattened small children and offered them as a sacrifice. His Latin nature was filled with disgust at their intolerance, their iconoclastic rage, their brutal, stumbling bearing. The proconsul wished to depart, but Aulus refused to accompany him.

The exaltation of the people increased. They abandoned themselves to dreams of independence. They recalled the glory of Israel, and a Syrian spoke of all the great conquerors they had vanquished,— Antigone, Crassus, Varus.

"Miserable creatures!" cried the enraged proconsul, who had overheard the Syrian's words.

In the midst of the uproar Antipas remembered the medallion of the emperor that Herodias had given to him; he drew it forth and looked at it a moment, trembling, then held it up with its face turned towards the throng.

At the same moment, the panels of the gold-railed balcony were folded back, and, accompanied by slaves bearing wax tapers, Herodias appeared, her coiffure crowned with an Assyrian mitre, which was held in place by a band passing under the chin. Her dark hair fell in ringlets over a scarlet peplum with slashed sleeves. On either side of the door through which one stepped into the gallery, stood a huge stone monster, like those of Atrides; and as Herodias appeared between them, she looked like Cybele supported by her lions. In her hands she carried a patera, a shallow vessel of silver used by the Romans in pouring libations; and, advancing to the front of the balcony and pausing just above the tetrarch's chair, she cried:

"Long live Cæsar!"

This homage was repeated by Vitellius, Antipas, and the priests.

But now, beginning at the farthest end of the banqueting-hall, a murmur of surprise and admiration swept through the multitude. A beautiful young girl had just entered the apartment, and stood motionless for an instant, while all eyes were turned upon her.

Through a drapery of filmy blue gauze that veiled her head and throat, her arched eyebrows, tiny ears, and ivory-white skin could be distinguished. A scarf of shot-silk fell from her shoulders, and was caught up at the waist by a girdle of fretted silver. Her full trousers, of black silk, were embroidered in a pattern of silver mandragoras, and as she moved forward with indolent grace, her little feet were seen to be shod with slippers made of the feathers of humming-birds.

When she arrived in front of the pavilion she removed her veil. Behold! she seemed to be Herodias herself, as she had appeared in the days of her blooming youth.

Immediately the damsel began to dance before the tetrarch. Her slender feet took dainty steps to the rhythm of a flute and a pair of Indian bells. Her round white arms seemed ever beckoning and striving to entice to her side some youth who was fleeing from her allurements. She appeared to pursue him, with movements light as a butterfly; her whole mien was like that of an inquisitive Psyche, or a floating spirit that might at any moment dissolve and disappear.

Presently the plaintive notes of the gingras, a small flute of Phœnician origin, replaced the tinkling bells. The attitudes of the dancing nymph now denoted overpowering lassitude. Her bosom heaved with sighs, and her whole being expressed profound languor, although it was not clear whether she sighed for an absent swain or was expiring of love in his embrace. With half-closed eyes and quivering form, she caused mysterious undulations to flow downward over her whole body, like rippling waves, while her face remained impassive and her twinkling feet still moved in their intricate steps.

Vitellius compared her to Mnester, the famous pantomimist. Aulus was overcome with faintness. The tetrarch watched her, lost in a voluptuous reverie, and thought no more of the real Herodias. In fancy he saw her again as she appeared when she had dwelt among the Sadducees. Then the vision faded.

But this beautiful being before him was no vision. The dancer was Salome, the daughter of Herodias,

who for many months her mother had caused to
be instructed in dancing, and other arts of pleasing,
with the sole idea of bringing her to Machærus and
presenting her to the tetrarch, so that he should fall
in love with her fresh young beauty and feminine
wiles. The plan had proved successful, it seemed; he
was evidently fascinated, and Herodias felt that at last
she was sure of retaining her power over him!

And now the graceful dancer appeared transported
with the very delirium of love and passion. She
danced like the priestesses of India, like the Nubians
of the cataracts, or like the Bacchantes of Lydia.
She whirled about like a flower blown by the tempest. The jewels in her ears sparkled, her swift
movements made the colors of her draperies appear to
run into one another. Her arms, her feet, her clothing even, seemed to emit streams of magnetism, that
set the spectators' blood on fire.

Suddenly the thrilling chords of a harp rang
through the hall, and the throng burst into loud acclamations. All eyes were fixed upon Salome, who paused
in her rhythmic dance, placed her feet wide apart,
and without bending the knees, suddenly swayed her
lithe body downward, so that her chin touched the
floor; and her whole audience, — the nomads, accustomed to a life of privation and abstinence, the Roman
soldiers, expert in debaucheries, the avaricious publicans, and even the crabbed, elderly priests — gazed
upon her with dilated nostrils.

Next she began to whirl frantically around the
table where Antipas the tetrarch was seated. He
leaned towards the flying figure, and in a voice half
choked with the voluptuous sighs of a mad desire, he
sighed: "Come to me! Come!" But she whirled on,

while the music of dulcimers swelled louder and the excited spectators roared their applause.

The tetrarch called again, louder than before: "Come to me! Come! Thou shalt have Capernaum, the plains of Tiberias! my citadels! yea, the half of my kingdom!"

Again the dancer paused; then, like a flash, she threw herself upon the palms of her hands, while her feet rose straight up into the air. In this bizarre pose she moved about upon the floor like a gigantic beetle; then stood motionless.

The nape of her neck formed a right angle with her vertebræ. The full silken skirts of pale hues that enveloped her limbs when she stood erect, now fell to her shoulders and surrounded her face like a rainbow. Her lips were tinted a deep crimson, her arched eyebrows were black as jet, her glowing eyes had an almost terrible radiance; and the tiny drops of perspiration on her forehead looked like dew upon white marble.

She made no sound; and the burning gaze of that multitude of men was concentrated upon her.

A sound like the snapping of fingers came from the gallery over the pavilion. Instantly, with one of her movements of bird-like swiftness, Salome stood erect. The next moment she rapidly passed up a flight of steps leading to the gallery, and coming to the front of it she leaned over, smiled upon the tetrarch, and, with an air of almost childlike naïveté, pronounced these words:

"I ask my lord to give me, placed upon a charger, the head of —" She hesitated, as if not certain of the name; then said: "The head of Iaokanann!"

The tetrarch sank back in his chair as if stunned.

He had bound himself by his promise to her; and the people awaited his next movement. But the death that night of some conspicuous man that had been predicted to him by Phanuel,—what if, by bringing it upon another, he could avert it from himself, thought Antipas. If Iaokanann was in very truth the Elias so much talked of, he would have power to protect himself; and if he were only an ordinary man, his murder was of no importance.

Mannæus stood beside his chair, and read his master's thoughts. Vitellius beckoned him to his side and gave him an order for the execution, to be transmitted to the soldiers placed on guard over the dungeon. This execution would be a relief, he thought. In a few moments all would be over!

But for once Mannæus did not perform a commission satisfactorily. He left the hall but soon returned, in a state of great perturbation.

During forty years he had exercised the functions of the public executioner. It was he that had drowned Aristobulus, strangled Alexander, burned Mattathias alive, beheaded Zozimus, Pappus, Josephus, and Antipater; but he dared not kill Iaokanann! His teeth chattered and his whole body trembled.

He declared he had seen, standing before the dungeon, the Angel of the Samaritans, covered with eyes and brandishing a great sword, glowing and quivering like a flame. He appealed to two of the guards, who had entered the hall with him, to corroborate his words. But they said they had seen nothing except a Jewish captain who had attacked them, and whom they had killed.

The fury of Herodias poured forth in a torrent of invective against the populace. She clenched the rail-

ing of the balcony so fiercely as to break her nails;
the two stone lions at her back seemed to bite her
shoulders and join their voices to hers.

Antipas followed her example; and priests, soldiers,
and Pharisees cried aloud together for vengeance, echoed
by the rest of the gathering, who were indignant that
a mere slave should dare to delay their pleasures.

Again Mannæus left the hall, covering his face
with his hands.

The guests found the second delay longer than the
first. It seemed tedious to every one.

Presently a sound of footsteps was heard in the
corridor without; then silence fell again. The sus-
pense was becoming intolerable.

Suddenly the door was flung open and Mannæus
entered, holding at arm's length, grasping it by the
hair, the head of Iaokanann. His appearance was
greeted with a burst of applause, which filled him
with pride and revived his courage.

He placed the head upon a charger and offered it
to Salome, who had descended the steps to receive
it. She remounted to the balcony, with a light step;
and in another moment the charger was carried about
from one table to another by the elderly female slave
whom the tetrarch had observed in the morning on
the balcony of a neighboring house, and later in the
chamber of Herodias.

When she approached him with her ghastly burden, he turned away his head to avoid looking at it.
Vitellius threw upon it an indifferent glance.

Mannæus descended from the pavilion, took the
charger from the woman and exhibited the head to
the Roman captains, then to all the guests on that
side of the hall.

They looked at it curiously.

The sharp blade of the sword had cut into the jaw with a swift downward stroke. The corners of the mouth were drawn, as if by a convulsion. Clots of blood besprinkled the beard. The closed eyelids had a shell-like transparency, and the candelabra on every side lighted up the gruesome object with terrible distinctness.

Mannæus arrived at the table where the priests were seated. One of them turned the charger about curiously, to look at the head from all sides. Then Mannæus, having entirely regained his courage, placed the charger before Aulus, who had just awakened from a short doze; and finally he brought it again to Antipas and set it down upon the table beside him. Tears were running down the cheeks of the tetrarch.

The lights began to flicker and die out. The guests departed, and at last no one remained in the great hall save Antipas, who sat leaning his head upon his hands, gazing at the head of Iaokanann; and Phanuel, who stood in the centre of the largest nave and prayed aloud, with uplifted arms.

At sunrise the two men who had been sent on a mission by Iaokanann some time before, returned to the castle, bringing the answer so long awaited and hoped for.

They whispered the message to Phanuel, who received it with rapture.

Then he showed them the lugubrious object, still resting on the charger amid the ruins of the feast. One of the men said:

"Be comforted! He has descended among the dead in order to announce the coming of the Christ!"

And in that moment the Essene comprehended the words of Iaokanann: "In order that His glory may increase, mine must diminish!"

Then the three, taking with them the head of John the Baptist, set out upon the road to Galilee; and as the burden was heavy, each man bore it awhile in turn.

A SIMPLE SOUL

A SIMPLE SOUL

OR half a century the housewives of Pont-l'Evêque had envied Madame Aubain her servant Félicité.

For a hundred francs a year, she cooked and did the housework, washed, ironed, mended, harnessed the horse, fattened the poultry, made the butter and remained faithful to her mistress — although the latter was by no means an agreeable person.

Madame Aubain had married a comely youth without any money, who died in the beginning of 1809, leaving her with two young children and a number of debts. She sold all her property excepting the farm of Toucques and the farm of Geffosses, the income of which barely amounted to 5,000 francs; then she left her house in Saint-Melaine, and moved into a less pretentious one which had belonged to her ancestors and stood back of the market-place. This house, with its slate-covered roof, was built between a passage-way and a narrow street that led to the river. The interior was so unevenly graded that it caused people to stumble. A narrow hall separated the kitchen from the parlour, where Madame Aubain sat all day in a straw armchair near the window. Eight mahogany chairs stood in a row against the white wainscoting. An old piano, standing beneath a barometer, was covered with a pyramid of old books and boxes. On either side of the yellow marble mantelpiece, in Louis XV. style, stood a tapestry armchair. The clock represented a temple of Vesta; and the whole room smelled musty, as it was on a lower level than the garden.

On the first floor was Madame's bed-chamber, a large room papered in a flowered design and containing the portrait of Monsieur dressed in the costume of a dandy. It communicated with a smaller room, in which there were two little cribs, without any mattresses. Next, came the parlour (always closed), filled with furniture covered with sheets. Then a hall, which led to the study, where books and papers were piled on the shelves of a book-case that enclosed three quarters of the big black desk. Two panels were entirely hidden under pen-and-ink sketches, Gouache landscapes and Audran engravings, relics of better times and vanished luxury. On the second floor, a garret-window lighted Félicité's room, which looked out upon the meadows.

She arose at daybreak, in order to attend mass, and she worked without interruption until night; then, when dinner was over, the dishes cleared away and the door securely locked, she would bury the log under the ashes and fall asleep in front of the hearth with a rosary in her hand. Nobody could bargain with greater obstinacy, and as for cleanliness, the lustre on her brass sauce-pans was the envy and despair of other servants. She was most economical, and when she ate she would gather up crumbs with

the tip of her finger, so that nothing should be
wasted of the loaf of bread weighing twelve pounds
which was baked especially for her and lasted three
weeks.

Summer and winter she wore a dimity kerchief
fastened in the back with a pin, a cap which concealed her hair, a red skirt, grey stockings, and an
apron with a bib like those worn by hospital nurses.

Her face was thin and her voice shrill. When she
was twenty-five, she looked forty. After she had
passed fifty, nobody could tell her age; erect and
silent always, she resembled a wooden figure working
automatically.

II.

Like every other woman, she had had an affair of
the heart. Her father, who was a mason, was killed by
falling from a scaffolding. Then her mother died and
her sisters went their different ways; a farmer took
her in, and while she was quite small, let her keep
cows in the fields. She was clad in miserable rags,
beaten for the slightest offence and finally dismissed
for a theft of thirty sous which she did not commit.
She took service on another farm where she tended
the poultry; and as she was well thought of by her
master, her fellow-workers soon grew jealous.

One evening in August (she was then eighteen
years old), they persuaded her to accompany them to
the fair at Colleville. She was immediately dazzled
by the noise, the lights in the trees, the brightness
of the dresses, the laces and gold crosses, and the
crowd of people all hopping at the same time. She

was standing modestly at a distance, when presently a young man of well-to-do appearance, who had been leaning on the pole of a wagon and smoking his pipe, approached her, and asked her for a dance. He treated her to cider and cake, bought her a silk shawl, and then, thinking she had guessed his purpose, offered to see her home. When they came to the end of a field he threw her down brutally. But she grew frightened and screamed, and he walked off.

One evening, on the road leading to Beaumont, she came upon a wagon loaded with hay, and when she overtook it, she recognised Théodore. He greeted her calmly, and asked her to forget what had happened between them, as it "was all the fault of the drink."

She did not know what to reply and wished to run away.

Presently he began to speak of the harvest and of the notables of the village; his father had left Colleville and bought the farm of Les Écots, so that now they would be neighbors. "Ah!" she exclaimed. He then added that his parents were looking around for a wife for him, but that he, himself, was not so anxious and preferred to wait for a girl who suited him. She hung her head. He then asked her whether she had ever thought of marrying. She replied, smilingly, that it was wrong of him to make fun of her. "Oh! no, I am in earnest," he said, and put his left arm around her waist while they sauntered along. The air was soft, the stars were bright, and the huge load of hay oscillated in front of them, drawn by four horses whose ponderous hoofs raised clouds of dust. Without a word from their driver they turned to the right. He kissed her again and she went home. The following week, Théodore obtained meetings.

They met in yards, behind walls or under isolated trees. She was not ignorant, as girls of well-to-do families are —— for the animals had instructed her; — but her reason and her instinct of honour kept her from falling. Her resistance exasperated Théodore's love and so in order to satisfy it (or perchance ingenuously), he offered to marry her. She would not believe him at first, so he made solemn promises. But, in a short time he mentioned a difficulty; the previous year, his parents had purchased a substitute for him; but any day he might be drafted and the prospect of serving in the army alarmed him greatly. To Félicité his cowardice appeared a proof of his love for her, and her devotion to him grew stronger. When she met him, he would torture her with his fears and his entreaties. At last, he announced that he was going to the prefect himself for information, and would let her know everything on the following Sunday, between eleven o'clock and midnight.

When the time drew near, she ran to meet her lover.

But instead of Théodore, one of his friends was at the meeting-place.

He informed her that she would never see her sweetheart again; for, in order to escape the conscription, he had married a rich old woman, Madame Lehoussais, of Toucques.

The poor girl's sorrow was frightful. She threw herself on the ground, she cried and called on the Lord, and wandered around desolately until sunrise. Then she went back to the farm, declared her intention of leaving, and at the end of the month.

after she had received her wages, she packed all her belongings in a handkerchief and started for Pont-l'Evêque.

In front of the inn, she met a woman wearing widow's weeds, and upon questioning her, learned that she was looking for a cook. The girl did not know very much, but appeared so willing and so modest in her requirements, that Madame Aubain finally said:

"Very well, I will give you a trial."

And half an hour later Félicité was installed in her house.

At first she lived in a constant anxiety that was caused by "the style of the household" and the memory of "Monsieur," that hovered over everything. Paul and Virginia, the one aged seven, and the other barely four, seemed made of some precious material; she carried them pig-a-back, and was greatly mortified when Madame Aubain forbade her to kiss them every other minute.

But in spite of all this, she was happy. The comfort of her new surroundings had obliterated her sadness.

Every Thursday, friends of Madame Aubain dropped in for a game of cards, and it was Félicité's duty to prepare the table and heat the foot-warmers. They arrived at exactly eight o'clock and departed before eleven.

Every Monday morning, the dealer in second-hand goods, who lived under the alley-way, spread out his wares on the sidewalk. Then the city would be filled with a buzzing of voices in which the neighing of horses, the bleating of lambs, the grunting of pigs, could be distinguished, mingled with the sharp sound of wheels on the cobble-stones. About twelve o'clock, when the market was in full swing, there appeared at the front door a tall, middle-aged peasant, with a hooked nose and a cap on the back of his head; it was Robelin, the farmer of Geffosses. Shortly afterwards came Liébard, the farmer of Toucques, short, rotund and ruddy, wearing a grey jacket and spurred boots.

Both men brought their landlady either chickens or cheese. Félicité would invariably thwart their ruses and they held her in great respect.

At various times, Madame Aubain received a visit from the Marquis de Grémanville, one of her uncles, who was ruined and lived at Falaise on the remainder of his estates. He always came at dinner-time and brought an ugly poodle with him, whose paws soiled the furniture. In spite of his efforts to appear a man of breeding (he even went so far as to raise his hat every time he said "My deceased father"), his habits got the better of him, and he would fill his glass a little too often and relate broad stories. Félicité would show him out very politely and say: "You have had enough for this time, Monsieur de Grémanville! Hoping to see you again!" and would close the door.

She opened it gladly for Monsieur Bourais, a retired lawyer. His bald head and white cravat, the ruffling of his shirt, his flowing brown coat, the manner in which he took snuff, his whole person, in fact, produced in her the kind of awe which we feel when we see extraordinary persons. As he managed Madame's estates, he spent hours with her in Monsieur's study; he was in constant fear of being compromised, had a great regard for the magistracy and some pretensions to learning.

In order to facilitate the children's studies, he presented them with an engraved geography which represented various scenes of the world: cannibals with feather head-dresses, a gorilla kidnapping a young girl, Arabs in the desert, a whale being harpooned, etc.

Paul explained the pictures to Félicité. And, in fact, this was her only literary education.

The children's studies were under the direction of a poor devil employed at the town-hall, who sharpened his pocket-knife on his boots and was famous for his penmanship.

When the weather was fine, they went to Geffosses. The house was built in the centre of the sloping yard; and the sea looked like a grey spot in the distance. Félicité would take slices of cold meat from the lunch basket and they would sit down and eat in a room next to the dairy. This room was all that remained of a cottage that had been torn down. The dilapidated wall-paper trembled in the drafts. Madame Aubain, overwhelmed by recollections, would hang her head, while the children were afraid to open their mouths. Then, "Why don't you go and play?" their mother would say; and they would scamper off.

Paul would go to the old barn, catch birds, throw stones into the pond, or pound the trunks of the trees with a stick till they resounded like drums. Virginia would feed the rabbits and run to pick the wild flowers in the fields, and her flying legs would disclose her little embroidered pantalettes. One autumn evening, they struck out for home through the meadows. The new moon illumined part of the sky and a mist hovered like a veil over the sinuosities of the river. Oxen, lying in the pastures, gazed mildly at the passing persons. In the third field, however, several of them got up and surrounded them. "Don't be afraid," cried Félicité; and murmuring a sort of lament she passed her hand over the back of the nearest ox; he turned away and the others followed. But when they came to the next pasture, they heard frightful bellowing.

It was a bull which was hidden from them by the fog. He advanced towards the two women, and Madame Aubain prepared to flee for her life. "No, no! not so fast," warned Félicité. Still they hurried on, for they could hear the noisy breathing of the bull close behind them. His hoofs pounded the grass like hammers, and presently he began to gallop! Félicité turned around and threw patches of grass in his eyes. He hung his head, shook his horns and bellowed with fury. Madame Aubain and the children, huddled at the end of the field, were trying to jump over the ditch. Félicité continued to back before the bull, blinding him with dirt, while she shouted to them to make haste.

Madame Aubain finally slid into the ditch, after shoving first Virginia and then Paul into it, and though she stumbled several times she managed, by dint of courage, to climb the other side of it.

The bull had driven Félicité up against a fence; the foam from his muzzle flew in her face and in another minute he would have disembowelled her. She had just time to slip between two bars and the huge animal, thwarted, paused.

For years, this occurrence was a topic of conversation in Pont-l'Evêque. But Félicité took no credit to herself, and probably never knew that she had been heroic.

Virginia occupied her thoughts solely, for the shock she had sustained gave her a nervous affection, and the physician, M. Poupart, prescribed the salt-water bathing at Trouville. In those days, Trouville was not greatly patronised. Madame Aubain gathered information, consulted Bourais, and made preparations as if they were going on an extended trip.

The baggage was sent the day before on Liébard's cart. On the following morning, he brought around two horses, one of which had a woman's saddle with a velveteen back to it, while on the crupper of the other was a rolled shawl that was to be used for a seat. Madame Aubain mounted the second horse, behind Liébard. Félicité took charge of the little girl, and Paul rode M. Lechaptois' donkey, which had been lent for the occasion on the condition that they should be careful of it.

The road was so bad that it took two hours to cover the eight miles. The two horses sank knee-deep into the mud and stumbled into ditches; sometimes they had to jump over them. In certain places, Liébard's mare stopped abruptly. He waited patiently till she started again, and talked of the people whose estates bordered the road, adding his own moral reflections to the outline of their histories. Thus, when they were passing through Toucques, and came to some windows draped with nasturtiums, he shrugged his shoulders and said: "There's a woman, Madame Lehoussais, who, instead of taking a young man——" Félicité could not catch what followed; the horses began to trot, the donkey to gallop, and they turned into a lane; then a gate swung open, two farm-hands appeared and they all dismounted at the very threshold of the farm-house.

Mother Liébard, when she caught sight of her mistress, was lavish with joyful demonstrations. She got up a lunch which comprised a leg of mutton, tripe, sausages, a chicken fricassée, sweet cider, a fruit tart and some preserved prunes; then to all this the good woman added polite remarks about Madame, who appeared to be in better health, Mademoiselle, who had grown to be "superb," and Paul, who had become singularly sturdy; she spoke also of their deceased grandparents, whom the Liébards had known, for they had been in the service of the family for several generations.

Like its owners, the farm had an ancient appearance. The beams of the ceiling were mouldy, the walls black with smoke and the windows grey with dust. The oak sideboard was filled with all sorts of utensils, plates, pitchers, tin bowls, wolf-traps. The children laughed when they saw a huge syringe. There was not a tree in the yard that did not have mushrooms growing around its foot, or a bunch of mistletoe hanging in its branches. Several of the trees had been blown down, but they had started to grow in the middle and all were laden with quantities of apples. The thatched roofs, which were of unequal thickness, looked like brown velvet and could resist the fiercest gales. But the wagon-shed was fast crumbling to ruins. Madame Aubain said that she would attend to it, and then gave orders to have the horses saddled.

It took another thirty minutes to reach Trouville. The little caravan dismounted in order to pass Les Ecores, a cliff that overhangs the bay, and a few minutes later, at the end of the dock, they entered the yard of the Golden Lamb, an inn kept by Mother David.

During the first few days, Virginia felt stronger, owing to the change of air and the action of the sea-baths. She took them in her little chemise, as she had no bathing suit, and afterwards her nurse dressed her in the cabin of a customs officer, which was used for that purpose by other bathers.

In the afternoon, they would take the donkey and go to the Roches-Noires, near Hennequeville. The path led at first through undulating grounds, and thence to a plateau, where pastures and tilled fields alternated. At the edge of the road, mingling with the brambles, grew holly bushes, and here and there stood large dead trees whose branches traced zigzags upon the blue sky.

Ordinarily, they rested in a field facing the ocean, with Deauville on their left, and Havre on their right. The sea glittered brightly in the sun and was as smooth as a mirror, and so calm that they could scarcely distinguish its murmur; sparrows chirped joyfully and the immense canopy of heaven spread over it all. Madame Aubain brought out her sewing, and Virginia amused herself by braiding reeds; Félicité wove lavender blossoms, while Paul was bored and wished to go home.

Sometimes they crossed the Toucques in a boat, and started to hunt for sea-shells. The outgoing tide exposed star-fish and sea-urchins, and the children tried to catch the flakes of foam which the wind blew away. The sleepy waves lapping the sand unfurled themselves along the shore that extended as far as the eye could see, but where land began, it was limited by the downs which separated it from the "Swamp," a large meadow shaped like a hippodrome. When they went home that way, Trouville, on the slope of a hill below, grew larger and larger as they advanced, and, with all its houses of unequal height, seemed to spread out before them in a sort of giddy confusion.

When the heat was too oppressive, they remained in their rooms. The dazzling sunlight cast bars of light between the shutters. Not a sound in the village, not a soul on the sidewalk. This silence intensified the tranquillity of everything. In the distance, the hammers of some calkers pounded the hull of a ship, and the sultry breeze brought them an odour of tar.

The principal diversion consisted in watching the return of the fishing-smacks. As soon as they passed the beacons, they began to ply to windward. The sails were lowered to one third of the masts, and with their fore-sails swelled up like balloons they glided over the waves and anchored in the middle of the harbour. Then they crept up alongside of the dock and the sailors threw the quivering fish over the side of the boat; a line of carts was waiting for them, and women with white caps sprang forward to receive the baskets and embrace their men-folk.

One day, one of them spoke to Félicité, who, after a little while, returned to the house gleefully. She had found one of her sisters, and presently Nastasie Barette, wife of Léroux, made her appearance, holding an infant in her arms, another child by the hand, while on her left was a little cabin-boy with his hands in his pockets and his cap on his ear.

At the end of fifteen minutes, Madame Aubain bade her go.

They always hung around the kitchen, or approached Félicité when she and the children were out walking. The husband, however, did not show himself.

Félicité developed a great fondness for them; she bought them a stove, some shirts and a blanket; it was evident that they exploited her. Her foolishness annoyed Madame Aubain, who, moreover did not like the nephew's familiarity, for he called her son "thou";—and, as Virginia began to cough and the season was over, she decided to return to Pont-l'Evêque.

Monsieur Bourais assisted her in the choice of a college. The one at Caen was considered the best. So Paul was sent away and bravely said good-bye to them all, for he was glad to go to live in a house where he would have boy companions.

Madame Aubain resigned herself to the separation from her son because it was unavoidable. Virginia brooded less and less over it. Félicité regretted the noise he made, but soon a new occupation diverted her mind; beginning from Christmas, she accompanied the little girl to her catechism lesson every day.

III.

After she had made a curtsey at the threshold, she would walk up the aisle between the double lines of chairs, open Madame Aubain's pew, sit down and look around.

Girls and boys, the former on the right, the latter on the left-hand side of the church, filled the stalls of the choir; the priest stood beside the reading-desk; on one stained window of the side-aisle the Holy Ghost hovered over the Virgin; on another one, Mary knelt before the Child Jesus, and behind the altar, a wooden group represented Saint Michael felling the dragon.

The priest first read a condensed lesson of sacred history. Félicité evoked Paradise, the Flood, the Tower of Babel, the blazing cities, the dying nations, the shattered idols; and out of this she developed a great respect for the Almighty and a great fear of His wrath. Then, when she listened to the Passion, she wept. Why had they crucified Him who loved little children, nourished the people, made the blind see, and who, out of humility, had wished to be born among the poor, in a stable? The sowings, the harvests, the wine-presses, all those familiar things which the Scriptures mention, formed a part of her life; the word of God sanctified them; and she loved the lambs with increased tenderness for the sake of the Lamb, and the doves because of the Holy Ghost.

She found it hard, however, to think of the latter as a person, for was it not a bird, a flame, and sometimes only a breath? Perhaps it is its light that at night hovers over swamps, its breath that propels the clouds, its voice that renders church-bells harmonious. And Félicité worshipped devoutly, while enjoying the coolness and the stillness of the church.

As for the dogma, she could not understand it and did not even try. The priest discoursed, the children recited, and she went to sleep, only to awaken with a start when they were leaving the church and their wooden shoes clattered on the stone pavement.

In this way, she learned her catechism, her religious education having been neglected in her youth;

and thenceforth she imitated all Virginia's religious practices, fasted when she did, and went to confession with her. At the Corpus-Christi Day they both decorated an altar.

She worried in advance over Virginia's first communion. She fussed about the shoes, the rosary, the book and the gloves. With what nervousness she helped the mother dress the child!

During the entire ceremony, she felt anguished. Monsieur Bourais hid part of the choir from view, but directly in front of her, the flock of maidens, wearing white wreaths over their lowered veils, formed a snow-white field, and she recognised her darling by the slenderness of her neck and her devout attitude. The bell tinkled. All the heads bent and there was a silence. Then, at the peals of the organ the singers and the worshippers struck up the Agnus Dei; the boys' procession began; behind them came the girls. With clasped hands, they advanced step by step to the lighted altar, knelt at the first step, received one by one the Host, and returned to their seats in the same order. When Virginia's turn came, Félicité leaned forward to watch her, and through that imagination which springs from true affection, she at once became the child, whose face and dress became hers, whose heart beat in her bosom, and when Virginia opened her mouth and closed her lids, she did likewise and came very near fainting.

The following day, she presented herself early at the church so as to receive communion from the curé. She took it with the proper feeling, but did not experience the same delight as on the previous day.

Madame Aubain wished to make an accomplished girl of her daughter; and as Guyot could not teach

English nor music, she decided to send her to the Ursulines at Honfleur.

The child made no objection, but Félicité sighed and thought Madame was heartless. Then, she thought that perhaps her mistress was right, as these things were beyond her sphere. Finally, one day, an old *fiacre* stopped in front of the door and a nun stepped out. Félicité put Virginia's luggage on top of the carriage, gave the coachman some instructions, and smuggled six jars of jam, a dozen pears and a bunch of violets under the seat.

At the last minute, Virginia had a fit of sobbing; she embraced her mother again and again, while the latter kissed her on her forehead, and said: "Now, be brave, be brave!" The step was pulled up and the *fiacre* rumbled off.

Then Madame Aubain had a fainting spell, and that evening all her friends, including the two Lormeaus, Madame Lechaptois, the ladies Rochefeuille, Messieurs de Houppeville and Bourais, called on her and tendered their sympathy.

At first the separation proved very painful to her. But her daughter wrote her three times a week and the other days she, herself, wrote to Virginia. Then she walked in the garden, read a little, and in this way managed to fill out the emptiness of the hours.

Each morning, out of habit, Félicité entered Virginia's room and gazed at the walls. She missed combing her hair, lacing her shoes, tucking her in her bed, and the bright face and little hand when they used to go out for a walk. In order to occupy herself she tried to make lace. But her clumsy fingers broke the threads; she had no heart for anything, lost her sleep and "wasted away," as she put it.

In order to have some distraction, she asked leave to receive the visits of her nephew Victor.

He would come on Sunday, after church, with ruddy cheeks and bared chest, bringing with him the scent of the country. She would set the table and they would sit down opposite each other, and eat their dinner; she ate as little as possible, herself, to avoid any extra expense, but would stuff him so with food that he would finally go to sleep. At the first stroke of vespers, she would wake him up, brush his trousers, tie his cravat and walk to church with him, leaning on his arm with maternal pride.

His parents always told him to get something out of her, either a package of brown sugar, or soap, or brandy, and sometimes even money. He brought her his clothes to mend, and she accepted the task gladly, because it meant another visit from him.

In August, his father took him on a coasting-vessel.

It was vacation time and the arrival of the children consoled Félicité. But Paul was capricious, and Virginia was growing too old to be thee-and-thou'd, a fact which seemed to produce a sort of embarrassment in their relations.

Victor went successively to Morlaix, to Dunkirk, and to Brighton; whenever he returned from a trip he would bring her a present. The first time it was a box of shells; the second, a coffee-cup; the third, a big doll of ginger-bread. He was growing handsome, had a good figure, a tiny moustache, kind eyes, and a little leather cap that sat jauntily on the back of his head. He amused his aunt by telling her stories mingled with nautical expressions.

One Monday, the 14th of July, 1819 (she never forgot the date), Victor announced that he had been engaged on a merchant-vessel and that in two days he would take the steamer at Honfleur and join his sailer, which was going to start from Havre very soon. Perhaps he might be away two years.

The prospect of his departure filled Félicité with despair, and in order to bid him farewell, on Wednesday night, after Madame's dinner, she put on her pattens and trudged the four miles that separated Pont-l'Evêque from Honfleur.

When she reached the Calvary, instead of turning to the right, she turned to the left and lost herself in coal-yards; she had to retrace her steps; some people she spoke to advised her to hasten. She walked helplessly around the harbour filled with vessels, and knocked against hawsers. Presently the ground sloped abruptly, lights flitted to and fro, and she thought all at once that she had gone mad when she saw some horses in the sky.

Others, on the edge of the dock, neighed at the sight of the ocean. A derrick pulled them up in the air and dumped them into a boat, where passengers were bustling about among barrels of cider, baskets of cheese and bags of meal; chickens cackled, the captain swore and a cabin-boy rested on the railing, apparently indifferent to his surroundings. Félicité, who did not recognise him, kept shouting: "Victor!" He suddenly raised his eyes, but while she was preparing to rush up to him, they withdrew the gangplank.

The packet, towed by singing women, glided out of the harbour. Her hull squeaked and the heavy waves beat up against her sides. The sail had turned and nobody was visible;—and on the ocean, silvered by the light of the moon, the vessel formed a black spot that grew dimmer and dimmer, and finally disappeared.

When Félicité passed the Calvary again, she felt as if she must entrust that which was dearest to her to the Lord; and for a long while she prayed, with uplifted eyes and a face wet with tears. The city was sleeping; some customs officials were taking the air; and the water kept pouring through the holes of the dam with a deafening roar. The town clock struck two.

The parlour of the convent would not open until morning, and surely a delay would annoy Madame; so, in spite of her desire to see the other child, she went home. The maids of the inn were just arising when she reached Pont-l'Evêque.

So the poor boy would be on the ocean for months! His previous trips had not alarmed her. One can come back from England and Brittany; but America, the colonies, the islands, were all lost in an uncertain region at the very end of the world.

From that time on, Félicité thought solely of her nephew. On warm days she feared he would suffer from thirst, and when it stormed, she was afraid he would be struck by lightning. When she harkened to the wind that rattled in the chimney and dislodged the tiles on the roof, she imagined that he was being buffeted by the same storm, perched on top of a shattered mast, with his whole body bent backward and covered with sea-foam; or,—these were recollections of the engraved geography—he was being devoured by savages, or captured in a forest by apes, or dying on some lonely coast. She never mentioned her anxieties, however.

Madame Aubain worried about her daughter.

The sisters thought that Virginia was affectionate but delicate. The slightest emotion enervated her. She had to give up her piano lessons. Her mother insisted upon regular letters from the convent. One morning, when the postman failed to come, she grew impatient and began to pace to and fro, from her chair to the window. It was really extraordinary! No news since four days!

In order to console her mistress by her own example, Félicité said:

"Why, Madame, I haven't had any news since six months!"—

"From whom?"—

The servant replied gently:

"Why—from my nephew."

"Oh, yes, your nephew!" And shrugging her shoulders, Madame Aubain continued to pace the floor as if to say: "I did not think of it.—Besides, I do not care, a cabin-boy, a pauper!—but my daughter —what a difference! just think of it!—"

Félicité, although she had been reared roughly, was very indignant. Then she forgot about it.

It appeared quite natural to her that one should lose one's head about Virginia.

The two children were of equal importance; they were united in her heart and their fate was to be the same.

The chemist informed her that Victor's vessel had reached Havana. He had read the information in a newspaper.

Félicité imagined that Havana was a place where people did nothing but smoke, and that Victor walked around among negroes in a cloud of tobacco. Could a person, in case of need, return by land? How far was it from Pont-l'Evêque? In order to learn these things, she questioned Monsieur Bourais. He reached for his map and began some explanations concerning longitudes, and smiled with superiority at Félicité's bewilderment. At last, he took his pencil and pointed out an imperceptible black point in the scallops of an oval blotch, adding: "There it is." She bent over the map; the maze of coloured lines hurt her eyes without enlightening her; and when Bourais asked her what puzzled her, she requested him to show her the house Victor lived in. Bourais threw up his hands, sneezed, and then laughed uproariously; such ignorance delighted his soul; but Félicité failed to understand the cause of his mirth, she whose intelligence was so limited that she perhaps expected to see even the picture of her nephew!

It was two weeks later that Liébard came into the kitchen at market-time, and handed her a letter from her brother-in-law. As neither of them could read, she called upon her mistress.

Madame Aubain, who was counting the stitches of her knitting, laid her work down beside her, opened the letter, started, and in a low tone and with a searching look said: "They tell you of a —— misfortune. Your nephew ——."

He had died. The letter told nothing more.

Félicité dropped on a chair, leaned her head against the back and closed her lids; presently they grew pink. Then, with drooping head, inert hands and staring eyes she repeated at intervals:

"Poor little chap! poor little chap!"

Liébard watched her and sighed. Madame Aubain was trembling.

foot-warmer, my purse and my gloves; and be quick about it," she said.

Virginia had congestion of the lungs; perhaps it was desperate.

"Not yet," said the physician, and both got into the carriage, while the snow fell in thick flakes. It was almost night and very cold.

Félicité rushed to the church to light a candle. Then she ran after the coach which she overtook after an hour's chase, sprang up behind and held on to the straps. But suddenly a thought crossed her mind: "The yard had been left open; supposing that burglars got in!" And down she jumped.

The next morning, at daybreak, she called at the doctor's. He had been home, but had left again. Then she waited at the inn, thinking that strangers might bring her a letter. At last, at daylight she took the diligence for Lisieux.

The convent was at the end of a steep and narrow street. When she arrived about at the middle of it, she heard strange noises, a funeral knell. "It must be for some one else," thought she; and she pulled the knocker violently.

After several minutes had elapsed, she heard footsteps, the door was half opened and a nun appeared. The good sister, with an air of compunction, told her that "she had just passed away." And at the same time the tolling of Saint-Léonard's increased.

Félicité reached the second floor. Already at the threshold, she caught sight of Virginia lying on her back, with clasped hands, her mouth open and her head thrown back, beneath a black crucifix inclined toward her, and stiff curtains which were less white than her face. Madame Aubain lay at the foot of the couch, clasping it with her arms and uttering groans of agony. The Mother Superior was standing on the right side of the bed. The three candles on the bureau made red blurs, and the windows were dimmed by the fog outside. The nuns carried Madame Aubain from the room.

For two nights, Félicité never left the corpse. She would repeat the same prayers, sprinkle holy water over the sheets, get up, come back to the bed and contemplate the body. At the end of the first vigil, she noticed that the face had taken on a yellow tinge, the lips grew blue, the nose grew pinched, the eyes were sunken. She kissed them several times and would not have been greatly astonished had Virginia opened them; to souls like these the supernatural is always quite simple. She washed her, wrapped her in a shroud, put her into the casket, laid a wreath of flowers on her head and arranged her curls. They were blond and of an extraordinary length for her age. Félicité cut off a big lock and put half of it into her bosom, resolving never to part with it.

The body was taken to Pont-l'Evêque, according to Madame Aubain's wishes; she followed the hearse in a closed carriage.

After the ceremony it took three quarters of an hour to reach the cemetery. Paul, sobbing, headed the procession; Monsieur Bourais followed, and then came the principal inhabitants of the town, the women covered with black capes, and Félicité. The memory of her nephew, and the thought that she had not been able to render him these honours, made her doubly unhappy, and she felt as if he were being buried with Virginia.

Madame Aubain's grief was uncontrollable. At first she rebelled against God, thinking that he was unjust to have taken away her child—she who had never done anything wrong, and whose conscience was so pure! But no! she ought to have taken her South. Other doctors would have saved her. She accused herself, prayed to be able to join her child, and cried in the midst of her dreams. Of the latter, one more especially haunted her. Her husband, dressed like a sailor, had come back from a long voyage, and with tears in his eyes told her that he had received the order to take Virginia away. Then they both consulted about a hiding-place.

Once she came in from the garden, all upset. A moment before (and she showed the place), the father and daughter had appeared to her, one after the other; they did nothing but look at her.

During several months she remained inert in her room. Félicité scolded her gently; she must keep up for her son and also for the other one, for "her memory."

"Her memory!" replied Madame Aubain, as if she were just awakening, "Oh! yes, yes, you do not forget her!" This was an allusion to the cemetery where she had been expressly forbidden to go.

But Félicité went there every day. At four o'clock exactly, she would go through the town, climb the hill, open the gate and arrive at Virginia's tomb. It was a small column of pink marble with a flat stone at its base, and it was surrounded by a little plot enclosed by chains. The flower-beds were bright with blossoms. Félicité watered their leaves, renewed the gravel, and knelt on the ground in order to till the earth properly. When Madame Aubain was able to visit the cemetery she felt very much relieved and consoled.

Years passed, all alike and marked by no other events than the return of the great church holidays: Easter, Assumption, All Saints' Day. Household happenings constituted the only data to which in later years they often referred. Thus, in 1825, workmen painted the vestibule; in 1827, a portion of the roof almost killed a man by falling into the yard. In the summer of 1828, it was Madame's turn to offer the hallowed bread; at that time, Bourais disappeared mysteriously; and the old acquaintances, Guyot, Liébard, Madame Lechaptois, Robelin, old Grémanville, paralysed since a long time, passed away one by one. One night, the driver of the mail in Pont-l'Evêque announced the Revolution of July. A few days afterward a new sub-prefect was nominated, the Baron de Larsonnière, ex-consul in America, who, besides his wife, had his sister-in-law and her three grown daughters with him. They were often seen on their lawn, dressed in loose blouses, and they had a parrot and a negro servant. Madame Aubain received a call, which she returned promptly. As soon as she caught sight of them, Félicité would run and notify her mistress. But only one thing was capable of arousing her: a letter from her son.

He could not follow any profession as he was absorbed in drinking. His mother paid his debts and he made fresh ones; and the sighs that she heaved while she knitted at the window reached the ears of Félicité who was spinning in the kitchen.

They walked in the garden together, always speaking of Virginia, and asking each other if such and such a thing would have pleased her, and what she would pr bably have said on this or that occasion.

All her little belongings were put away in a closet of the room which held the two little beds. But Madame Aubain looked them over as little as possible. One summer day, however, she resigned herself to the task and when she opened the closet the moths flew out.

Virginia's frocks were hung under a shelf where there were three dolls, some hoops, a doll-house, and a basin which she had used. Félicité and Madame Aubain also took out the skirts, the handkerchiefs, and the stockings and spread them on the beds, before putting them away again. The sun fell on the piteous things, disclosing their spots and the creases formed by the motions of the body. The atmosphere was warm and blue, and a blackbird trilled in the garden; everything seemed to live in happiness. They found a little hat of soft brown plush, but it was entirely moth-eaten. Félicité asked for it. Their eyes met and filled with tears; at last the mistress opened her arms and the servant threw herself against her breast and they hugged each other and giving vent to their grief in a kiss which equalized them for a moment.

It was the first time that this had ever happened, for Madame Aubain was not of an expansive nature. Félicité was as grateful for it as if it had been some favour, and thenceforth loved her with animal-like devotion and a religious veneration.

Her kind-heartedness developed. When she heard the drums of a marching regiment passing through the street, she would stand in the doorway with a jug of cider and give the soldiers a drink. She nursed cholera victims. She protected Polish refugees, and one of them even declared that he wished to marry her. But they quarrelled, for one morning when she returned from the Angelus she found him in the kitchen coolly eating a dish which he had prepared for himself during her absence.

After the Polish refugees, came Colmiche, an old man who was credited with having committed frightful misdeeds in '93. He lived near the river in the ruins of a pig-sty. The urchins peeped at him through the cracks in the walls and threw stones that fell on his miserable bed, where he lay gasping with catarrh, with long hair, inflamed eyelids, and a tumour as big as his head on one arm.

She got him some linen, tried to clean his hovel and dreamed of installing him in the bake-house without his being in Madame's way. When the cancer broke, she dressed it every day; sometimes she brought him some cake and placed him in the sun on a bundle of hay; and the poor old creature, trembling and drooling, would thank her in his broken voice, and put out his hands whenever she left him. Finally he died; and she had a mass said for the repose of his soul.

That day a great joy came to her: at dinner-time, Madame de Larsonnière's servant called with the parrot, the cage, and the perch and chain and lock. A note from the baroness told Madame Aubain that as her husband had been promoted to a prefecture, they were leaving that night, and she begged her to accept the bird as a remembrance and a token of her esteem.

Since a long time the parrot had been on Félicité's mind, because he came from America, which reminded her of Victor, and she had approached the negro on the subject.

the passers-by to inquire of them: "Haven't you perhaps seen my parrot?" To those who had never seen the parrot, she described him minutely. Suddenly she thought she saw something green fluttering behind the mills at the foot of the hill. But when she was at the top of the hill she could not see it. A hod-carrier told her that he had just seen the bird in Saint-Melaine, in Mother Simon's store. She rushed to the place. The people did not know what she was talking about. At last she came home, exhausted, with her slippers worn to shreds, and despair in her heart. She sat down on the bench near Madame and was telling of her search when presently a light weight dropped on her shoulder — Loulou! What the deuce had he been doing? Perhaps he had just taken a little walk around the town!

She did not easily forget her scare; in fact, she never got over it. In consequence of a cold, she caught a sore throat; and some time afterward she had an earache. Three years later she was stone deaf, and spoke in a very loud voice even in church. Although her sins might have been proclaimed throughout the diocese without any shame to herself, or ill effects to the community, the curé thought it advisable to receive her confession in the vestry-room.

Imaginary buzzings also added to her bewilderment. Her mistress often said to her: "My goodness, how stupid you are!" and she would answer: "Yes, Madame," and look for something.

The narrow circle of her ideas grew more restricted than it already was; the bellowing of the oxen, the chime of the bells no longer reached her intelligence. All things moved silently, like ghosts. Only one noise penetrated her ears; the parrot's voice.

As if to divert her mind, he reproduced for her the tick-tack of the spit in the kitchen, the shrill cry of the fish-vendors, the saw of the carpenter who had a shop opposite, and when the door-bell rang, he would imitate Madame Aubain: "Félicité! go to the front door."

They held conversations together, Loulou repeating the three phrases of his repertory over and over, Félicité replying by words that had no greater meaning, but in which she poured out her feelings. In her isolation, the parrot was almost a son, a lover. He climbed upon her fingers, pecked at her lips, clung to her shawl, and when she rocked her head to and fro like a nurse, the big wings of her cap and the wings of the bird flapped in unison. When clouds gathered on the horizon and the thunder rumbled, Loulou would scream, perhaps because he remembered the storms in his native forests. The dripping of the rain would excite him to frenzy; he flapped around, struck the ceiling with his wings, upset everything, and would finally fly into the garden to play. Then he would come back into the room, light on one of the andirons, and hop around in order to get dry.

One morning during the terrible winter of 1837, when she had put him in front of the fire-place on account of the cold, she found him dead in his cage, hanging to the wire bars with his head down. He had probably died of congestion. But she believed that he had been poisoned, and although she had no proofs whatever, her suspicion rested on Fabu.

She wept so sorely that her mistress said: "Why don't you have him stuffed?"

She asked the advice of the chemist, who had always been kind to the bird.

He wrote to Havre for her. A certain man named Fellacher consented to do the work. But, as the diligence driver often lost parcels entrusted to him, Félicité resolved to take her pet to Honfleur herself.

Leafless apple-trees lined the edges of the road. The ditches were covered with ice. The dogs on the neighboring farms barked; and Félicité, with her hands beneath her cape, her little black sabots and her basket, trotted along nimbly in the middle of the sidewalk. She crossed the forest, passed by the Haut-Chêne and reached Saint-Gatien.

Behind her, in a cloud of dust and impelled by the steep incline, a mail-coach drawn by galloping horses advanced like a whirlwind. When he saw a woman in the middle of the road, who did not get out of the way, the driver stood up in his seat and shouted to her and so did the postilion, while the four horses, which he could not hold back, accelerated their pace; the two leaders were almost upon her; with a jerk of the reins he threw them to one side, but, furious at the incident, he lifted his big whip and lashed her from her head to her feet with such violence that she fell to the ground unconscious.

Her first thought, when she recovered her senses, was to open the basket. Loulou was unharmed. She felt a sting on her right cheek; when she took her hand away it was red, for the blood was flowing.

She sat down on a pile of stones, and sopped her cheek with her handkerchief; then she ate a crust of bread she had put in her basket, and consoled herself by looking at the bird.

Arriving at the top of Ecquemanville, she saw the lights of Honfleur shining in the distance like so many stars; further on, the ocean spread out in a confused mass. Then a weakness came over her; the misery of her childhood, the disappointment of her first love, the departure of her nephew, the death of Virginia; all these things came back to her at once, and, rising like a swelling tide in her throat, almost choked her.

Then she wished to speak to the captain of the vessel, and without stating what she was sending, she gave him some instructions.

Fellacher kept the parrot a long time. He always promised that it would be ready for the following week; after six months he announced the shipment of a case, and that was the end of it. Really, it seemed as if Loulou would never come back to his home. "They have stolen him," thought Félicité.

Finally he arrived, sitting bolt upright on a branch which could be screwed into a mahogany pedestal, with his foot in the air, his head on one side, and in his beak a nut which the naturalist, from love of the sumptuous, had gilded. She put him in her room.

This place, to which only a chosen few were admitted, looked like a chapel and a second-hand shop, so filled was it with devotional and heterogeneous things. The door could not be opened easily on account of the presence of a large wardrobe. Opposite the window that looked out into the garden, a bull's-eye opened on the yard; a table was placed by the cot and held a wash-basin, two combs, and a piece of blue soap in a broken saucer. On the walls were rosaries, medals, a number of Holy Virgins, and a holy-water basin made out of a cocoanut; on the bureau, which was covered with a napkin like an altar, stood the box of shells that Victor had given her; also a watering-can and a balloon, writing-books,

the engraved geography and a pair of shoes; on the
nail which held the mirror, hung Virginia's little plush
hat! Félicité carried this sort of respect so far that
she even kept one of Monsieur's old coats. All the
things which Madame Aubain discarded, Félicité
begged for her own room. Thus, she had artificial
flowers on the edge of the bureau, and the picture
of the Comte d'Artois in the recess of the window.
By means of a board, Loulou was set on a portion of
the chimney which advanced into the room. Every
morning when she awoke, she saw him in the dim
light of dawn and recalled bygone days and the
smallest details of insignificant actions, without any
sense of bitterness or grief.

As she was unable to communicate with people,
she lived in a sort of somnambulistic torpor. The
processions of Corpus-Christi Day seemed to wake
her up. She visited the neighbours to beg for candlesticks and mats so as to adorn the temporary altars
in the street.

In church, she always gazed at the Holy Ghost,
and noticed that there was something about it that
resembled a parrot. The likeness appeared even more
striking on a colored picture by Espinal, representing the baptism of our Saviour. With his scarlet
wings and emerald body, it was really the image of
Loulou. Having bought the picture, she hung it
near the one of the Comte d'Artois so that she could
take them in at one glance.

They associated in her mind, the parrot becoming
sanctified through the neighbourhood of the Holy
Ghost, and the latter becoming more lifelike in her
eyes, and more comprehensible. In all probability the
Father had never chosen as messenger a dove, as the

latter has no voice, but rather one of Loulou's ancestors. And Félicité said her prayers in front of the colored picture, though from time to time she turned slightly toward the bird.

She desired very much to enter in the ranks of the "Daughters of the Virgin." But Madame Aubain dissuaded her from it.

A most important event occurred: Paul's marriage.

After being first a notary's clerk, then in business, then in the customs, and a tax collector, and having even applied for a position in the administration of woods and forests, he had at last, when he was thirty-six years old, by a divine inspiration, found his vocation: registrature! and he displayed such a high ability that an inspector had offered him his daughter and his influence.

Paul, who had become quite settled, brought his bride to visit his mother.

But she looked down upon the customs of Pont-l'Evêque, put on airs, and hurt Félicité's feelings. Madame Aubain felt relieved when she left.

The following week they learned of Monsieur Bourais,' death in an inn. There were rumours of suicide, which were confirmed; doubts concerning his integrity arose. Madame Aubain looked over her accounts and soon discovered his numerous embezzlements; sales of wood which had been concealed from her, false receipts, etc. Furthermore, he had an illegitimate child, and entertained a friendship for "a person in Dozulé."

These base actions affected her very much. In March, 1853, she developed a pain in her chest; her tongue looked as if it were coated with smoke, and the leeches they applied did not relieve her oppression; and on the ninth evening she died, being just seventy-two years old.

People thought that she was younger, because her hair, which she wore in bands framing her pale face, was brown. Few friends regretted her loss, for her manner was so haughty that she did not attract them. Félicité mourned for her as servants seldom mourn for their masters. The fact that Madame should die before herself perplexed her mind and seemed contrary to the order of things, and absolutely monstrous and inadmissible. Ten days later (the time to journey from Besançon), the heirs arrived. Her daughter-in-law ransacked the drawers, kept some of the furniture, and sold the rest; then they went back to their own home.

Madame's armchair, foot-warmer, work-table, the eight chairs, everything was gone! The places occupied by the pictures formed yellow squares on the walls. They had taken the two little beds, and the wardrobe had been emptied of Virginia's belongings! Félicité went upstairs, overcome with grief.

The following day a sign was posted on the door; the chemist screamed in her ear that the house was for sale.

For a moment she tottered, and had to sit down. What hurt her most was to give up her room,—so nice for poor Loulou! She looked at him in despair and implored the Holy Ghost, and it was this way that she contracted the idolatrous habit of saying her prayers kneeling in front of the bird. Sometimes the sun fell through the window on his glass eye, and lighted a great spark in it which sent Félicité into ecstasy.

Her mistress had left her an income of three hundred and eighty francs. The garden supplied her with vegetables. As for clothes, she had enough to last her till the end of her days, and she economised on the light by going to bed at dusk.

She rarely went out, in order to avoid passing in front of the second-hand dealer's shop where there was some of the old furniture. Since her fainting spell, she dragged her leg, and as her strength was failing rapidly, old Mother Simon, who had lost her money in the grocery business, came every morning to chop the wood and pump the water.

Her eyesight grew dim. She did not open the shutters after that. Many years passed. But the house did not sell or rent. Fearing that she would be put out, Félicité did not ask for repairs. The laths of the roof were rotting away, and during one whole winter her bolster was wet. After Easter she spit blood.

Then Mother Simon went for a doctor. Félicité wished to know what her complaint was. But, being too deaf to hear, she caught only one word: "Pneumonia." She was familiar with it and gently answered:—"Ah! like Madame," thinking it quite natural that she should follow her mistress.

The time for the altars in the street drew near.

The first one was always erected at the foot of the hill, the second in front of the post-office, and the third in the middle of the street. This position occasioned some rivalry among the women and they finally decided upon Madame Aubain's yard.

Félicité's fever grew worse. She was sorry that she could not do anything for the altar. If she could, at least, have contributed something toward it! Then she thought of the parrot. Her neighbors objected that it would not be proper. But the curé gave his consent and she was so grateful for it that she begged him to accept after her death, her only treasure, Loulou. From Tuesday until Saturday, the day before the event, she coughed more frequently. In the evening her face was contracted, her lips stuck to her gums and she began to vomit; and on the following day, she felt so low that she called for a priest.

Three neighbors surrounded her when the dominie administered the Extreme Unction. Afterwards she said that she wished to speak to Fabu.

He arrived in his Sunday clothes, very ill at ease among the funereal surroundings.

"Forgive me," she said, making an effort to extend her arm, "I believed it was you who killed him!"

What did such accusations mean? Suspect a man like him of murder! And Fabu became excited and was about to make trouble.

"Don't you see she is not in her right mind?"

From time to time Félicité spoke to shadows. The women left her and Mother Simon sat down to breakfast.

A little later, she took Loulou and holding him up to Félicité:

"Say good-bye to him, now!" she commanded.

Although he was not a corpse, he was eaten up by worms; one of his wings was broken and the wadding was coming out of his body. But Félicité was blind now, and she took him and laid him against her cheek. Then Mother Simon removed him in order to set him on the altar.

V.

The grass exhaled an odour of summer; flies buzzed in the air, the sun shone on the river and warmed the slated roof. Old Mother Simon had returned to Félicité and was peacefully falling asleep.

The ringing of bells woke her; the people were coming out of church. Félicité's delirium subsided. By thinking of the procession, she was able to see it as if she had taken part in it. All the school-children, the singers and the firemen walked on the sidewalks, while in the middle of the street came first the custodian of the church with his halberd, then the beadle with a large cross, the teacher in charge of the boys and a sister escorting the little girls; three of the smallest ones, with curly heads, threw rose leaves into the air; the deacon with outstretched arms conducted the music; and two incense-bearers turned with each step they took toward the Holy Sacrament, which was carried by M. le Curé, attired in his handsome chasuble and walking under a canopy of red velvet supported by four men. A crowd of people followed, jammed between the walls of the houses hung with white sheets; at last the procession arrived at the foot of the hill.

A cold sweat broke out on Félicité's forehead. Mother Simon wiped it away with a cloth, saying inwardly that some day she would have to go through the same thing herself.

The murmur of the crowd grew louder, was very distinct for a moment and then died away. A volley of musketry shook the window-panes. It was the postilions saluting the Sacrament. Félicité rolled her eyes and said as loudly as she could:

"Is he all right?" meaning the parrot.

Her death agony began. A rattle that grew more and more rapid shook her body. Froth appeared at the corners of her mouth, and her whole frame trembled. In a little while could be heard the music of the bass horns, the clear voices of the children and the men's deeper notes. At intervals all was still, and their shoes sounded like a herd of cattle passing over the grass.

The clergy appeared in the yard. Mother Simon climbed on a chair to reach the bull's-eye, and in this manner could see the altar. It was covered with a lace cloth and draped with green wreaths. In the middle stood a little frame containing relics; at the corners were two little orange-trees, and all along the edge were silver candlesticks, porcelain vases containing sun-flowers, lilies, peonies, and tufts of hydrangeas. This mound of bright colours descended diagonally from the first floor to the carpet that covered the sidewalk. Rare objects arrested one's eye. A golden sugar-bowl was crowned with violets, earrings set with Alençon stones were displayed on green moss, and two Chinese screens with their bright landscapes were near by. Loulou, hidden beneath roses, showed nothing but his blue head which looked like a piece of lapis-lazuli.

The singers, the canopy-bearers and the children lined up against the sides of the yard. Slowly the priest ascended the steps and placed his shining sun on the lace cloth. Everybody knelt. There was deep silence; and the censers slipping on their chains were swung high in the air. A blue vapour rose in Félicité's room. She opened her nostrils and inhaled it with a mystic sensuousness; then she closed her lids. Her lips smiled. The beats of her heart grew fainter and fainter, and vaguer, like a fountain giving out, like an echo dying away;—and when she exhaled her last breath, she thought she saw in the half-opened heavens a gigantic parrot hovering above her head.